DO[N] McHALE
Under a Broken Sky

VINCI BOOKS

Vinci Books

vinci-books.com

Published by Vinci Books Ltd in 2025

1

Copyright © Dougie McHale 2024

The author has asserted their moral right to be identified as the author of this work in accordance with the Copyright, Designs and Patents Act 1988
This work is a work of fiction. Names, characters, places and incidents are the product of the author's imagination or are used fictitiously. Any resemblance to actual persons, living or dead, places and incidents is entirely coincidental.
All rights reserved. No part of this publication may be copied, reproduced, distributed, stored in any retrieval system, or transmitted in any form or by any means, including photocopying, recording, or other electronic or mechanical methods, nor used as a source for any form of machine learning including AI datasets, without the prior written permission of the publisher.
The publisher and the author have made every effort to obtain permissions for any third party material used in this book and to comply with copyright law. Any queries in this respect should be brought to the attention of the publisher and any omissions will be corrected in future editions.
A CIP catalogue record for this book is available from the British Library.
Paperback ISBN: 9781036700812

Printed and bound in Great Britain by Clays Ltd, Elcograf S.p.A.

BY DOUGIE MCHALE

The Hellenic Collection

The Girl in the Portrait

The Flight of the Dragonfly

The Boy Who Hugs Trees

The Homecoming

A Moth to the Flame

Where the Sky Falls

Beneath a Burning Sky

Under a Broken Sky

CHAPTER ONE

A LIFETIME AGO

Edinburgh 2002

Rosa Koumeris has been putting it off for some time. She is not sure if her old bones are up to the task, but she is too proud to ask her daughter for help. Years of clutter need to be thrown out, destined for the local tip. During this spurt of energy, Rosa catches sight of a nineteen thirties camera languishing in a cardboard box. A 16mm Swiss-made Bolex H16. It is the chrome trims and leatherette panels that catch her eye. It belonged to an uncle, who in the early nineteen thirties, emigrated to the United States and returned to the Greek island of Corfu to visit his family a year before the outbreak of the Second World War. Rosa remembers him taking footage of the town, and the locals in the Jewish quarter. She remembers everyone being fascinated by the camera and wanting to be captured by its lens.

In a cruel twist of fate, the uncle suffered a coronary arrest and died a week into his stay. The camera remained in the family house in Corfu Town. Rosa's father kept it as a memento of his brother's visit and sad passing.

Rosa sits transfixed. Her pale and sunken eyes are alert, focused and searching. Behind her, a white light projects a beam that illuminates fine dust motes, like snowflakes, falling silent and weightless. She takes a sharp intake of breath. Black and white images project onto the screen, illuminated faces of boys and girls, men and women resurrected through smiles and laughter. They stare into the camera lens where, for decades, they have languished, ageless ghosts confined to her memory.

Rosa knew each one. She shared in their lives, their hopes and dreams, their happiness and joy, their sadness and pain. Rosa lived among them as a daughter and a sister, a friend and confidant, an enemy and lover. She knows each smile and expression from the faces that flit in and out of the camera lens. Remnants caught in a moment of time. A glimpse of another life, where every second of every day now hangs on her, as lucid in this very moment as it was back then.

Amongst every smile, gesture, and waving hand to the camera, no one could have conceived then the events that were about to unfold and change the lives they knew forever.

For years, she banished that time to a dark corner of her mind and there it remained but an echo of her past.

It strikes her like a blow to the stomach. She tries to catch her breath. The rush of memory is like a raging river. It flows and consumes every sense, so that sound and smell and touch and vision, and taste are not but a whisper but are as vivid and real as the whir of the projector behind her.

It is a lifetime ago, yet it feels like only yesterday. The world was different then, and it was about to change. They were told it would, but only some believed it, and even fewer acted upon it.

CHAPTER TWO

AN INVITATION

The invitation comes by mail. The clatter of the letter box announces that morning's post deposited on her mat. Rosa shuffles from the kitchen and tuts at the sight of more junk mail scattered along her hall floor and now destined to join yesterday morning's pile in the bin. She bends stiffly to gather up the mail and hobbles back into the kitchen. Rosa is about to drop the mail into the bin when a white envelope catches her eye. She turns it over in her hand, speckled with age spots and blue veins, and the words immediately snag her attention. *If undelivered, return to The Municipality and Jewish Community of Corfu.* Rosa covers her mouth with her hand. Like opening a door, a rush of images pulls at her.

She leans a hand on the work surface as the air sucks from her. She struggles for a breath. Eventually, Rosa gathers herself and pulls her hand through her grey and silvered hair. She deposits the junk mail into the pedal bin and eases herself into a chair. Rosa looks down at the cup of tea and digestive biscuit, reminders of the world she has returned to.

When she considers it, she has had a good life. She cannot complain. Only the last few years have tested her. She was married for fifty-seven years, not only to a husband but to her best friend, her confidant, her soulmate. He was as much a part of her as the air she breathed. Without him, life has been empty. Each day holds no purpose, only an insurmountable loss that words struggle to define and that fills the endless hours.

Her breathing quickens with each rush of breath and the pound of her heart. Rosa stares at the envelope that now lies on the table in front of her.

How long will she endure this stand off? The envelope won't open itself.

And that's when she makes the decision just as the front door opens.

'It's just me, Grandma.'

'Elly. I'm in here.'

Elly sweeps into the kitchen, bends towards Rosa and kisses her forehead. 'How are you today?' she asks, peeling her rucksack from her back and balancing it next to a table leg.

'I'm fine,' Rosa answers, chewing her bottom lip. 'There's tea in the pot.'

'Lovely. Oh! And biscuits too,' Elly says, leaning over and plucking one from the plate. She takes a mouthful of biscuit and pours herself a cup of tea. Pulling a chair back, she sits opposite Rosa, her smile warm as she settles into the chair. 'So, what have you got planned for today?'

'Never mind me. Tomorrow's your last day at university. Are you celebrating?'

'A few of us are going into town for a meal and some drinks.'

'That'll be nice. Where are you going?'

'There's a new Greek restaurant just opened in East Claremont Street. Julie recommended it. It seems popular. I'm looking forward to it, though I can't imagine it will be anywhere as good as your cooking.'

'Nonsense.' Rosa glances at the envelope. 'If it's as popular as you say, the food will be good.'

'I suppose so. If it's not, I can always come back here and get some real authentic Greek cooking.'

'You and your friends are welcome anytime. Any news on the job front?'

'I've applied for a few, but to be honest, Grandma, after four years of studying, I'm looking forward to a rest.'

'You'll need money, especially if you still want your own place. When have you to be out of your flat?'

'In a week's time.'

'What about the girls you shared with? Have they found somewhere else?'

'Julie's moving in with her boyfriend and Sharon's going back to live with her parents for now.'

'Would you?'

'Mum's already offered. I might, just until I get my own place.'

'Then you'll need a job.'

'I've been thinking of taking a year off.'

'Off from what?'

Elly takes a sip of tea and puts her cup down. She grins. 'I'd like to do some travelling and work as I go. Lots of graduates do it.'

'Where would you go?'

'Europe, Australia maybe. I don't know yet.'

'Have you told your parents? That's quite a commitment, but I can see the appeal of it. Would you be looking for company?' Rosa smiles.

'Oh, Grandma, I'd love if you could come.'

'I wish. These old bones of mine do enough creaking just having to walk around this house, never mind halfway around the world.'

Elly grins. 'We could stop off in Greece for a while. Wouldn't you like to go back? Mum said you never did go back to Greece, even just to visit.'

'Edinburgh became my home, and this is where I made a life with your Grandad, and then, eventually, when the children came along, I was too busy being a mother and a wife and then…' Rosa's face creases into a smile. 'A grandma.'

Elly smiles too. 'And the best one ever.'

Rosa smiles at this and then glances at the envelope.

'You haven't touched your tea, Grandma. Are you feeling all right?'

'I'm just a little tired. Nothing to worry about,' Rosa says, trying to sound convincing.

'Do you need anything from the shops… food, milk?'

'I've just filled the fridge. Yesterday was the Tesco delivery. So, I'm fine. No need to worry.' She picks the thin skin of her hand.

'You know you just need to ask and if you're not up to it, it's not a problem. That's not just the shopping. If you need me to do anything, just ask.'

'I know. And I'm grateful, but honestly, I'm fine.'

Elly is quiet for a moment. 'What's in the envelope? You haven't opened it, and I can't help but notice you keep looking at it.'

She doesn't want to worry her. 'It's just a bill, that's all.'

Elly's eyes widen. 'Do you have money worries?'

Rosa laughs. 'No. I've got more money than I know what to do with. When you get to my age, there's not much left to spend it on.'

'That's a relief.'

'In fact. That's given me an idea.'

'What has?'

'I'm going to give you some money.'

'But I don't want your money.'

'Consider it a gift to help finance your year of travel.'

'It's your money.'

'But if I don't spend it, it just gets taxed. Who would I rather it went to? The government who doesn't need it but will take it anyway, or my grandchild who will need it and if she accepts my offer, will reduce my need to worry about her.' Rosa stares at her expectantly.

'I know that look.'

'Then there's no need to argue any further. Is there?'

Reluctantly, Elly nods her head in agreement.

'Good. That's settled then.'

Elly glances at her watch. 'I better get going. I've got some books I need to hand back to the uni library. I've already had to pay a fine and I don't want another one before I leave the uni. I'll wash the cups before I go.'

Rosa waves her hand dismissively. 'Just leave them. You get yourself off.'

Elly stands then, grabs her rucksack and kisses Rosa's forehead. 'See you tomorrow morning, then. Love you.'

'Love you too.'

When the rattle of the front door fades, Rosa sits in the silence of her kitchen. She sighs as she gets up from her chair, clears the table and puts the cups and plate in the sink. She stares out into the garden. It is a space full of memories, a haven where her children played, a host for birthday parties and family barbeques, a place of solitude to read and relax. It was where she stood for the first time in her new country, in her new home, in the safety of an enclosed garden, and cried as she wrapped her arms around her stomach in disbelief. She was starting a new life, a new beginning.

Rosa turns, picks up the envelope and weighs it in her hand. She can feel the weight of the past seep through her fingers. She opens a drawer, takes out a knife, and cursing her arthritic grip, she takes a deep breath and slices under the fold of the envelope.

When the letter is between her fingers, Rosa can feel the quality of the paper. She unfolds it and peers at the contents. She rubs the side of her head just above the leg of her spectacles and begins to read.

Rosa has barely read a few lines when, with a slight intake of breath; she slides a chair back and sinks into it. She returns her attention to the letter, her eyes on the words.

As one of the few living survivors, it is an invitation to attend the unveiling of a memorial statue in Corfu, Greece. The statue by the sculptor Georgios Karahalios was a commission dedicated to the 2,000 Jews who lived in Corfu Town and, when deported, met their deaths in the Nazi concentration camps of Auschwitz and Birkenau in June 1944. Rosa is invited to attend. The Municipality and Jewish Community of Corfu will arrange and pay for her flight with one travelling companion, transfer from the airport to Corfu Town, and stay in the Corfu Palace Hotel.

CHAPTER THREE

RUNNING

'Are you feeling all right, Grandma? You're not your usual self. You haven't touched your biscuit. That's not like you.' Elly gives her that look that Rosa knows only too well. She is on a mission to get the truth.

Rosa is reluctant to discuss the letter, even when found out.

'It's nothing. I think I might be getting a cold. I'm sure I'll be fine in a day or two,' Rosa says, staring at her mug of tea.

'You don't look yourself. In fact, it's like you're not even here. You were the same yesterday. You've been staring out of that window most of the time I've been here. What is it? Tell me.'

'It's nothing for you to worry about.'

'Whatever it is, it's something that's troubling you. I can tell.'

The last thing Rosa wants is to mention the reason she is not herself. She thought her veneer of pretence was working. Damn, she should have eaten the biscuit, even though the thought of it makes her stomach churn. Tea and biscuits have always characterised Elly's daily visits. It has been a ritual of theirs since Elly started university. Rosa's house is close by the buildings Elly frequents to attend her lectures.

'Is it bad news? If you're ill, I need to know. You can't hide something like that for long, so there's no point in trying.'

'No. I'm not ill,' Rosa says, cutting Elly off. 'I'm not going to die. I am, but not anytime soon. Not that I know of, anyway.' She's rambling, trying to give herself time in the hope she can redirect the conversation.

'But you can tell me anything, you know that,' Elly says defensively.

Well, that didn't work. 'Sometimes, there are things words can't describe. What I mean by that is…' Rosa rubs her forehead. 'It's difficult for me to talk about. The point is, I haven't spoken about it, not for a long time.'

'I don't know what you're talking about,' Elly says, confused.

Rosa's shoulders sag. 'I'm sorry. I know I'm not making much sense.'

She has kept her past from her family, with only a select few who knew the truth. They are all dead now. There is no one left from that time. The wounds have never healed. She has lived with them. Life had to continue. She busied herself with the fabric of living, raising her family and investing in the time and energy it took to make a new life for herself. Life has had its own equilibrium. Rosa cannot erase the memories. They have always been just below the surface and every so often they break the waterline. Like now.

She won't win this standoff. She's only prolonging the

inevitable. Rosa takes a deep intake of breath. 'Yesterday morning, I received a letter...'

When Rosa finishes, it's Elly who is now struggling to find the appropriate words.

'I don't know what to say.'

'You don't have to say anything. It was a long time ago.'

'I feel terrible now.'

'Don't. Telling you about the letter has helped me. I feel better about it now.'

'I knew you lived in Corfu when you were young, but I didn't know anything about what happened at that time. I didn't even know there were so many Jews living in Corfu during the war.'

'We were a community. We had our own synagogues and businesses. There were grocers, printers, tailors, and jewellers. There were two thousand people living in the Jewish quarter and after the war, less than a hundred returned from the death camps.'

'I feel ashamed. It's where I've come from. It's my history too. My identity.' Elly's frown creases her forehead.

Rosa shakes her head. 'Don't you dare think like that? Don't feel ashamed, ever. It's not your fault. You can't be blamed for something you didn't know. Your mum was born in Edinburgh, and like you, she has lived in Edinburgh all her life. Your dad is from Leith, and you were brought up a Catholic, just like he was. Life goes on, it moves and changes, it never sits still. Identity gets diluted through time. I am Greek first and then I am Jewish, but my family is Scottish, and this is my home. If I wanted to, I could have gone back to Corfu, but I didn't. I spent my holidays touring the highlands and towing a caravan. You can't get more Scottish than that.' Rosa grins.

Elly smiles then. 'But I never knew. I thought you left

Corfu before the war. I had no idea you were there during the German occupation.'

'It was a decision I took. I decided not to tell anyone. Everyone I knew, my mother, my father, our friends and neighbours, people I had known all my life, old and young, were dead, murdered by the Nazis. An entire community wiped out.'

'That's horrific.' Elly trembles.

'I was running away from hell and when I arrived in Edinburgh, it was a different world. It felt a new world. I had the chance to make a new life.' Rosa picks a crumb from the table and drops it onto her saucer. 'When the war ended, there was nothing left for me in Corfu.'

'Do Mum and dad know all this?'

Rosa shakes her head. 'Some, but not all of it. It was better that way. I never spoke to anyone about it. I tried not to think about it too much.'

'How did you manage to escape being deported with all the others? You survived. How did you survive?'

Rosa leans on the table and stands. She shuffles to the sink, pours the dregs of tea from her cup and places it alongside the breakfast dishes that have still to be washed. Rosa is quiet for a moment, considering her answer. She glances out of the window. There is a fine frost on the stone path and the shed roof is coated white where the low sun has not reached. She turns to face Elly. 'That is a story for another time.'

Elly decides not to pry further. 'So, what will you do? Are you going to accept the invitation?'

Rosa sighs. 'It has come as a shock. How did they know where to find me? If I had wanted to go back to Corfu, I would have done so by now. I'm not sure I want to be reminded of…'

'Your past is still who you are. It makes you the person you are today.'

'Do you really believe that?'

'Of course. You have lived longer in Scotland than you did in Greece, but that doesn't make you any less Greek. If you're running away from the past, it's not your Greekness you're running from, it never has been. It's what happened to you because you were a Jew. You can't change what has happened, and humanity should never forget those times, but you can only be healed by facing whatever it is you have avoided all these years.'

'That psychology degree is coming in handy. I see.'

'If you did go, when would that be?'

'In two weeks. November twenty-first. It's a Wednesday.'

'Not long then.'

'It's out of the question,' she says decisively. 'I can't travel all that way on my own. How would I get around the airport and then onto the plane? And then there's my luggage, and that's before I even set foot in Corfu.'

'You can take a companion. Someone to help you with all of that. It said so in the letter.'

Rosa waves her hand. 'Who? I'm not sure your mum would get the time off work at such short notice.'

Elly takes Rosa's hand. 'I would go with you. I'd love to. That's if you would want me to.'

Rosa's expression changes. 'You would?'

'Well, my passport is still in date and I'm not doing much else, am I?'

CHAPTER FOUR

CROSSING

Rosa settles herself in her favourite chair in the garden. She takes deep breaths of the fresh air. There is a definite chill, even though there is not a cloud in the sky and the sun is shining. It is a bright crisp November morning, and she loves days like these. Around the garden, the trees are skeletal and their branches dark against the pale icy blue sky. Above her, Rosa can see the silver trail of an airplane. Although it's long gone, she wonders where its destination might be.

She unfolds the letter and stares at the words. Her past has dropped through the letter box and landed on her hall floor. She sighs. Can she do this? Before the letter, she wouldn't have contemplated returning to Corfu. Such a thought would not have even entered her head. So, what has changed? In her mind, she has always been running from her memories. The milestones of her life and the raising of her family have not passed without the dark shadows casting their presence, but always extinguished by the light of a birthday gathering, her son and daughter's first day at school, a family holiday, her children's wedding days and becoming a grandmother.

Life moves forward, it regenerates, and from the past, new beginnings emerge and solidify identity and belonging. Like the unfolding of buds from a flower, vibrant colours purify the world, a reminder that life can be, and is, beautiful, inspiring, and forever evolving, but like the flower, it's a fragile thing that can change in the blink of an eye.

Now with the letter in her hand, she scratches the paper with a fingernail. Life has offered a crossroads, and it demands a choice to be either acted upon or ignored. It could pull her in with warm arms or pierce her heart.

Even though she has not asked for it, an opportunity has presented itself. The reality is concrete. She can feel it between her fingers and read the words that jump out at her on the page, *Corfu, Jewish, June 1944.* She can stop running from them and embrace the moment that may just define her lifetime.

Alvertos, what would you do? Rosa asks out aloud and, in that moment, a slight breeze brushes over her, and she smiles. She is not normally one to look for signs, but even if it's not, she will view it as a response that has helped galvanise her choice. Rosa lifts her head and looks around the garden and her expression loosens. She feels a heavy weight lift from her. *Thank you, my darling.*

CHAPTER FIVE

BACK TO THE BEGINNING

'You look different today,' Elly says as she unpacks the shopping bag.

Rosa gives her finest smile. 'Did you get my favourite biscuits?'

Elly pulls a packet from the bag. 'Of course. Fox's salted caramel. How could I forget?'

'Lovely. Thank you, dear. I'll put the kettle on.' Rosa shuffles to the sink and fills the kettle with water.

Elly looks at her curiously.

Rosa turns to her and smiles. 'I thought I'd put a little makeup on today.'

'I can see that, and it suits you.'

'I'm not sure if that's a compliment or not.'

'It is. It brings out the colour of your eyes.'

'Well, thank you.'

'It's really busy out there today. Scotland is playing Ireland at Murrayfield. The pubs will be bursting at the seams.'

'Is that football?' Rosa asks as she sets two cups and saucers on the table.

'No, Grandma. It's rugby. Murrayfield is the national stadium.'

Rosa frowns. 'I thought Hampden was the national stadium.'

'That's football.'

Rosa makes a dismissive noise. 'Seems silly to have two.'

'They're two different sports.'

'Your grandad never liked rugby.'

'He never liked football either,' Elly reminds Rosa.

Now finished putting the shopping away, Elly sits down and asks. 'Golf was his thing, wasn't it?'

'It was. We both played. Your grandad spent more time on the golf course than he did in the house.' Rosa laughs. 'Not so much in the winter, though. He hated the cold.'

Elly smiles. 'I do too. It must be the Greek blood in me.'

Rosa raises her eyebrows. 'I haven't heard you mention that before.'

'I know. Because of dad's Italian descent, it was always the Italian side of the family that has been prominent in my life. The Italian side of the family has always been a big part of my upbringing. The other day, when you told me about the letter and about what happened in Corfu, I suddenly realised there is a part of my family I know nothing about, and that history of my family is who I am as well, even though I know nothing about it. It shamed me. Do you remember what I said to you the other day, when you told me about the letter? I said, *your past is still who you are. It makes you the person you are today.*'

She nods with understanding. 'Yes, I remember.'

'Since then, I've thought a lot about it, and I don't know

my past, not like I thought I did. There's a hole in it, and I can't fill that hole.'

Rosa inhales deeply and lets it go. 'When I came to Scotland, I made the decision that if I was going to make a life for myself in Scotland, I had to fit in. I needed to be part of the community. After the war, when I came to Edinburgh, there were no Greek churches or synagogues, and in a way that didn't matter, it was what was in my heart that mattered. It was enough just to feel secure and safe in my home.'

Elly nods. 'It must have been difficult. I can't imagine what it must have been like coming to a strange country, especially after the war. I've always wondered about what you must have gone through trying to make a life for yourself and because it was never spoken about, I just assumed it was a taboo subject. But now I know there was always more to it than that. Mum knew a little, but she's never spoken about it to me.'

Rosa shakes her head sadly and Elly sees something in her grandma's face, but can't quite detect it.

Rosa serves the tea and as she sits opposite Elly, she looks down at her hands. 'I've come to a decision.' Rosa lifts her head. 'I'm going to accept the offer to go to the ceremony in Corfu and if you're still in agreement, I'd like you to come with me. Maybe then you can start to fill that hole.'

Elly gives her a bright smile even though tears prick her eyes. 'We can do it together.'

She will need to tell Charlie she is going away for a few days. He works in the garden every two weeks. He is due to do some repairs to the slabs that have cracked and see to the flower beds the day after she will have left for Corfu. Charlie has worked in the garden for years. Rosa chose him from a possible five potential candidates.

She asked around the neighbours and at her local golf club, quizzing them on reliable gardeners. *'They're not coming for a job interview,'* Edwina, one of her golfing friends, reminded her, *'They already have a job. It's called gardening. That's why you contacted them in the first place.'*

Rosa was having none of it. She liked to potter in the garden, nothing serious. Planting a few flowers was her limit, but she'd rather spend her spare time playing a round of golf than tending to weeds. If someone was going to tend to her garden, then they needed to be up to the job and surpass her expectations. That's why she insisted on her *five special questions*, as she called them.

Rosa knew Charlie was her choice the second she finished interrogating him with the *five special questions*.

'He's the one.' She beamed. *'Very impressive, and he's been gardening for thirty years. You can't replace experience with someone who has just started to shave. The last one was just out of school.'*

'He had a beard, though,' Edwina reminded her.

'Well, you know what I mean. I liked that man, Charlie, and he's agreed to come every second Tuesday. The others could only come every three weeks, which is no good.'

Charlie is in his early seventies now. He doesn't take payment for his work, not anymore. He has become a good friend of the family and nothing is any trouble for him. Over the years, Rosa has nicknamed him *Accommodating Charlie*.

A lot has changed now. She no longer plays golf; her arthritis has seen to that. To her annoyance, Rosa has become more dependent on her family. She has told them she will not have them wash and toilet her. If it comes to that, professionals will nurse her. She won't put that burden on her family. Thankfully, she is not at that stage just yet. Rosa is still independent in most things, especially around the house. She can vacuum downstairs and dust and make her meals, but her daughter, Elly's mum, insists on doing a *deep clean* every two weeks, washing the bed linen and vacuuming the bedrooms. She has even approached the subject of putting the house up for sale so that Rosa can downsize, or God forbid, move into a retirement housing complex. Rosa is not ready for that, and she will hold off as long as she can. The only way she'll leave her house is in a coffin if she has her way.

Rosa is grateful for her family's help. She knows how fortunate she is that she still has her family around her. Loneliness is the silent killer. She looks forward to Elly's almost daily visits. Now that Elly has completed her degree and not just around the corner at the university anymore, Rosa has wondered how long her visits will continue. It is selfish of her to expect them to do so. She will miss Elly's conversations and her company. They have become closer, and Rosa has grown to look upon her as a close friend, as well as her grandchild. If she is honest with herself, she relies on Elly, not just for her company, but for the companionship as well. She reminds Rosa so much of her younger self. It's like looking at her own reflection.

She will have to pack a suitcase. It has been so long since she has been away from the house. Rosa has to remind herself where the suitcase is. She wonders if she will need to buy a new one. Hers must be over ten years old now and may not be fit for the purpose. She won't be packing much. At this time of year, Corfu will still be cold and wet. A few jerseys, maybe a cardigan or two and trousers. Yes, she will need to keep warm. What will she wear on the day of the ceremony? She hasn't thought about that. Something practical but fitting for the occasion. She will have to think about that. Maybe she will ask Elly and see what she thinks.

The thought of accepting the invitation and going to Corfu after all these years is as bizarre to her as a Jewish couple marrying in a church. Rosa is a mixture of emotions and contradictions. She is unsettled but curious, scared and trepidatious, but eager to be in the place she once called home. She is fraught with dread, panicked at the thought of it, but stirred to confront it, as it has incited a desire to lay the ghosts of her past to rest.

It is a peculiar thing, but now that it has begun and set in motion, she feels she has no control over it.

Not for the first time, she wonders what her husband would make of it all. She wishes he was with her. Maybe he will be. He will be in her heart and a constant presence in her thoughts. Even now, after all this time, his passing is as raw today as the second he breathed his last breath.

She is going back to the place where it all began. Amongst the incarnation of evil, she found love, and lost everything she held dear and sacred. There is still the retching in her guts and the sense of immense loss in her heart.

Rosa inhales deeply, tears pricking her eyes. How can she go back? She must, she tells herself. She closes her eyes and covers her mouth, and to her horror she remembers, she can recall it all, as if it was yesterday.

CHAPTER SIX

RETURNING

Corfu

A middle-aged woman dressed in a dark suit with flowing blonde hair and wide rimmed spectacles meets Rosa and Elly in the hotel foyer. Rosa shakes the woman's outstretched hand, who, in Greek, welcomes Rosa and Elly to Corfu. She informs Rosa her name is Marianna, and it's her job to make sure Rosa's stay is as comfortable as possible before the ceremony and after it. Rosa asks Marianna if she speaks English. This way, Rosa won't have to interpret everything she says to Elly.

'Of course. This is not a problem. Forgive me, I just assumed your granddaughter spoke Greek. I'll speak English from now on.'

Rosa smiles. 'Thank you.'

'Once you have checked in, we can sit in the bar area, and I'll go over the itinerary for your stay. Reception will take care of your luggage and take it to your rooms. Would you like a drink?'

'A water would be fine,' Rosa replies. 'What about you Elly?'

'I wouldn't mind a lemonade.'

Marianna smiles. 'Perfect. I'll see to them now.'

Rosa is relieved there is no expectation for her to attend the unveiling of the statue and speak publicly about her experience during the Nazi occupation of Corfu and the persecution and deportation of its Jewish population. Marianna relays this to her as they sit in the bar with their drinks.

'Have you visited Corfu since…'Marianna hesitates.

'No. I've not been back. This is my first time,' Rosa says, sipping her drink.

'Well, it's an honour to have you here. After the ceremony tomorrow there will be an informal reception, just drinks and a buffet. Also, the local newspaper will be taking some photographs. Are you okay with getting your photograph taken? They might want to interview you as well, just a few questions. Would you be okay with that?'

Rosa can feel her stomach churn at the thought. 'A photograph maybe, but I'm not sure about an interview. No. I wouldn't be comfortable with that.'

Marianna nods, but Rosa can see she is disappointed. 'It's fine.' Marianna tries to force a smile. 'You might change your mind.'

'I won't.'

'The reception will be a relaxed affair and I'm sure the reporter will be discreet.'

'If it's okay with you. I'd like to go to my room now.'

'Of course. You must be tired after your journey.'

Marianna hands Rosa a sheet of paper. 'This is the

timetable for tomorrow's events. I'll pick you up at ten tomorrow morning.'

Rosa takes the sheet without looking at it. 'Thank you.'

'I've been told the food is nice here in the hotel. Are you planning on having dinner here or are you going out to eat in the town? I could recommend a few restaurants.'

Rosa looks at Elly, who leans forward. 'I think we might have an early night. Tomorrow will be a busy day for Grandma.'

'In that case, I'll meet you at the reception tomorrow morning. A car will take you to the ceremony.' And with that, Marianna shakes Rosa's and Elly's hands and is gone.

'Thank you, Elly. I thought that woman had more than a written agenda, an interview, indeed. I'll be straight back on the first plane out of here if she starts that tomorrow.'

Elly offered Rosa her hand. 'Come on, let's see what your room looks like.'

'I hope there's a bath. I've never got used to a shower. You can't take a long soak standing up.'

Elly helps Rosa out of her seat and steadying herself, Rosa says, 'During the war there was no airport, so it was strange to see how Corfu has changed. I knew it would. It has been nearly sixty years. What I wasn't prepared for was how much the town has grown. It's a lot bigger than when I was here. There are so many more streets and houses, and the traffic, well, there was hardly any traffic back then. The old town looks the same. It hasn't changed.'

'How do you feel being back?'

'I'm here, but I'm not. It's difficult to take in. It's like a dream. It doesn't feel real. Not yet anyway, but here I am. I thought I'd be bombarded with memories. Maybe it's too soon and I haven't been outside walking. I'm scared but also anxious to see the old streets and see what I recognise. That's when I'll know what I'll feel.'

Elly leads Rosa out of the bar, and they walk into the spacious foyer. A few people linger, a couple consult a map, another is checking in at the reception desk.

Rosa turns to Elly. 'I wonder if there'll be other survivors attending tomorrow. Very few returned to Corfu from the concentration camps.'

'Marianna didn't mention anyone else. If there is, I suspect they'll be staying in this hotel as well,' Elly says.

Rosa takes Elly's arm. 'I've changed my mind. I think I'll go for a walk.'

'Are you sure? We could see the town tomorrow after the ceremony.'

'I'm sure,' Rosa insists. 'It's been a long time. A lifetime. I'm ready to get reacquainted with an old friend.'

'Let's go then,' Elly smiles.

As they step outside the hotel, Rosa pulls the collar of her coat around her.

Elly glances at her. 'Are you sure this is a good idea? I don't want you getting a chill. It will be dark soon.'

'I've been cold before. I've lived most of my life in Edinburgh. I think I'm used to it by now.'

Elly can tell Rosa is nervous, and why wouldn't she be? This is a huge juncture of her life.

They turn towards the Liston, a wide and straight pedestrian street where arcade terraces shelter diners and couples enjoying drinks.

Elly locks her arm in Rosa's and glances around the street. 'Oh. That looks grand. I wasn't expecting that.'

'It was designed to look like the Rue de Rivoli in Paris.'

'I thought it had a French look to it.'

'The town has been influenced by the Venetians, the

French and British over the centuries. All have left their mark on the architecture of the buildings. You'll see what I mean when we get further down this way.' Rosa falls silent and then says sadly, 'The Germans left a different mark.'

They turn left, past the shop fronts of Evgeniou Voulgares, and further, where multi storied and muted red buildings tower over a labyrinth of narrow streets and lanes paved with colourful cobblestones.

Not for the first time, Rosa is aware of the discord inside her. A simultaneous rise of keenness and a deeper twinge of trepidation seeps into her with every step. She is thankful Elly has said few words. As they walk further, the years have changed little the streets and buildings around her. She has the sense that she is walking into her past and the feeling grows more intense with each familiar scene, lane and square that opens in front of her.

It starts to rain, a steady soft rain, and the cobbled street shines wet and polished.

They turn a corner and the sense of something being wrong strikes Elly hard. Rosa, suddenly apprehensive, takes a sharp intake of breath and panic seizes her chest.

Elly looks around. 'What is it, Grandma? Are you feeling unwell?'

Rosa doesn't meet Elly's eyes. Instead, her fingernails dig into her palm as she sways slightly, and then, comfortingly she is aware of Elly's reassuring arm around her. Rosa can hardly speak. 'Take me back to the hotel.'

It is a relief to step into the warm and dry surroundings of their hotel.

Although Elly is eager to ask Rosa why she reacted in the way she did, she does not want to pry, especially since she can see Rosa is not herself.

'You're soaking, Grandma.' Elly frowns. 'We should

have taken an umbrella, look there're plenty over there that the hotel has provided for guests.'

'Don't fuss, Elly. We're back now. I hope there is a bath because I need a long hot bath and sleep.'

Rosa is grateful that Elly has not asked her why she reacted in the way she did. It was stupid of her. She should have known this would happen. After all the years that have passed, the street had changed little. It looked much the same as it did on that day. It caught her by surprise. She was not aware she was so close. It must have been the dim light and the rain that affected her judgement. Has she done the right thing coming back after all these years?

Tomorrow looms large and right now, she feels so small, and unprepared for what the day might bring.

CHAPTER SEVEN

HAUNTED

Rosa opens her eyes, but it's not the familiarity of her own bedroom that she wakes up to, but the grey outlines of a hotel room that heavy curtains conceal. Throughout the night she has floated in and out of sleep and it has only been in the last hour that a deep sleep enfolded her. She reaches for her glasses and inspects the time on the bedside clock she has brought with her. It is 6.30.

'Did you sleep well?' Elly asks as she sits down at the table in the dining room and pours herself a tea from a silver pot.

Rosa nods. 'I did, thank you.' It is a lie. A small one. She doesn't want Elly to worry about her more than she already is.

'That's good. A good night's sleep can be like medicine. It sets you up for the day ahead.'

Rosa lifts her head from her eggs and toast and smiles. She adjusts her spectacles on the bridge of her nose and peers at the sheet of paper on the table in front of her. 'I think I'm going to need it. Have you seen the day's itinerary?'

'No, but I suspect it will be well organised.'

'You can say that again. It looks like a military operation…10 o'clock, pick up, 10.30, assemble and seated in the square, 10.45, speakers and unveiling of the statue, 11.45, reception and lunch 1.00, drinks 1.30…I'm exhausted just reading it.'

'I'm sure it will be restrained, given the reason we're here.'

'I haven't forgotten.'

Elly shifts in her chair. 'I didn't mean it like that. I'm sorry.'

'It should be me that's apologising. I'm nervous and, to tell you the truth, a little scared.'

'Of what?'

She decides it's time to tell Elly. 'How I might react? Last night was difficult for me. I've spent a lifetime telling myself tomorrow will be different, but it never is. I've never forgotten what happened. How can I forget? It haunts me every day. Like a tattoo, it remains a permanent part of me. And I am here, sitting eating my breakfast, among the buildings and streets where I played as a child in the warmth of a loving family and community and where I grew into a young woman with dreams and aspirations. I was happy and delirious with the prospects of what could be achieved and the possibilities of my whole life in front of me. And here I am now, I have returned, and I promised myself I never would. But I have done so as an old woman with her memories and her secrets, and even now, the evil that was inflicted upon us with all its vileness and hatred, its desire to murder babies, children, men and women, old and young, entire families, because they were seen as inferior and more unclean and worthless as the dirt on their boots is still present today. Last night, I saw the faces of those children, those men and women my past reinvented itself on every street, every building, every house. It has not left this place. It is still living inside me.

'I don't know what I was thinking. I shouldn't have come. It was an error of judgement. I can see that now.'

'But you're here. I've always believed that things happen for a reason. We might not see that at the time, but when we look back, nearly always, we can see a positive side to why things turned out as they did. You are here for a reason, Grandma. It just hasn't shown itself yet.'

Rosa smiles at Elly.

'What?'

'You remind me so much of myself when I was your age.'

'I do?'

'Just like you, I was emboldened by the prospects of what life had to offer and consumed by a youthful exuberance and optimism. As I've got older...' Her forehead creases. 'I sometimes struggle to feel as confident in myself as I used to be.'

'You are one of the most self-assured people I know. You have never let your age define you or restrict you.'

'I'm a wonderful actor, that's all.' Rosa rubs just below her ear and her earring tumbles onto the table. 'Look at me, I'm falling apart.'

Elly's laughter is tinged with sadness. 'If you're worried about today, I'm here for you. You don't have to do this on your own.'

'I know, Elly. I haven't thanked you for coming. If it wasn't for you, I wouldn't be here now and that's the truth of it.' She shifts her chair backwards and, using the table as leverage, she pulls herself to her feet. 'I'm ready.'

'You've forgotten your earring.'

Rosa lifts the earring from the table and secures it in place.

Elly smiles then. 'There. You're ready now.'

'As ready as I'll ever be.'

CHAPTER EIGHT

GHOST

Rosa lifts her head. She looks at the sky and listens to the voice inside her. *You are doing this for them. This is not about you. By being present, you are their witness that the world has not forgotten.* An old Jewish prayer comes to mind, and she whispers the words, 'They will be remembered.'

Elly lays her hand over Rosa's hand and gives her a warm smile. It feels like a tender hug.

Around her, seated in rows in front of the walls of the New Fortress in the Jewish quarter of the town, dignitaries and relatives of the two thousand people, the entire Jewish population of Corfu that perished in the camps of Auschwitz and Birkenau listen to the speeches in respectful silence. Eventually, standing on a stone base, the sculpture is revealed and as the cloth slides from the memorial, there is an audible gasp.

Bronze figures, naked, stripped of their dignity and denied their humanity, depict a mother cradling her infant and a boy hiding his face in his father's thigh. On a plaque on the memorial are the sentiments *"Never again for any nation."*

Rosa leans forward, struck by contrasting but distinguishable emotions. The memorial seizes her and pulls her in with warm arms and simultaneously pierces her heart with unimaginable pain.

As she feels tears welling in her eyes, Rosa understands it now. For years, she has been looking for permission to forgive herself. She has agonised over the horrifying consequences brought by the choices, and forced to make as a young woman. There are things she cannot forget and time cannot heal. She has felt them all, shock, horror, and revulsion. There will never be peace until she faces that which she has spent a lifetime pretending has been a long time dead to her. Now she must face its resurrection. Rosa has locked it away far too long. She needs to be in control. She needs to give it a different place to live, not inside her where it has been, but in the past, where it is finite.

They are all sitting or standing in small groups, holding and munching neatly cut sandwiches, tipping cups of coffee into their mouths, placing napkins and spreading them on laps, a crescendo of voices, nodding heads, sweeping hands, concentrated looks, scratching of necks, flicking of hair. She is an imposter. She doesn't belong here. Her vulnerability is crushing her.

Elly has gone to get them some food from the buffet laid out on tables at the far end of the room. They sit at a table next to the windows, the view over the rooftops of the town a distraction that Rosa needed. She can see the sea and the undulating hills of the mainland, grey on a background of a sky.

As Rosa stares out of the window, she is aware of someone standing close by. She turns. The woman's gaze is uncomfortably intense, and it feels her eyes are absorbing every detail of Rosa.

'It is you, isn't it?' the old woman asks in Greek.

'I'm sorry, but do I know you?' Rosa answers her with a question.

The old woman, pale and thin and slightly bowed, leans heavily on her walking stick as she makes slow progress towards Rosa.

There is something familiar about her, but Rosa can't put her finger on it.

'It is me Rosa, surely you haven't forgotten me?'

Rosa searches the face of the woman who is now in front of her, looking at her long and hard. It was the eyes that finally sparked a recognition. She could never forget those eyes. 'Josefina!'

Josefina Kalamenios smiles in satisfaction. 'Look at us both, together again. After all these years, who would have thought it possible?'

'Josefina,' she says again in disbelief. 'You're alive.' A hundred questions swarm inside her head.

Josefina pinches her forearm, her eyes not leaving Rosa. 'I do believe I am.'

'I wasn't sure if there would be anyone here, I'd know. To tell you the truth, I struggled with the decision to come.'

'Where do you live?'

'In Edinburgh. Alvertos and I have lived there since, well, since we left Corfu. And you?'

'Israel. I came back, but it wasn't the same. Only a handful of us survived and even fewer returned. I've been in Israel ever since. Have you come on your own?'

'No. I'm here with my granddaughter.'

'Oh. I'm sorry. Was that who I saw you with? The young woman.'

'Yes, Elly. She persuaded me to come. Are you with anyone?'

'No. It's just me. It always has been. I never married, never had children, but all in all, I've had a good life: how could it have been any worse? It was a time like no other, wasn't it? Some things remain ingrained, forever. Like an incurable disease.'

Around them, people sit at tables and eat food from the buffet. Rosa catches sight of Elly making her way along the tables, filling two plates with food. Her appetite has deserted her.

'I envied you Rosa Koumeris.' Josefina's face hardens and Rosa's name spills from her mouth as if laced with poison. 'But most of all, what stirred in me, was, I hated you.' Josefina looks across the space between them, her face expressionless apart from the heat that grew in her cheeks, and for a moment, Rosa feels struck by an invisible force, quelling the sensation of suddenly wanting to rise to her feet. Josefina turns and shuffles away. Her slight frame, for once, seems towering, leaving Rosa unusually insecure, her nerves unsettled.

'Here we are, Grandma. I've got a selection of sandwiches. I wasn't sure what you'd like, so I went for a full sweep.' Elly places the plate on the table and sits opposite Rosa. 'They'll be coming round with coffee and tea as well.' Elly looks at Rosa and her smile falls from her face. 'Are you all right, Grandma? You look like you've seen a ghost.'

CHAPTER NINE

HER STORY

They are sitting outside Mikro café with its stylish terraces among a mixture of young people, smoking and drinking coffee, an older couple enjoying a light meal and a young woman, cradling her sleeping baby with one arm, and with the other, holding a book that she is reading.

'You look tired,' Elly says, while sipping her coffee.

'It's been a long day. A different kind of day, for many reasons.'

'We could eat in the hotel if you'd prefer. We don't have to go out for dinner tonight.'

'It would seem such a waste not to go out. After all, we're leaving tomorrow,' Rosa sighs. 'There's so much I would like to have seen, but these old bones restrict me in a way my mind never has. I would like to have shown you, Corfu. The town has always had its own character, but there is so much more to see. The island was beautiful. It still is, I suspect, but it will undoubtedly have changed. The town looks much the same, even after all these years. Although the area where we stayed, I was told our apartment was not there anymore. Nor is the synagogue. There used to be four, you know, now there is only one left.'

'We can still go and look. It can't be far.'

'It's not. In fact, it's virtually around the corner.'

'It would have been nice to have stayed a few days longer. I should have thought about that. Imagine coming all this way just for two days. I could have hired a car and taken you around the island.'

'I would have liked that.'

'After the ceremony, when we were at the lunch, did you see anyone you knew? I saw you talking to someone, a woman.'

'Her name is Josefina.'

'That must have been nice, seeing someone you haven't seen since you were…'

'It was a shock.'

'Oh, I see. A good shock then? She seemed a nice woman,' Elly says, fishing with bait.

'The last time I saw her was just before the deportations.'

'She was one of the few that survived Auschwitz, then.'

'Apparently so. She told me she returned to Corfu but later made her home in Israel. She was invited to the ceremony, just like me.'

'You sound like that was a surprise to you.'

'We were forced to make choices… impossible choices.'

'I can't imagine how that must have been. The psychological trauma alone… well, how can that be put into words?'

Rosa pulls her handbag close to her.

'It has been a difficult time for you, Grandma. You've been quiet most of the day. To be fair, I was worried about how you'd react to today. It can't have been easy, finally being back and given the reason why.'

'There was a tailor just over there where the fruit shop is. He had a good reputation. I remember my father being measured for a suit for my brother's bar mitzvah and next to the tailor was a baker. I was sent by my mother to get bread most mornings. We lived not far from here. I wasn't sure how I would feel coming back, and I was scared of that. But now that I'm here, I'm ready to see my home.'

Elly must concentrate and slow her pace to keep walking by Rosa's side. She is grateful for the walking stick Rosa leans heavily on. Elly is sure Rosa is not as steady on her feet as she used to be, even a few weeks ago, and since then, she has slowed considerably when walking.

'I can remember everything,' Rosa is saying. 'It's like watching a film. I can still recall the smells. In the mornings, the air was heavy with the aroma of freshly baked bread. The butcher always had carcasses hanging outside, a feast for flies in the summer and goodness knows what else. Then there were the fruit stalls that always seemed to blossom in colour, and vegetables of every variety. A woman walked the streets with a cart. I can't remember what she sold. Bread, that was it. She walked around the lanes and narrow streets selling bread. The cafes bustled with conversations, people met over a coffee or a drink and ate cakes and enjoyed what the menus offered. There were several hotels, too. We had a good life. It was hard at times. There wasn't always enough money, but we managed. My father owned a cafe with his brother, my uncle, who emigrated to America before the war. In the same street, there was a cheese shop, the barber's and a handmade hat store.

'Even when the Italians invaded, they saw us as Greeks. To them, it didn't matter that we were Jewish. On the whole, they were friendly and even civilised. They ate at our cafes and restaurants and drank at our bars. They laughed a lot and sang when they were drunk.

'The heart of the Jewish district was almost completely destroyed by the German bombardment and when they invaded, life would never be the same again. Everything changed. I'll never forget the feeling of terror that seized us.'

Rosa gazes at the people filing the narrow street. Her eyes widen. 'It's so hard to imagine a time like that, especially today. Everything is normal. People are eating and enjoying each other's company. The small streets are full of locals, young and old, families and tourists. There are shops, cafes, restaurants, people taking photographs, others glued to their phones. It feels so normal.'

Elly removes her sunglasses and surveys the people around her. 'As it should be. Imagine a world if everything stood still. What's important is that in the present, the past is not forgotten.'

Eventually, Rosa announces, 'We're here. This is where I lived.'

Elly's expression sinks. She didn't know what to expect, but it was not this.

Rosa is quiet now as she surveys the dilapidated and crumbling buildings. An eruption of weeds colonises the windows that protrude into the daylight where once glass protected the occupants who lived inside.

These are shells of buildings, an affront to the memory of the once prosperous and proud community. Every corner, every doorway and narrow lane holds a memory, personal stories. It is a place that moulded Rosa into the person she grew up to be.

Rosa stares around her and shakes her head. 'There's nothing left of the building we lived in. It was home to many families. I even remember their names, Battinous and Giannoukakis, Constantinis and Andras, just a few of the families that lived here. How can they have let it become so rundown? Where is the respect?'

'What was it like?' Elly asks. 'The buildings are so close together; you were almost living on top of each other.'

A sudden memory makes Rosa smile with affection. 'Everyone was your auntie and uncle, even though they weren't related to you. It was full of children playing and laughing, even crying when knees were bruised or grazed.

'Everyone knew each other. It was a thriving community. I can still see them all, and I can still hear them. Every voice in my head is accompanied by memories that have never faded.

'It was here we celebrated our festivals, keeping our traditions alive and passing them on to the next generation. Everyone worked hard and tried to make a good living. We had lived and prospered in Corfu since the twelfth century. We were as Greek as those that went to pray in their churches to the same God we did.'

Rosa's drawn and tired appearance accentuates the lines on her face. 'There's so much of the town that remains similar. Whole streets and buildings are still as they were when I was here as a young woman, but it feels, not only did the Nazis erase us from Greece, but there also doesn't seem to be any attempt to make any permanence that so many Jews lived and worked here. Our homes and our synagogues were reduced to rubble. I even heard the Germans used one of the synagogues as a stable for their horses.

'I've spent my whole life running from this place. Why would I do that, Elly? The guilt is crippling at times. I've lived a full life and raised a family. So many of my friends, relations and neighbours were murdered, extinguished. Everything they owned, every material possession gone. There is no trace that they ever existed. Yet here I am and because of what I did all those years ago, you Elly, are able to stand here with me, because I did not suffer that fate. Some good has come out of it. Life has continued. I had children, and they too had their own children and life continues to prevail with all its beauty and ugliness, with all its joy and pain, as it should be. Grief is the price of love, and that's the other side we have to pay.

'I'm tired of running. I'm exhausted with the guilt. I know now I was always going to return. It has just taken me a lifetime to realise it.'

They eat their evening meal outside in M Theotoki Square with its paved terraces, fountain and Catholic Cathedral. Elly has imagined the younger Rosa living and working among the narrow alleys and cobble streets in a world far removed from her own. She has realised Rosa would have been exactly her age during the German occupation. She is also aware Rosa hasn't revealed any personal detail or experience. Elly is mindful the infrastructure of the tightly compact town has changed little since Rosa was last here and she can sense the magnitude of this in Rosa's demeanour. She knows Rosa is reliving the events of that time and although she has not given much away, Elly is reluctant to push the issue.

'More wine, Grandma?'

'Not for me. One is enough these days. I think I'll just stick with water.'

Elly fills her own glass, and taking a sip, she looks around the square. Above them, several shutters are open to small balconies where the interior of the apartments is visible in shaded light.

'This is such a lovely spot. Do you think those are people's homes or are they rented out to holiday makers?'

'I wouldn't know. They would have been apartments built for families. In my day, there were a few hotels that only those with money could afford. It's different now, of course.'

'I wish we didn't have to leave tomorrow.'

'You should come back in the summer when it's hotter with your friends.'

'I might just do that. A week would be great, or even two.'

Rosa smiles with sudden affection. 'It sounds like a good plan.'

Elly glances at her watch. 'We're getting picked up at nine in the morning. We'd better get back to the hotel.'

'I'm packed already. I've just got my make-up and toothbrush to put in the case.'

'I wish I was as organised as you. I'll have to do mine when we get back to the hotel.'

Rosa looks around her. She remembers it all vividly. It is now beginning to make sense. She has lived far too long in the shadow of the past. A past she now must exorcise. And how is she to do this? The answer has been with her all along. It is sitting in front of her.

When they return to the hotel, Rosa invites Elly to her room. When they're seated, Rosa feels excited but also apprehensive about disclosing things she will find difficult to articulate. A thread of grief will be stitched into her words, and like a snake's venomous bite, parts will be painful, but there is also the beginning of a life that was shared in love and communion.

It is time to share her story. She does not want it to die with her. It is part of the fabric of her past, but it also needs to be known when she is gone. It needs to be a living presence in her family's present and where better to start than with her family's future... Elly.

Without her story, Rosa wouldn't be the person she is today. It is the embodiment of the unthinkable, existing in the face of evil. It is the story of family, of community, of courage and of dreadful choices, and importantly, it is her story, but much more...

CHAPTER TEN

EVERYTHING HAS CHANGED

Corfu 1943

The street below was awakening into life as Rosa peered from the second-floor window and smiled as she saw Sophia filling stalls with onions, carrots and potatoes, in the shop opposite her father's cafe where the first customers of the day sat outside drinking their morning coffee.

'Are you going to spend the entire morning looking out of that window? Your breakfast is getting cold, and your father will be expecting you downstairs.'

Rosa could hear the irritation in her mother's voice. 'I'm coming,' Rosa replied as she turned from the window.

After breakfast, and once she'd helped her mother wash and put away the dishes, Rosa descended the flight of stairs that led from the apartment to her family's cafe.

Salamo Matsas strode into the cafe with a tray of empty

cups and saucers and welcomed his daughter with a warm smile. 'There you are, Rosa. One Metrios and one Glykos for…'

'Yes, I know. It's the same every morning.'

'Just as well. It keeps the food on our table. I've heard many people talking about cutbacks. Look at Sophia's stall and her shop. She only has half the produce she used to sell. The Germans are not like the Italians, they want everything for themselves. Our supply of coffee will run out soon. In the villages, they are making coffee by roasting and boiling chicory and dandelion.'

Rosa inhales the rich, dark coffee she has just poured into a cup. 'That sounds horrible. Why would you want to drink something like that?'

Salamo's eyes clouded with sadness. 'Because that's all they have. They're desperate. It's already happening here.'

Rosa knew her father was right. She was aware how scarce certain foods had become and that the shelves in the shops were mostly empty these days.

Salamo sighed. 'Just yesterday, Minos the tailor, told me he can no longer buy fabrics and merchandise for making suits and clothes. There are no longer supplies coming from Athens. The shops he relied on have all closed.'

Rosa frowned. 'That's terrible.'

She had sensed for herself a profound unease among her friends and the town's people, and like most, she knew the Germans were a very different proposition to the defeated Italians who had previously occupied Corfu.

Still embroiled with such thoughts, Rosa deposited the two coffees with a forceful clunk on the table where the two regular customers sat. She apologised and wiped the small spillage of coffee from the tablecloth, dreading the prospect that her father had been watching her. To her relief, the seconds passed without a reprimand.

After a while, her young brother appeared in the cafe dressed for school, a satchel slung over his shoulder and his hair coaxed into a side parting. There were ten years between them. Andras was a late child, a result of Yvette, her mother, longing for another child when her second born died of tuberculosis.

Rosa glanced over to where her father stood behind the counter. 'I'm just taking Andras to school.'

She held her brother's hand, much to his disapproving looks, as they moved through the narrow lanes, and above them, lines of washing coloured the sliver of blue sky between the shutter clad tenements. They rounded a corner and entered a square. Immediately, Rosa heard the guttural shout of a German soldier, followed by a terrifying scream. Her eyes widened in shock. A man cowered at the soldier's feet, one eye swelling and Rosa glimpsed blood trailing down the man's cheekbone. The soldier raised the butt of his rifle and plunged it into the man's side, who instinctively pulled his knees to his chest and covered his head with his hands.

Rosa yanked on Andras' hand and caught sight of the man's eyes glazed in fear, and the shock that filled her sparked panic in Rosa. Andras was asking innocently why the soldier was hurting the man lying on the ground. On lookers stand and watch in astonishment, flinching with fear at the sound of another blow striking bone. Appalled, Rosa hurried across the square. She pulled Andras into her thigh, to shield him from the horror they were witnesses to.

As she watched Andras enter the small school building, Rosa suddenly realised she was shaking, numbed and in shock.

Rosa had been sitting in her father's cafe nursing a glass of water, her hazel eyes clouded in disbelief. 'I don't understand how this can happen. Even when they saw Andras, it did not stop them. They continued to beat the man. What could he have done to deserve such a beating and in broad daylight, with people looking on and…'

'Shh, try to drink some water.' Salamo urged Rosa, trying to stem the flow of words from his daughter's lips.

'Poor, Andras. I was in two minds about sending him to school, but what would be the point of him returning home? I thought I should keep everything as normal as possible, even though it wasn't. Did I do the right thing, Patera? Should I have brought Andras home?'

Salamo rested his hand on his daughter's head, and it helped to stem the flow of her thoughts. 'It was the right thing to do. He's too young to understand what is going on. His youthfulness is a defence against what the war has done to our country. His ignorance is a blessing.'

Rosa looked up at her father and Salamo could see worry shadow her hazel eyes.

'This man you saw, he must have committed a crime that was serious to have warranted such a reaction from the soldiers.' Salamo's quiet air of assurance made his words sound convincing, even though his blood chilled in his veins.

'Do you think so, Patera?'

'I'm sure of it. Go upstairs and help your mother. I can manage the cafe on my own for the rest of the day.'

'I'm fine, Patera. I can still work.'

'I'm sure you can. But you might feel worse as the day goes on. Shock tends to creep up on you. Your mother is making soup. You can help with chopping the vegetables.'

'That won't take long. We only have garlic, potato, and onion.'

'It will be made with the best ingredient of all.'

Rosa's brow ceased. 'And what would that be?'

Salamo smiled. 'It will be made with love, of course.'

When Andras returned from school, there was no mention of the beating in the square. That evening, they ate the soup with challah bread and potato Latkes. And, although Andras was uncharacteristically quiet, Salamo did not broach the matter.

As the table was being cleared, there was a knock at the door.

'Who can that be at this time of night?' Yvette asked.

Salamo laid his ear to the door. 'Who is it?'

'It is me, Lazaros.'

Salamo felt a surge of relief. 'It's late. Why are you calling at this time?' He turned the key in the lock and opened the door. 'My God! What has happened to you? Come in Lazaros.'

Lazaros shuffled into the apartment, clenching the collar of his coat with bloodstained fingers.

Rosa stared white faced and almost dropped the plate she was drying. She recognised the man's sallow face as that of the poor wretched soul beaten in the square. His eye swollen and closed, his face bruised purple and crimson. Salamo pulled out a chair and Lazaros eased himself into it. As he did, he grunted in pain.

'Forgive the intrusion, Salamo. I know it's late.'

'Nonsense, you're welcome in my home anytime. What has happened to you? Have you been robbed?'

Lazaros shook his head slowly. 'I wish that's all it was. This was the work of the Germans.'

Salamo glanced at Rosa and, seeing his daughter's wide

eyes, he knew Lazaros was the man in the square. 'Would you like a drink?'

Lazaros raised his hand.

'Water perhaps?'

'Water...yes some water.'

Yvette handed Lazaros a glass of water and he drank it thirstily and wiped his mouth with the back of his hand.

'Thank you.'

'Have you seen a doctor?'

'Later, perhaps.'

'You are in pain and your face...'

'A few broken ribs, I suspect. Nothing that won't heal with time.'

'Why has this happened?'

'Because I am the only Jewish lawyer, I was asked to make a directory of names, ages, occupation and addresses of all the Jews living in the town and, also a list of real estate. They also wanted other inventories and catalogues. I told them I did not have the means to do such a thing, it would take several people to undertake such a task. Because I am a lawyer and have two employees, they gave me ten days to hand over the information. This is the result of my initial refusal. Then they forced me to look at the sun without turning my head and when it became impossible to do so and I closed my eyes, they struck me with the butt of their rifles. If I fail to hand over the required information, I will be shot.'

Yvette covered her gaping mouth with her hand.

'What will you do? Surely, you can make a deal with them. Surely, everything is subject to negotiation.'

'These are not Jews, Salamo. They do not know our ways. These are Germans.'

'Then we must do as they say in order to protect our families and our businesses.'

'There's a boat leaving tonight for Athens. I will be on it. I have a cousin who lives there. It has all been arranged with the assistance of a lot of money on my part. My cousin has friends in the Athens Greek Police. They will supply us both with new identity cards. I will stay with him until this can be arranged and then together, we will travel by bus to Euboea with permission from the police to leave Athens so that we can pass through the German checkpoints and then by boat, where many are making the crossing, I will be in Turkey soon and God willing, safe.

'My cousin has told me that in Athens, things are getting worse, as they are all over Greece, but especially for Jews. They have to register and report every second day for registration or be shot, and there is a curfew, no Jew can walk the streets at night. The Germans have pillaged houses and thrown furniture into the streets. The need to cross the Aegean and reach the safety of Turkey is getting stronger by the day, and as more Jews take that option, it's getting more expensive to charter boats. I have to take my chance now. I might die trying, but if I stay, I'll be signing my death certificate, anyway.'

'This is awful Lazaros.'

'I don't have time to say goodbye to anyone. I'm leaving my home, friends, and my business.'

He reached into his jacket and pulled out an envelope. 'I need to ask you a favour, Salamo. There's no other person I would trust. It pains me greatly that because of what I have chosen to do, Isaak and Jacob, my employees, will no longer have work. Give them this envelope first thing tomorrow. There is enough money in it to see them for two months. By that time, I hope they will have found jobs.'

Lazaros placed the envelope on the table. 'There will be questions asked about my disappearance. I'm well aware that the Germans will ransack my office when it's known that I've left. I have one more ask of you, Salamo.'

Salamo placed his hand on Lazaros's shoulder. He smiled weakly. 'Anything, my friend.'

'I have placed in my safe documents that will be of interest to the Germans. It has the names of all my clients and their financial interests. In the envelope, there are instructions for Isaac and Jacob. They will know what to do.'

'Don't worry, it will be done.'

'My only worry is that Isaac and Jacob will be interrogated. I could not live with myself if anything was to happen to them because of what I have done.'

Salamo squeezed Lazaros's shoulder. 'You have no choice. You are doing the right thing.'

Lazaros tried to stand, but faltered. Salamo took his friend's weight and, grasping him around the waist, helped him to the door.

'God be with you,' Salamo said with a heavy heart.

Lazaros smiled wryly. 'I think I might need more than his company, but thank you all the same.'

That night, Rosa lay in her bed, staring at the ceiling. Even though the air was warm, she shivered under the sheet. It had felt like a dream, but it was as real as the blood pounding in her ears. She recalled her father's face drawn with anguish, wearied and exhausted and her mother fluttering around the apartment, her nerves on edge.

As a wave of nausea burnt her throat, Rosa realised with horrible clarity their lives had changed.

CHAPTER ELEVEN

INQUISITION

'I saw you with a young man. Who is he? I didn't recognise him.' Salamo's face looked stern.

Rosa is quiet for a moment. 'His name is Alvertos.'

'Who is his father?'

'You won't know him.'

'Why not? I know everyone. Even if they go to the other synagogues. If I don't know him by name, I'll know him by face.'

'You won't. His father is dead.'

'His mother then.'

'Why all the questions? I'm a grown woman.'

'Where does he live? What street?'

'You are being absurd and stupid.'

Salamo stared at her as if she'd thrown a knife at him. 'I'm only trying to protect you. If it is serious, then I want to meet this young man.'

'He is not the first man I have had relations with.'

'No, he is not and see how that one turned out.'

'I can make my own choices. I don't have to seek your approval for everything I do.'

'That's enough, Rosa. I know what these boys are like, what they are after.'

'He's not like that.'

'Maybe not to begin with, but he will. Believe me, I know.'

'He's not like that. He respects me for who I am. He loves me.'

'Love! What does he know of love?'

'You are being impossible.' Rosa turned away from him.

'Impossible! I only want what is best for you.'

'I'm a grown woman. I'm not a child. You would think he had asked me to marry him.'

'What synagogue does he go to? … I've never seen him.'

'No, you won't have seen him. In fact, you won't see him pray in the synagogue.'

"He doesn't go to the synagogue?' Salamo shakes his head. 'I knew it. How can you associate with such a person?'

'He doesn't go to the synagogue because if he prays, which I don't know if he does, but if he did, it would be in a church.'

CHAPTER TWELVE

A LESSON

'You said that to him?' Alvertos couldn't believe what he was hearing.

'I did.'

'And what did he say? How did he react?'

'As I expected.'

Alvertos frowned. 'He told you to never see me again.'

'Which, since I'm standing here talking to you, I ignored.'

He brushed her hand with his. 'I'm glad you did.'

'Why should it matter that I'm Jewish and you're not? We believe in the same God.'

'I think it's more complicated than that.'

'Then it shouldn't be.' She tugged at her sleeve. 'We are all born from a womb. It shouldn't matter to him. It's my happiness that should matter.'

'I'm sure he wants you to be happy. Every father wants that.'

'Then he has a funny way of showing it.'

'The important thing is that you're here with me.'

She held his gaze, and he could see a question forming in her eyes. 'Would your mother act like my father?'

'She…she does not believe religion defines a person. Look at the Germans and before them the Italians. They are Christians, just like the majority of Greeks, but that did not stop them from invading and killing us. My mother prays to the icons and attends church, but to her, you would have just as much right to pray in the synagogue and read from the Torah. She would not think anything less of you.'

'I would like to meet her. She sounds nice.'

He smiled at her. 'Why don't you? We've been seeing each other for months now. It's about time I introduced you to her.'

Rosa's eyes lifted in surprise. 'I'm not sure.'

'But you just said you'd like to meet her.'

Her expression grew serious. 'I know, but saying and then doing are two completely different things.'

'She won't bite, well… maybe just a little nip.'

'You're making a fool of me.'

He leaned closer to her face and kissed her full on the mouth. Reluctantly, he tore himself from her lips. 'Let's go now. I want her to see how beautiful you are.'

'Stop it. Now I know you're making a fool of me.'

'Never, I'd never do that Rosa. In fact, I've never been surer of this. I've never felt this way about anyone. I love you, Rosa. I want to spend the rest of my life with you. There, I've said it. It's in the open now.'

She was silent for a few moments. Mesmerised by his words, that enveloped in a warm embrace. In that moment, she knew what it felt like to be loved and she didn't want it to end. Then, to Alvertos' relief, she lifted her hand to his face and her touch melted the tightening panic from his throat.

Visibly relieved, Alvertos smiled. 'For a second, I thought I'd said too much, and I was the one being the fool.'

Just then, a group of German soldiers disembarked from a truck across from where they sat. The soldiers were hot and sweating, their uniforms caked in dust. They were fresh faced and young, not much older than Rosa herself. She could feel Alvertos' gaze slide from her as one soldier laughed and ripped the moment from them.

Alvertos shifted in his seat. 'Look at them. They think they can do anything. They hide behind their guns, without them how brave would they feel. They think they can just roll into Greece and take anything they want, kill who they want. They are pieces of shit.'

'Alvertos. Watch what you're saying.'

'They can't hear me.' Alvertos curled his hand into a fist, his knuckles white against the skin. 'What I'd give to have one of them in a room, just me and him, without his gun.'

'They're coming this way. Keep your voice down.'

'They can't speak Greek.'

'You don't know that.'

As they neared, Rosa glanced at them. One of the Germans lit a cigarette. He grinned when he saw Rosa. Rosa caught sight of his rifle slung over his shoulder. She knew they were a patrol returning from hours in the sun, further inland towards the hills and small villages. Her heart thumped at the thought of the terror they would have brought to the young, the old and the men and women going about their ordinary daily lives, or what that had now become.

The cafe was almost full and as the soldiers approached, some customers vacated their seats, preferring to leave before forcefully made to do so. When the German with the cigarette reached their table, he gestured for Alvertos to stand and give up his chair. Rosa held her breath, her blood chilled in her veins.

Alvertos reached for his cup, deliberately, and slowly he raised it to his lips. What was he doing? Rosa shook her head, silently pleading with him. She knew he was making a point, but at what cost?

The soldier spat at Alvertos in German and even before Alvertos could lay his cup back on the table, the butt of the soldier's rifle collided with his head, sending Alvertos tumbling from his chair. Before he had even hit the ground, a jackboot thudded into his chest. Rosa screamed, and it was enough to force the other Germans to intervene and cause a halt to the beating. The German was breathing heavily like a panting dog. He scowled at Alvertos and took a long victorious drag on his cigarette clamped between his teeth the whole time as he moved to another table.

Rosa hunched beside Alvertos. A trail of blood oozing from a gash on his cheekbone. 'Oh my God, you're bleeding. Are you all right?'

Alvertos grunted and then coughed. He screwed his eyes in pain. 'I'll live.'

Rosa's concern evaporated. 'You fool. What were you thinking? I can't believe you did that.'

'Something came over me. I don't know what. I'm sorry Rosa.'

Like a newborn lamb, Alvertos struggled to his feet.

A wave of laughter erupted from the soldiers, who were now sitting at a hastily vacated table.

'Don't you dare turn around and look at them,' she warned him.

Alvertos clutched his chest with a hand. 'I feel like I've been trampled by a horse.'

'That would have been the lesser of the two. We need to get you home. You are going to have to see a doctor for that cut.' Rosa swiped a napkin from the table and attempted to wipe the flow of blood from Alvertos's wound. 'It's deep. You'll need stitches.'

'This wasn't the introduction to my mother I had anticipated for you.'

'My knees are shaking.' Her voice was almost a sob.

'In relief?'

'No,' Rosa corrected him. 'At the thought of seeing your mother.'

CHAPTER THIRTEEN
MELINA

Alvertos pushed open a weathered wooden door and Rosa followed him into the modestly spaced apartment, her pulse fluttering with nerves at meeting Alvertos' mother and also with worry over his cut that had now thankfully stopped bleeding. The shutters were not fully open, but left at an angle, just enough to allow sunlight to cast dappled patterns on the hardwood floor and highlight the imperfections of dark wooden furnishing that sat under a high stuccoed ceiling.

Rosa observed a radio, resembling her father's, on top of a mahogany side table and she pondered if someone had adjusted it to receive the BBC broadcasts, which her father would listen to nightly as a routine he had adopted.

The kitchen, unlike her own, was larger than Rosa had anticipated. Polished copper pots hung from a row of hooks above an impressive range where the most mouthwatering aromas floated infused with an assortment of herbs that lined the wall in glass containers.

Hearing footsteps, Alvertos' mother turned from the

kitchen sink and faced them. Her mouth fell open when she saw Alvertos' bloodstained shirt and face. 'What has happened to you?'

'I fell,' Alvertos blurted out sheepishly.

'After a German soldier hit you with his gun,' Rosa reminded him.

She rushed over to them. 'Why would he do such a thing?'

'I pissed him off. It doesn't take much for them to show their hatred for us.'

'Alvertos! He could have killed you.'

'He wanted my seat, and I was making a point.'

'Well, from where I'm standing, it looks like he was making a point too, and his was the most successful of the two.'

'I wasn't going to let him sit next to Rosa.'

She turned to Rosa. 'And I presume this is Rosa?'

'I am, Mrs Koumeris.'

She waved a hand. 'Please, call me Melina. If my son had any manners, which he should have, because he has been taught them, he would have introduced us.'

Alvertos looked hurt. 'I'll just stand here bleeding.'

Melina gave a little shrug. 'You can walk and talk. I think you'll live.'

Melina filled a basin with water and, wetting a cloth, she wiped the blood from Alvertos' face. He pulled away and winced under his breath.

Seeing that her son was not in any danger of bleeding to death, Melina smiled for the first time. 'It has stopped bleeding, thankfully. You will have a nasty bruise, but I don't think you will need stitches, which is a good thing really, as I've used the last of the gut wire.' She dropped the cloth into the water. 'Please sit, Rosa. I'll make us all a coffee, then Alvertos, you can introduce me properly.'

Rosa and Alvertos sat at the wooden table, and she glided her hand over its worn smooth surface. She could see stocked cabinets with canned goods, dried herbs, and jars of home-made preserves.

As Alvertos nursed his pride, Melina boiled water in a pot over a gas stove. The coffee made, she brought to the table three slices of Portokalopita - orange cake.

'I hope you like cake. I made it myself. I could only get three eggs, it should really have four eggs, but since it's the first cake I've been able to make in months, it's a little sacrifice. It still tastes sweet. That's all that matters.'

'It looks delicious.'

'Please, take some. Don't wait to be asked.'

Taking a slice, Rosa took a conservative mouthful, and savouring its sweet taste, with a fingertip, she consciously wiped crumbs from the side of her mouth.

Melina sighed. 'It's a luxury I know, but even in times like these, now and again, if we can, we should treat ourselves.'

'I agree, especially when it tastes so nice. The syrup just sets it off.'

'Thank you.' Melina settled in her chair. 'So, Rosa, where do you stay?'

'In Velissariou Street. We live above my father's cafe.'

'I know it well. I have a friend who lives not far from there. You might know her. Maria Finneta, her husband, owned the bakery. It was hit by a German bomb. It was dreadful. He was killed. That area suffered a lot of damage.'

'It did. We were lucky, others weren't.'

'It was an awful time. Just the start of things to come.

The Italians were civilised in comparison to the Germans, although it didn't always feel like that.'

Alvertos sniffed. 'An occupier is an occupier. One is no better than the other.'

'Maybe so, but life was a lot easier when the Italians were around,' Melina said.

On the wall, Rosa noticed a photograph. The resemblance was striking. It was Alvertos' father, dressed in his best suit and beside him was a younger and beautiful Melina.

Melina saw Rosa looking at the photograph. 'Spiros and I didn't know it at the time, but I was pregnant with Alvertos.'

'You look so young…Oh! I didn't mean you look old now.'

Melina smiled indulgently. 'You don't have to apologise. I know what you mean. I was nineteen. We had only been married for six months when that photograph was taken. It's been six years now since he was taken from us.'

Rosa didn't know what to say. She wanted to know what caused Spiros' death but felt it was a too personal question to ask given she was a guest in Melina's house and the thought of offending her didn't bear thinking about.

To her surprise, Melina answered her thoughts.

'It was a tumour. There was nothing that could be done.'

Sometimes, a silent pause can be strained, uncomfortable even, but when Rosa saw Melina's eyes fall upon the image of Spiros, they radiated a love that mesmerised her.

'I've often wondered what he would have thought of what has become of Greece.' Alvertos said.

'I can tell you exactly how he would have felt. If it was

me that German wanted to sit beside, your father would have done exactly the same as you.'

Alvertos' eyes brimmed with an upwelling of emotion, and he drew in a breath.

Rosa glanced at her watch. 'I need to go. I'm expected in the cafe in ten minutes. It's the busiest time of the day.'

'Is business good?' Melina asked.

'It was before the war. Now we just get by. Most of the customers are regulars who have been drinking my father's coffee for years. He doesn't say as much, but I know he is worried how long it will remain open.'

'I used to have my own shop. I'm a seamstress. Alvertos' father was a tailor. We made clothes for both men and women. We were a good team and business thrived. Fabric is in such short supply and people can't afford the luxury of new clothes anymore. It is what it is. I can't change that.' Lines of sorrow creased her face. 'We're luckier than most. These days, people bring me their old clothes to patch and sew. With that money and what Alvertos earns, we get by most weeks. We're all in the same boat together, and at least we have the sanctuary of our homes, unlike some. Well then, here I am going on about my woes and in doing so, I'm going to make you late. You'd better get yourself off. It was lovely to meet you, Rosa. Now we have met, I'll expect to see a lot more of you.'

'You will, and thank you for the cake. It was delicious.'

Melina grinned. 'Just don't expect it on every visit.'

CHAPTER FOURTEEN

A QUESTION OF IDENTITY

Several days later, Rosa was tidying cups and saucers from a table outside her father's cafe when she heard a verbal commotion and rising panicked voices, where a flock of pigeons fluttered towards the mustard terraced buildings and the safety of the terracotta slate roofs. The few customers still sitting at tables risked unnerved glances.

Despite their protestations, two men were being led away from a doorway by German soldiers, and it wasn't until they emerged from the shadows and into the blistering sun that Rosa saw one soldier pull his revolver from its holster and strike one man. The unfortunate man's head snapped sideways and blood spattered the wall, like paint flicked from a brush. His legs gave way, and he crumpled onto the cobbled street. A soldier shrieked at him and hauled the man to his feet, his lips and chin covered in blood.

'What's going on?' Salamo emerged from inside the

cafe, wiping his hands on the white apron tied around his waist.

'German soldiers are taking two men away. And look, there's Greek police as well. They're involved too.'

It was then that Salamo's expression turned to stone. 'It's Lazaros' colleagues Jacob and Isaac. I recognise them from when I went to Lazaros's office and delivered the envelope he gave me.'

'What does this mean?'

Salamo ran a hand over his beard. 'I'm not sure, but it will have something to do with Lazaros' disappearance and the information in the envelope.'

Rosa took a deep breath. Did this implicate her father? Was it just a matter of time before the soldiers came for him, too? She could feel the foundations of her life shift from under her feet as a surge of fear ran through her veins. The war had invaded the most precious and safe space she'd known, and until now, until threatened, she'd taken it for granted... her family.

'What will they do to them?' she asked, and her father's silence only emphasised what she already knew.

Early that evening, she met Alvertos in their usual place just off Mitropoleos Square. He reached out and gently traced the curve of her hand before curling his fingers around hers. He suggested they go for a walk. The setting sun's lingering rays still warmed the air, and around them, sun bleached buildings basked in the soft glow of a golden light.

They walked down to the Port and then continued along the outskirts of the Old Town. Instinctively, Rosa turned her eyes over the calm waters of the Ionian towards the brooding and forbidding mountains of the mainland. A truck laden with German soldiers passed them. One soldier looked at her and Rosa drew in a breath. The sight of their guns brought back a vivid memory of the arrest of Jacob and Isaac just hours before. Her stomach churned at the thought of what had become of them, and she tightened her grip on Alvertos' hand.

Alvertos examined her face with a searching look. He had been absently telling her about his day and suddenly realised how subdued she'd become.

'You've been quiet.'

'Have I?'

'You're not your usual self, that's all. Is everything all right?'

'Something has happened.'

'What?'

She tried to curb the surge of her thoughts. What horrified her was the threat that now hung over her family. Did it implicate her father, too?

She explained about Lazaros' visit, his request of her father and the Germans asking for a list of names of every Jew who lived in the town.

'My father is involved. He warned Jacob and Isaac. He gave them the money. There is a safe in the office. Lazaros said that Isaac and Jacob would know what to do. What if the Germans have tortured them and they have given them my father's name?'

Alvertos put his arm around her. 'It's the list of names they're after, not your father.'

'His name will be on the list, and because of this, my mother, my brother and my name will be just as well on that list, as will everyone who is a Jew.'

The realisation soaked into Alvertos. 'They can't question every Jew in Corfu Town.'

'It's not about that. It's about controlling us through fear. In Athens, every Jew has to register, or face being shot. There's a curfew on the streets at night. Lazaros told my father these things before he left. There have been rumours that this will happen in Corfu, too. Some say it's only a matter of time. Each day, the Germans are tying the rope tighter around every Jew's neck. We do not feel safe in our own communities anymore. When I saw what happened to Isaac and Jacob today, it was the first time I really became frightened, not just for myself and my family, but for everyone.' Rosa's mouth sets in a grim line. 'I fear we have not seen the worst. This is only the beginning.'

'I don't know what to say.'

'Then don't say anything.' She lowered her gaze, tears welling in her eyes.

A soft breeze carried a hint of salt that fused with the unease about them. Suddenly, they were no longer two lovers suffused in their own private world, the outside world with its hate and fear had tried to tarnish that love with ideology and evil.

Alvertos stared out over the shimmering waters. His brow furrowed. 'I can't imagine what you must be going through.'

'No. I don't suppose you can. It's different for us now. We are living side by side as neighbours, but our war has dramatically changed. We are not just being occupied; we face a threat that only a few weeks ago was unthinkable. Because I'm a Jew, I'm beneath you, worthless. I'm nothing but an object to be vilified. I am a degenerate. I am not human. My life is worthless.'

Alvertos' mouth fell open. 'Why are you saying these things? That's not who you are. You are beautiful and intelligent. You are caring and gentle. In my eyes, you are perfect, and I love you.'

Rosa reached for his face and ran a finger softly down his cheek. 'I'm not talking about you. That is what I am when a German looks at me.'

'Because you're Jewish? It has never been a thing between us, and it never will.'

Rosa could sense his anger simmering. 'I know that.'

'What does this mean? What is going to happen?'

'I'm not sure. But we are being targeted, and it's not because we are Greek, it's because of what we are. It can only be a matter of time before they knock on every door.'

Alvertos shook his head slowly. 'Then it will only get worse. We have to do something.'

'Like what?'

He touched her arm. 'We have to find a way. I'll think of something.'

They entered a street where several German soldiers stood around a truck, smoking cigarettes.

'Bastards.' Alvertos hissed under his breath. His eyes burnt into them.

'Don't look at them like that,' Rosa demanded as her stomach churned.

'Why not? Anyway, I can't help it. How could they think of you in such a way?'

'Staring at them is not going to change that.'

Reluctantly, Alvertos averted his eyes. As they passed, he couldn't help one more look, and his eyes flicked over the soldiers, who either ignored them or weren't even aware of their presence.

The light fading and narrow streets emptying of potential custom, shop owners closed their shutters and cleared their stalls of the meagre stock they tried to scrape a living from. Rosa's mind wandered to her father. He would be closing up the cafe for the day. She thought of Isaac and Jacob and the fear that strained their faces. She hoped with all her heart they had come to no harm, but she knew such hope to be futile.

Her life was changing and even if she had no influence over what was to come, she needed to have some control of the direction it took.

'I've never been to a synagogue before. Have you ever been inside a church?' Alvertos asked, pulling Rosa from her thoughts.

'No. I've seen the outside of a lot of churches. How could I not? They're everywhere, but I've never been inside one.'

'I've always thought we knew everything about one another. We have shared everything, but there is a gap in that sharing, and it's the most important gap of all. I know nothing of you as a Jew. It is part of your identity. It defines who you are. Just as the Orthodox faith is embedded in who I am. You don't have to believe in something for it to be a part of your life. Even if I wanted to, I can't escape it.'

'I know what you mean. My mother and father have always practised their faith, and as a young child, my earliest memories are filled with the rituals, beliefs and traditions. I suppose it's what being a Jew is all about. Our religion defines who we are and what we are.'

'It has been the same for me, too. As I got older, I was free to make up my own mind about what I believed and what I did not believe. Even in rejection, there is still a stronghold. Call it identity, or whatever you want. It's like paint, untouched. It takes a long time to peel, but there is still the undercoat that remains visible, even if it fades over time, it's still present. That's how I feel when I think about religion. I don't know, it's hard to explain. I don't even know if I'm making sense.'

She caught his eye. 'It makes perfect sense to me.'

They walked further and when they came to a little square, Alvertos' eyes lit up. 'You see this church here? It is the church of Saint Nikolas. It's my local church. Mum still goes every Sunday and most weekdays and I... well, I've not been for a while, but I'd love to show you it if it's something you would like to see.'

Rosa nodded. 'I would. I would like that.'

He stands and lets Rosa walk through the opened doors.

'When you enter a church, there are a few customs you need to perform. Even though I haven't been inside a church for a long time, it would feel odd not doing it. It's that undercoat of paint that's to blame,' Alvertos smiled.

Just to their right stood a golden candle stand where long, thin white candles rooted in a layer of sand flickered in yellow light. Alvertos reached for a candle and hovered it above a lit one, where the wick crackled into a flame. He secured the candle into the sand and, turning to the icon of St. Nikolas, he bent forward, kissed the icon, and made the sign of the cross.

He turned to Rosa, who was gazing at this new version of Alvertos, this deeper part of him who she'd never seen before.

'It's an automatic response. A learnt ritual. It just feels right. It's an act of respect and veneration.'

Rosa took a step back and lifted her eyes to the Iconostasis, a wall of icons lit in silver light. She lifted her eyes to the ceiling and the vivid paintings, with their intense colours, looking down on her.

'It's like an art gallery,' she said, feeling a potent sense of awe, as her eyes filled with wonder, flicked from one figure to another. 'I wasn't expecting there to be so much colour, even in this muted light. It's dazzling me.'

For the first time that evening, Rosa's shoulders relaxed as the horror of the world that lay outside the walls of the small church melted and her fear and worry abated. 'Who are these people?'

'You really don't know who they are?' Alvertos said, and then he reminded himself, why would she? They are as unfamiliar to her as the figures in the Torah are to him.

'They are the icons of Christ, the Virgin Mary. St Peter and Paul…' He stopped. Rosa looked baffled.

'I have heard of this, Christ. He was a Jew.'

'He was,' Alvertos ventured awkwardly.

She continued, 'As was this Mary the virgin, and Peter and Paul.'

'All of Christ's followers were Jewish, as were his disciples, who were close to him.'

'Interesting. Christians worship a Jew, yet the Germans, who are Christian, despise us.'

'I know. When you put it like that, it makes little sense. It confuses me too.'

Sensing his unease, Rosa's mood switched, and she smiled at him. 'Your church is beautiful.'

'I'm glad you like it. My parents were married here, and this is where I was baptised. It's part of my family's history.'

'Then it is a special place.'

'I don't come here that often, not anymore. It holds a lot of memories for me, warm memories. When I stand here, I feel a sense of security, the same feeling I had when I was younger, when I came here with my family. I wanted to feel that again, but I wanted to feel it with you next to me.'

'And do you feel it?' Rosa asked him.

Alvertos nodded, and the confirmation in his smile pleased her.

Alvertos reached out and took her hand in his. 'I have an idea. You might not like it, in fact you won't, not at first, anyway. I'm not expecting an answer from you just now, but all I'm asking is that you think about it.'

'Think about what?'

'I'm not even sure how to go about it, but I know it can be done with the help of the right people.'

'What?'

'Changing your identity.'

Suddenly, the colour drained from her face. Rosa looked shocked. Her eyes flashed with disbelief. In that moment, Alvertos' enthusiasm bled from him, like blood from a cut.

'It's extreme, I know, but just think about it, Rosa,' he said, desperate to retrieve the situation.

'I don't have to think about it. It's the worst idea I have heard,' Rosa snapped.

'But you of all people know why I would suggest it.'

'I'm not ashamed of who I am, and I'll not deny my heritage, not for anyone,' Rosa said, her words searing with anger. Then, turning on her heels, infuriated with Alvertos, she left the muted interior of the church and disappeared into the cluster of buildings and the soft evening light.

CHAPTER FIFTEEN

A MIND OF HER OWN

The next few days passed in a blur. Rosa waited at the tables and said few words to her father or his customers as her anger bubbled inside her like lava. Her father's curiosity got the better of him as he observed her closely, noticing her disposition.

'Is everything all right, Rosa? Lately, you haven't been your usual self.'

With a clatter, Rosa dropped the pile of dirty dishes she was carrying into the sink. What should she say? Tell him the real reason. No, that was not an option. With the threat of arrest still hanging over her father, she could use that as a diversion. It wouldn't be a lie. It had hung over them all for days now. Her mother was ill with worry, and although her father had not alluded to it, she knew it preyed upon his mind, too.

'I'm worried, that's all.' She felt a pang of guilt, but it was also true. 'What will happen if the Germans come for you? Isaac and Jacob have not been seen since they were arrested.'

The set of his shoulders was tense as Salamo wiped his hands on his white apron. 'It's been hard for us all. But as each day passes, so does the threat that I'll be questioned. It doesn't change our daily lives. We have to try to do the best we can with the little that we have got. We're more fortunate than most. At the moment, I can still make a living. If the worst came to the worst, you and your brother wouldn't go without. There is enough money to see to that. Your mother and I have savings. We have to live each day at a time. That is what we must do. I can't worry about something that might not happen.'

'*If the worst came to the worst*. What does that mean?'

Salamo sighed. 'Truthfully, I don't know. It wasn't so bad when the Italians were here, was it? So far, the Germans have allowed us all to still run our businesses. If anything were to happen to me, then you, your brother and your mother would still have a roof over your heads and have food on the table every day. That will not change.'

'Maybe not, but it changed for your friend Lazaros and for Isaac and Jacob. The Germans are not like the Italians. Why do they want a list of names? Why do they want to know what people do for a living? And why are they interested in their financial affairs?'

Lazaros scratched his beard. 'Such things are normal in times like these.'

'Then why do they just want a list that is specific? What does that tell you?'

'It tells me that they want to know about the local economy, how many businesses, trades and occupations serve the community, which ones are prosperous and which ones are not. It serves their interests to know such things.'

'Do you really believe that? What if it was more sinister?'

Salamo took a deep breath. In that moment, Rosa couldn't tell if it was of exasperation, or of worry.

Salamo threw up his hands. 'What is the alternative?'

'Lazaros knew. He told you about the curfews in Athens, Jew's being forced to register. That is why he is not here anymore. He could see what was coming. The Germans are beating us up in our own streets, humiliating us, arresting us, and others are disappearing. It has changed. We are no longer safe in our own homes, not because we are Greeks, but because we are Jewish.'

Salamo rubbed his forehead. 'The British and Americans are gaining ground day by day. The Russians, too, are winning back territories that were once occupied by the Germans. Every day, the broadcasts coming from the BBC confirm this. The course of the war is changing. The Germans are suffering losses that will soon determine their defeat. I'm convinced it's only a matter of time.'

'My fear is we don't have time.'

'When we talk of such things at the synagogue, we all share the same opinion. What is happening on the mainland won't transpire on the islands. And even if it did, the most destructive storm will always pass.'

Rosa took a step back. She tried to curtail it, but her voice growled with anger. 'What do you know of what is happening elsewhere? If it wasn't for people like Lazaros and his cousin, we wouldn't know what was happening. You listen to the BBC broadcast every night. When have you heard them reporting such things? You haven't because they are complicit with their silence. You are not telling me this has not gone on unnoticed. If it's happening in Athens, it's happening in other Greek cities as well. Greece is no longer safe for Jews.'

She had never spoken to her father in this way before,

but she felt compelled to do so. It had been an uncomfortable discussion, and although her mind hesitated, she now knew Alvertos' suggestion was not only *her* only option, but it was also every Jew's.

That night, it was a Friday evening, and all over the houses and apartments of the Jewish quarter, Sabbath was being greeted. Salamo had just returned from the synagogue and Rosa's mother, Yvette, covered the dinner table in a white tablecloth. She placed two candlesticks and two braided loaves of bread on the table.

Salamo secured his kippah on his head and placed his hand gently on Andras' shoulder. 'Now Andras, tell me why we place two candlesticks on the table?'

Andras cleared his throat. 'The candlesticks symbolise the words *Zahor*, remember the Sabbath day to keep it holy and *Shamor*, observe the Sabbath and keep it holy.'

'Excellent, Andras. Now, why do we have two loaves of bread?'

'The bread is called Hallahs, and it represents the double portion of manna the Lord sent to the Jews on the Sabbath on their way across the Canaan desert.'

Salamo nodded approvingly and ruffled Andras' hair.

Together, both Rosa and Yvette lit the Sabbath candles and recited the prayer blessing for the day. Salamo performed the ritual of sanctification (Kiddush) of the Sabbath. He offered blessings over wine and the bread, which they would cut into pieces and eat with salt.

Due to the prohibition of lighting a fire and cooking on the Sabbath day, Yvette prepared Cholent, a stew of potatoes, beans, meat, fat, and spices earlier, and she kept it overnight in the oven.

During the meal, conversation between Rosa and Salamo was strained, and it didn't go unnoticed by Yvette.

'Could you pass me the bread, Rosa?' Yvette asked. She took the bread from Rosa and took a bite out of it. 'You haven't eaten much. Are you feeling unwell?'

'I'm fine. I'm not hungry, that's all.'

'You can't afford to not eat, and you should be thankful we have food on our table. There are lots of families struggling. We are fortunate we are not one of them.'

'Leave her, Yvette. She is not a child anymore. She is a grown woman with a mind of her own, it would seem.'

'And what is wrong with that? I can have my own opinions and ideas and I can express them to who I see fit and in what way I please.'

'You have shown that already. As long as you are under my roof, you will respect the ways of this household.'

'You mean, I'm expected not to question your judgement. I'm to become blind to what I see around me.'

'What is going on, Salamo?' Yvette demanded.

Salamo slammed his cup of wine down onto the table. 'I will not be spoken to like that in my own home, and especially not by you. Remember who I am. You are a daughter, and I am your father.'

'You have made that clear and what is expected of me, but you can't control what is going on outside this house. Not even you, nor your friends at the synagogue, can change what is happening.'

Yvette raised her eyebrows in surprise. 'Rosa, what are you talking about? Have you gone mad?'

'No, I've not gone mad. The world has.' She stood, and her chair fell backwards, crashing to the floor. She turned and headed for the door.

'Rosa, where are you going?' Yvette called after her and reached out to grab Rosa's arm, who pulled it away and slammed the door behind her.

'Leave her, Yvette.'

Yvette struggled to speak. 'Your daughter is leaving the house at the start of the Sabbath.'

Salamo was silent for a moment. 'Yes, I am aware of that. It would seem, she is telling us, she has a mind of her own.'

CHAPTER SIXTEEN

A CHANGE IN THE AIR

Rosa walked briskly through the empty streets. Behind the closed shutters, most families ate their evening meal to celebrate the start of the Sabbath. She rounded a corner, replaying in her head the argument with her father. Even if the Germans were like the Italians, which they undoubtably were not, it would still feel like she was a prisoner. Because of the occupation, the entire island feels like a prison. How can he not see that? There has been a definite change in the Germans' posturing towards the Jewish population. There is an arrogance about them. It was aways there, but something has changed. There has been a tangible shift. She had witnessed the beginning of the persecutions. She had seen this with her own eyes. It was now becoming a daily occurrence. Their lives were now filled with fear. People were being arrested; people were now disappearing. A feeling of sick dread clawed at the inside of her stomach.

Knowing what happened to his friend, Lazaros, and the action forced upon him, her father, of all people, had experienced the fear and dread their community was suffering. How could he be so blind to what was going on around him? And he was not the only one. There were others too, who are like her father in their belief that the war wouldn't last long and eventually force the Germans to abandon Greece and retreat to Germany.

As she left the Jewish district behind her, the narrow streets and lanes began to pulse with activity. Shops were still open, selling whatever was available, now that food, clothes, and anything of commerce were getting more difficult to come by. Even her father's customers had stopped complaining about the second-grade coffee he sold them.

Rosa felt the beginnings of a dull pain in her head. All she wanted now was to be with Alvertos. It had been days since they last saw each other. She had been angry with him then. Now, she was angry with her father. It seemed to her that lately she had enough anger in her to last a lifetime.

Soon, she was standing outside Alvertos' mother's apartment. She rapped on the door and waited. She pulled her fingers through her hair and straitened her dress. Should she apologise to him? She felt a twinge of guilt. As she waited, she traced her fingers along the grain of the door and flakes of paint fell from her fingertips.

When Alvertos opened the door and saw Rosa standing there, his eyes widened. 'Rosa.'

'Can I come in?'

'Of course.'

When Alvertos closed the door behind her, she turned to him and spoke without taking a breath. 'I'm sorry for the other day. It was unforgivable. I know you were only trying to help. I don't know what got into me.'

'Don't say sorry, Rosa. It was a stupid thing to ask you. You're here now and that's all that matters to me.'

She flung her arms around him and leaned into his chest. She promised herself she would keep her resolve, but she couldn't help her tears burning her eyes, nor the choking sob.

'Rosa, what is it? What has happened?' he asked in a state of puzzlement and panic.

'Don't worry, it's not me. There's nothing wrong with me.'

'Then what is it? You're worrying me, Rosa.'

She could hear the tension in his voice and in that moment, all she wanted was to feel safe. She longed to feel secure. Lifting her face to him, she kissed his mouth. His arms tightened around her, and she pressed her lips against his, the kiss becoming deeper, infused by a passion that burnt in her chest.

'Is your mother home?' her breath was hot on his lips.

He gasped, trying to find the words. 'She's visiting a friend.'

'Then we have time.'

'Time for what?'

She took Alvertos' hand and led him to the bedroom.

CHAPTER SEVENTEEN
RECONCILED

Rosa was sitting by the window while Alvertos was waiting on water boiling from a pot on the stove. After the distraction their love making provided, his concern returned and Rosa's silence on the matter only increased his brooding.

'We're running low on coffee now, that's if you can call it coffee. It looks like and tastes like black water. It'll taste nothing like your father's coffee.'

'He won't be serving it much longer.'

'Is it getting that bad?'

'Only his regular customers come. Those that have come for years. There are not enough of them to make ends meet. My parents are living off their savings. No matter what, they'll still have a roof over their heads. Dad was always good with his money. Some would say he was frugal, but when he bought the cafe, the apartment above it came with the sale. Seemingly, it was in a terrible state. It virtually cost him nothing. He said that when he saw it, even though every room needed a lot of work, he had the foresight to see what it could be... a family home.' She felt the twinge of guilty betrayal. 'I came here because of him. I needed to get out of that house and all I could think about was being with you.'

'What has happened?'

'He is blind to what is going on around him. Like us all, he is scared and worried too, but he thinks that in a couple of months the Germans will be driven out of Greece, and we have just to sit it out. He knows what is happening in places like Athens. His friend told him that Jews were being targeted. He knows all of this, yet he thinks it's more important that his authority in the house is taken as law and not to be questioned.'

'But what can he do, really? What can any of us do? At night, I've been going out with some friends of mine and we have been putting posters on the walls all over town.'

'I have seen them.'

Alvertos shrugged. 'It's not much, but it's active resistance. It lets the Germans know we will not just lie down to their occupation. It gives us a voice. Even if it means putting ourselves in danger for several nights, it has to be better than doing nothing.'

'Doing nothing won't get you caught. If the Germans find out what you're doing, I dread to think what would happen to you.'

'Nothing is going to happen to me. Anyway, I don't go out all the time with them.'

'If they get caught, they could name you too.'

'They wouldn't do that.'

'How do you know?'

'I just do.'

'Don't be foolish, Alvertos. Under interrogation, torture, even, someone would talk.'

'As quick as we put them up, the Germans take them down again.'

'So, they will be looking for those that are doing this. It's just a matter of time.' A spike of fear inched up the nape of Rosa's neck. 'I don't know what I'd do if something were to happen to you. You could get yourself killed. I've seen what they do to people in broad daylight. I saw what they did to my father's friend. Imagine what they would do to you behind closed doors.'

'I'm careful. We're all careful. Look, there's a printing press that we have access to. As long as we have ink and paper, we can be a thorn in the German side.'

'Just like I'm a thorn in my father's side.'

Alvertos sat beside her. 'You could never be a thorn, Rosa. To me, you're a rose and a beautiful one at that.'

She smiled tenderly. 'Be careful what you wish for. Even roses have thorns.'

He reached out and touched her face. 'See, nothing has happened. You don't prick my skin. In fact, instead of drawing blood, you make my blood rush in my veins whenever I touch you. You do know I love you, Rosa.'

His words closed around her heart, and she took his hand in hers and kissed it. 'I know it and every pore and every cell in my body feels it.'

He leaned into her and pressed his lips against hers. He placed his hand on her neck, and they parted breathlessly, astonished.

Outside, the light was fading. 'It's getting late. What will you do now?'

Rosa hesitated, then looked Alvertos in the eye. 'Go back home. What else can I do? My father is a good man, he just wants the best for us. By doing nothing, he thinks he is protecting us. And that's all a father can do.' She bit her lip and spoke through a knotted throat. 'He really believes that in time, things will go back to how they were before the war. I wish I could believe this. He is scared, like we all are, but fear clouds judgement, it stifles choice. But what can I do? What can we do as a community? Where would we go? All we know is our home, our street, our town, our island.'

CHAPTER EIGHTEEN

ERRIKOS

As the weeks wore on, life took on a rhythm of its own again, under an acknowledged but unsaid truce between Rosa and Salamo.

As she entered the house, she heard her father's voice, uncharacteristically hushed and whispery. He was sitting at the kitchen table and talking to another man whose back was to Rosa.

Salamo looked up in surprise and straightened in his chair. 'Rosa, I didn't hear you come in. We have a visitor. You remember your uncle Errikos?'

Errikos turned in his chair and smiled nervously through his thick beard. 'Yasas, Rosa, it's so good to see you.'

'Uncle Errikos!' It was then she noticed the small suitcase, his matted hair stuck to his scalp, the dishevelled appearance of his trousers and jacket and his dust ingrained shoes.

'How old are you now?'

'I'm nineteen.'

Errikos glanced an appraising eye over her. 'My, how time flies. It's scary. You were just a small girl when I last saw you.'

Salamo straightened his glasses. 'Errikos will be staying with us for a while.'

Errikos shifted in his chair. 'Just until I can find a place of my own. I don't want to be a burden.'

Rosa smiled. 'I doubt you will be that. You're family, after all.'

'That may be so, but I'll only stay as long as I need to. What I need now is to wash the weeks of dirt off me. My hair feels like it's stuck to my head.'

'You'll feel better when you're washed and have had something to eat. Then we can talk. You can tell me how you have ended up in Corfu.'

Just then, Yvette entered the room, drying her hands on a towel. 'Your bath is ready, Errikos.'

Errikos lowered his eyes to the floor. 'I've dreamed of lying in a hot bath for so long now, I thought I'd never feel clean again.'

Yvette rested her hand on his shoulder. 'Well, you get yourself washed while I make you something to eat. I don't suppose you've had a decent meal inside you for some time.'

'Don't go to any trouble, Yvette. Anything will do.'

'Nonsense, I don't just cook anything. Even though we don't have the luxury of buying quality food anymore, I still take a pride in my cooking.'

'I'm grateful and I can't thank you both enough for taking me in without knowing I was coming and at such short notice.'

'You would do the same for us,' Salamo reminded him.

'I've put trousers and a clean shirt out for you. You can't

wear those clothes again,' Yvette said, before disappearing into the kitchen.

Once Errikos had washed, they sat together and ate a simple but filling meal. Although his stomach demanded to be filled with food, Errikos took his time, indulging in every mouth full and savouring every flavour until he had cleaned his plate. He sat back in his chair and sighed in contentment.

'There's more left in the pot, several spoonfuls at least?' Rosa asked.

Errikos grinned. 'I never thought I'd say this, but I couldn't eat another mouthful. I think my stomach must have shrunk. I've had a bath and a lovely meal; it surely has been a day of firsts.'

'You looked tired, Errikos. You don't have to explain what has brought you here. It can wait until the morning.'

'No. It's better to tell you now and get everything out in the open. The problem is, I don't know where to start,' Errikos said gravely.

'Start at the beginning.' Salamo encouraged him.

Errikos scratched his head. 'The trouble is, I can't even remember the beginning. Let me think. As you know, I was living in Salonika with Katarina. We were living with her mother just until we could find a place of our own. It was difficult. I'd just returned from fighting in Albania and had left the army to find work to support Katarina, who was pregnant. I found work easily. Salonika is… or was a special place. Have you ever visited the city, Salamo?'

Salamo shakes his head. 'No. I've heard a lot of good things about it. Maybe one day I will walk its streets.'

Rosa knows it was important. Even the sound of the word and how Errikos delivered it radiated its stature.

'A Jewish city in Greece. Can you believe it? We all knew

it as the *mother of Israel*. Fifty thousand Jews called the city their home. At first, when the Germans arrived, there was no indication of what was to come. It didn't take long. The Germans abandoned their soft diplomacy and sent their henchmen to deport the fifty thousand Jews of Salonika.'

Rosa covered her mouth with a hand and Salamo looked away and swore under his breath.

'Let me see. It started in the first weeks the Germans entered the city and shut down Jewish newspapers. Before long, Jewish slogans were being posted all over the city, in tavernas, cafes and shops. Even by then, families were being thrown out of their homes to make way for the Germans. Then came the order to mobilise the male Jewish population under the pretext of civilian labour. We gathered at Eleftheria Square, ironically named *Freedom Square*.'

Errikos hesitated and narrowed his eyes. 'It was here that we were publicly humiliated. It was a circus, a human circus. A large crowd soon emerged and surrounded by armed guards. Hundreds of us. I've heard some say there were thousands. It was hard to tell. It looked like a sea of men, forced to stand in the blistering sun. We weren't allowed to wear hats, which added to our humiliation as it was a Saturday, the Sabbath. Some were forced to do exercises for hours, many collapsed exhausted in the heat while the crowd laughed and cheered. To add to the entertainment, the German soldiers kicked and beat us with their guns.

'After that time, we were forced to work, building roads and airfields. The conditions were terrible, a pittance of bread and cabbage soup were all we were given to eat each day. It didn't take long for many to get sunstroke and for the less fortunate poor souls, malaria. We suffered daily beatings. It wasn't until the Jewish community raised a vast sum of money to pay the German authorities that our nightmare ended. Seven thousand men returned home to Salonika, but it was not the end of our suffering. It was just the beginning.'

'That's awful. We had no idea,' Yvette said and wiped a tear from her eye.

'Oh, it gets worse.' Errikos took a drink of water and cleared his throat. 'Once you start to desecrate the dead, there is no turning back.'

Salamo's eyes widened in horror. 'What do you mean?'

'There was a large Jewish cemetery in Salonika that lay on the eastern side of the city, and it was here that the Nazis' disdain for the Jewish people was visibly demonstrated. They flattened it to the ground, taking away the tombstones to be used as material for roads and buildings.' Errikos' mouth tightened. 'When they had finally finished, the cemetery was erased, like toppling a stack of dominoes.

'Six thousand families were forced to leave their homes and move into the ghettos. Curfews were enforced, and we were instructed to wear the yellow star blazoned with the words *Jude* and *Evraios*.'

Salamo sighed. 'In German and Greek.'

'We were among the first wave of people sent to the Baron Hirsch camp. By that time Katrina was not well. She had a nasty cough that grew worse by the day. It was chaos. The streets thronged with families, women, men and children and the old clenching sacks of belongings to their chest. No one was allowed to bring suitcases with them. Soldiers and the police were everywhere, both German and Greek. They randomly chose victims for their beatings – old, young, disabled. It didn't matter. Almost ten thousand people were cramped into a district that normally housed two thousand people. There was squalor everywhere, on every street. Floodlights turned night into day, and we were watched by soldiers with machine guns stationed at the gates. We were forced to hand over all the money we had, our valuables and jewellery. If I could laugh, I would. How could we have been so naïve? The Germans gave us receipts and told us we could cash them in the new Jewish state we were being sent to in Poland.'

Errikos struggled to speak. He closed his eyes and wiped away a tear. 'Not long after that, Katrina was killed by a stray bullet in the street from a soldier's gun who shot at a group of men who had attacked a policeman.'

Yvette clutched her chest. 'Oh, Errikos. I'm so sorry. Poor Katrina.' She gasped; her eyes were full of pity.

'Days later I was in a crowded and putrid freight car with another seventy-six people that stank with the fetid reek of urine and excrement. There was no drinking water, and the lack of air felt suffocating. At one point, they stopped the train, and hundreds of hands thumped the wooden sides of the wagons. When the doors slid open, the sun was blinding. Under the threat of being shot, they forced people to hand over their valuables and money to the soldiers. A young man jumped from a wagon and ran towards the trees. The soldiers shot him in each leg and dragged him back to the wagons. They kneeled him in front of his parents and shot him in the head. I can't get the screams of his mother out of my mind. They're stuck there.'

Yvette clinched her hand over her mouth.

Errikos continued. 'In the panic that followed, there were several more shots fired and as some people fell from my wagon, I too stumbled and was thrown out. Somehow, among the panic and hysteria, I managed to crawl under the wagon and hide. When the train finally moved off, I lay as close to the ground as I could, wishing it to swallow me up. Then I could feel the sun on my back and the train was heading away from me. Getting smaller and smaller. I'd escaped my hellish confinement as had the young man whose dead body lay where he was shot.'

Errikos held his head in his hands. 'Under certain circumstances, we're no longer the person we think we are. To my shame, I searched the young man's body to see if he had any food on him.'

'Don't blame yourself, Errikos, you were desperate. Anyone in your position would have done the same. You went through a terrible ordeal,' Salamo said, trying to comfort his brother.

'He didn't deserve it. He was just a boy, really. I couldn't even bury him, so I carried him to some trees and covered him with branches. I tried to pray for him, but God had stopped listening to my prayers long before that day, so I told him I hoped he was at peace, wherever he was.

'I escaped to the mountains where I was fed and found shelter in isolated villages. It was there, I met with local *andartes* loyal to ELAS, the Greek People's Liberation Party and so I joined the armed resistant movement. I met several Jewish *andartes* who, like me, had escaped the Nazi deportations and joined their fellow Greeks in armed resistance.

'I spent many months living in the mountains. We travelled from village to village, blowing up bridges, ambushing German patrols and weeding out informers.

'Then, one day, with a group of others, I was sent to Athens. We weren't told what our mission would be, just that it was of high importance. There were several Jews among our number that day and it wasn't until we were eventually told what we were there to do that we understood why.

'Elias Barzilai, the Grand Rabbi of Athens, had been given three days to provide the Germans with names, addresses, and information of the Jewish community in Athens. The deportations of Salonika had by now reached the Jewish community in Athens and Barzilai knew what the fate of any man, woman or child would be if the Nazis' demands were acted upon.

'There were rumours that ELAS was behind his disappearance.' For the first time, Errikos grinned. 'We took the Rabbi, along with his wife and daughter, out of Athens, hiding in a mail truck to an undisclosed destination in the mountains in central Greece. After this, many other Jews went into hiding, or left Athens for the safety of the mountains. They were right to do so. Not long after, the Germans issued a decree that ordered every Jew to register and report every second day thereafter. They were forbidden to leave their homes during the hours of 5:00 p.m. and 7:00 a.m. Those that didn't report or give their names would be shot. Many refused to do so. From the round ups that followed, they were transported by train to the camps. I've heard of one called Auschwitz in Poland, and if the rumours are to be believed, no one has come out alive. I've heard terrible things. My blood boils over each time I think of it.'

Salamo's eyes widened in horror. 'My God, this is dreadful. How can such a thing happen?'

'This is why I'm here, to warn you, Salamo.'

'This is not the mainland. The Germans have not come down hard on the community. The tide of the war is turning. The British and Russians are closing in, the war is changing, and the Germans are on the back foot.'

'That may be so, but they're still here in Corfu. Believe me, Salamo, it will happen here. I have no doubt about that.

A frightened dog has a sharper bite than a dog that sleeps all day.'

Salamo laid his hand on Errikos's shoulder. 'You're safe now and that's all that matters.'

A silence hung over them like a heavy shroud, Errikos' words stealing their voices and numbing their tongues. Eventually, Yvette rose from her chair and busied herself with clearing the table. Salamo removed his glasses and methodically cleaned the lenses with his handkerchief. Rosa didn't know what to say, but something inside her was growing. She could feel it flutter inside her, a small seed of resolve.

For days afterwards, Rosa found it hard to do anything other than think of the desperation and horror her fellow Jews were suffering on the mainland. It would only be a matter of time before such horrors visited Corfu. Errikos had warned them, 'Believe me, the Nazis will not stop until every Jew has been erased from Greece.'

CHAPTER NINETEEN

LOVE RUNS DEEPER THAN FAITH

Several weeks passed and although at first it was strange having another person in the house, it didn't take long for everyone to grow accustomed to having Errikos there.

An equilibrium settled over them, new routines emerged and although Errikos slept on the sofa, in the morning when everyone awoke, he had already tidied away his bed linen and cooked breakfast for everyone. Errikos offered Salamo and Yvette money every week for his keep, which they refused every time, turning him down by reminding him he was family. He offered to work in the cafe for free, by way of paying them for their hospitality. Initially, Salamo refused but was persuaded by an insistent Errikos who said that he had to do something to stop his brain from seizing up. Even washing dishes was better than doing nothing all day. Eventually, Salamo gave in and, as a result, Errikos became absorbed into family and work life.

'Your mother tells me you have a boyfriend,' Errikos

asked Rosa one morning as they were laying chequered tablecloths on the tables outside.

Rosa grinned. 'I do.'

'Have you been seeing each other long?'

'Nearly two years now.'

'Wow! That's serious.' Errikos scratched his chin. 'If you have been seeing him all that time, why haven't I seen him around the house, or seen the two of you together?'

Rosa glided her hand over the table's surface, flattening the tablecloth. She straightened her back. 'Dad doesn't approve.'

'And the reason for that is?'

'He's not Jewish.'

'Ah! Your father was always the serious one when it came to religion. And what about your boyfriend's parents? What have they got to say about this relationship?'

'His mother takes me as I am, not what religion I was born into.'

'She seems like a sensible woman.'

'She is. I like her.'

'And his father?'

'He's passed away.'

'I see. So, you're going against your father's wishes.'

She nodded.

'Good for you. You're not a child anymore, you're a woman.'

Rosa smiled in relief. 'I'm glad you're of that opinion. I wish dad was.'

'Does he have a name?'

'He's called, Alvertos.'

'This young man, Alvertos, he must mean a lot to you.'

'He does. I couldn't imagine not seeing him.'

'So, it is love. Real love.'

Rosa didn't feel embarrassed speaking so intimately to Errikos. She found him easy to talk to. His presence relaxed her and, without thinking, she'd dropped her guard and exposed her true feelings. 'If this is what love feels like, then I'm in deep.'

'That's a nice way of putting it. And he feels the same way?'

Rosa nodded. 'He does.'

'Then it's only right that you keep seeing each other. Love runs deeper than faith.'

'Dad would never think like that. How can two brothers be so different?'

She could see sympathy in his eyes.

'Your father is a good man, Rosa, but even good men have their weaknesses. Sometimes, they are blind to what is in front of them. It's not a criticism of your father. Apart from your mother, I know him better than anyone. His faith is what sustains him. Even as a young boy, he was always reading the Torah, reciting verses and visiting the synagogue, while I, on the other hand, would have gladly suffered toothache, if it meant I didn't have to learn another word written in Hebrew.'

Rosa chuckled. 'Uncle Errikos, the young rebel.'

'I'd much prefer if you just called me Errikos. It would seem right. After all, I haven't exactly been around much.'

'Can I call you Errikos too?' Andras appeared from inside the cafe, smiling widely and evidently pleased with himself.

'I think your mother would have something to say about that and I want to stay in her good books, so you will have to call me uncle until you get older and then maybe we can drop the uncle.'

Andras's smile crumbled. 'That's not fair.'

'It's the rule.'

'That's a stupid rule.'

'Well, I'm sorry. I don't make the rules, I just follow them.'

Rosa grinned wryly. 'Somehow, I don't see you doing that.'

CHAPTER TWENTY

LIFELINE

They came without warning, like a storm in the morning, pounding on doors. If the doors weren't opened quick enough, they kicked them from their hinges with heavy boots. Weeping and sobbing filled the streets, insistent protests and words of defiance dowsed with the butt of a gun, bones broken, teeth smashed, hysterical mothers consoled young and old bleeding and dazed, terrified in a cacophony of confusion and fear. From every apartment and building, radios were thrown from windows, disintegrating on the cobblestones below and systematically crushed by German heels.

Errikos knew the agenda for the raid. 'They're destroying the radios.'

'But why would they do that?' Salamo asked in disbelief.

'They've just crushed our contact with the outside world. Even the BBC can be silenced.'

'It's an outrage. How will we know now if the war is to be lost or won?'

'That's the whole point. We will only know what the Germans want us to know.'

With haste, Salamo ran into the café and clambered up the stairs that led to the apartment.

'What in God's name is happening?' Yvette cried out in alarm with Andras by her side as she craned her neck down into the street.

'We need to hide the radio,' Salamo insisted, his eyes scanning the apartment.

'Where?'

Salamo stood for a moment, undecided.

'It's just a radio. Give them what they want, and they will be gone,' Yvette pleaded, her heart thumping.

'You don't understand Yvette. It is our lifeline to the outside world. They won't have it.'

'Quick, Salamo. The Germans will be here any second.' She placed a hand on Andras's shoulder. 'Andras, go to your room now, close the door, and don't come out until I say so.'

Salamo glanced at the sideboard; his mind made up. 'Beside the money.'

Yvette slid a sideboard from the wall and pulled at a wall panel. A section came away in her hand, revealing an empty space at floor level. She bent down and inspected the space behind the wall. 'It should be big enough.'

With the radio cradled in his arms, Salamo crouched before the opening and placed the radio inside the hollow, next to an old tin container. Once they secured the panel and the sideboard slid back into place, Salamo and Yvette stood in silence, gazing at the wall, listening to the fearful cries and chaotic commotion that rose from the street below.

The colour drained from Yvette's face. 'If they find the

radio, they'll discover the money and jewellery. Is it worth losing everything for a stupid radio?'

'It won't come to that. Once they see we don't have one, they'll move onto the next house.'

'How can you be so sure, Salamo? You are gambling away our security, our savings.'

'Quiet, Yvette. They're coming.'

The footfalls travelled up the stairs. The door creaked on its hinges as boots thudded along the hall. Yvette clutched Salamo's arm. Two soldiers loomed large in the small hall. They crossed the room with four long strides. The soldiers scanned the room from left to right. 'Where is the radio?' the one closest to Salamo barked in German.

Salamo did not understand a single word, but he knew what the German was looking for. 'There is no radio. We don't have one.'

'What is this Jew saying?' He bent forward, his face breathing down on Salamo like a raging bull. 'Radio!' This time he said the word in English.

'No radio,' Salamo replied in English, too.

The back of the German's hand whipped across Salamo's face. Yvette screamed and clamped her hand to her mouth. The other soldier moved through the apartment, searching every room, upending furniture and ransacking every cupboard. 'Nothing, there's no radio here.'

Salamo could see doubt in the soldier's eyes. 'It is here. This Jew is playing us for fools.'

'We need to move to the next house. There's no radio here.'

The soldier raised his rifle and pressed it against Salamo's forehead. 'Where is the fucking radio?'

Yvette's eyes widened in horror.

'We have no time for this. Shoot him or hit him,' the

other soldier said over his shoulder as he rushed towards the door.

Errikos watched the soldiers move from house to house, his blood ran chilled. He had witnessed similar scenes play out in Salonika and he knew what they would eventually lead to. This was the beginning and with every radio that disintegrated on impact on the street below, alarm flooded him.

The single gunfire came from above. Errikos gazed at the apartment windows above the café. *Salamo and Yvette! Please God, not this.*

A soldier exited the entrance to the apartment and pushed past Errikos. Errikos ran to the stairs, blood pounding in his head as he took two at a time. A second soldier appeared, exiting the apartment. He rushed at Errikos, his face red and sweating, his boots pounding the stairs. Then, with a roar, he raised the butt of his rifle and slammed it into Errikos' shoulder. The pain was searing. Errikos' back slammed against the wall and his legs gave way. To his relief, the soldier barged past him. Errikos staggered to his feet, his anguish terrorising his face. When he reached the apartment, a wailing Yvette was crouched over Salamo. Errikos stood at the top of the stairs and took a few tentative steps into the apartment. There was nothing he could have done. He approached Yvette. He hesitated for a moment, feeling helpless, his head swimming. Yvette looked up at him, her eyes puffy and red, her cheeks stained with tears. 'I told him not to hide that stupid radio. He wouldn't listen and it has killed him... it has...' her words evaded her.

Just then, Salamo's eyes fluttered and slowly opened, as he gave out a life affirming moan. Yvette clutched her chest with shaking hands and stared at Salamo in shock. She cried out. 'You're alive!'

Salamo nodded and moaned again, and it was then Errikos noticed the graze on Salamo's left temple.

Yvette smiled, and then it turned quickly into a frown. She shook Salamo by the shoulders, tears filming her eyes. 'I thought you were dead. I thought he had killed you.'

Salamo rubbed his head. 'On the contrary. He is either the worst shot in the German army, or one of God's angels was looking over me.'

Errikos smiled in relief. 'You scared the life out of me there, Salamo.'

Yvette sobbed. 'I hate them. I hate all of them. And you, Salamo, promise me you will never be so stupid again. I don't think my nerves can take any more.'

Salamo lifted his hand to her face and stroked it with his fingers. 'I promise,' he said, reassuring her with a smile. She hugged him tightly, pressing her face into his chest.

CHAPTER TWENTY-ONE

THE DECEPTION

One day, when Rosa was cleaning out the cupboards in the café, she came across an envelope that fell from the waste bin that was about to go out. Normally, she would have thought nothing of it, but when she saw the contents were still inside, she wondered if it had been put there by mistake. The Athens postage mark teased her interest.

She retrieved the envelope and from its confinement pulled out a half-folded sheet of paper. She opened it. As her eyes scanned the words, she didn't recognise the handwriting. She wrestled with a twinge of guilt. Despite this, she read the content. It immediately became clear the letter was from Lazaros informing Salamo he had made preparations for him to escape from Greece and take a chartered boat to Turkey. As she read on, Rosa's heart sank. Lazaros was inviting her father to accompany him. There was space for Salamo and his family on the boat. Lazaros would deal with the payment with the boat's owner and Salamo could reimburse him once they were all safe in Turkey. Lazaros explained the crossing wouldn't take place for a further two weeks, which gave Salamo time to organise his journey to Athens.

Immediately, Rosa's eyes went to the top of the letter and read the date. Lazaros had written the letter four weeks previous to the day. A wave of nausea pressed against Rosa's throat as the letter fell from her hand.

'How could you have done this?' Rosa yelled incredulously, waving the letter in front of Salamo as if it burnt her hand.

'I did it for you, for your brother and your mother. I was protecting you all,' Salamo replied defensively.

'What! You had the opportunity to leave Corfu, the Nazis, the uncertainty, this intolerable situation. You had the chance to give mother and Andras a new life.'

'I don't want a new life. This is my home. This is my family's home, and it has been that way for generations.'

She stared at him in disbelief. When she responded, her voice quaked with anger. 'You have condemned them. They could have left by now, they could have been in Turkey, safe and free of this nightmare.'

'It was not without risk. I could not put your mother and your brother through such a thing.'

'My God! You only had to travel to Athens, your friend had it all organised. He told you to join him. How many families in this town have had such an offer?' She raised her arms in the air.

'You don't understand, Rosa. You're thinking with the mind of a young woman. I have responsibilities. I am a father and a husband. My family is my priority. Taking them from everything they know to a life of a refugee… it's unthinkable.'

'You don't know what you have done.' She could feel the blood rushing in her veins. 'The Nazis will stop at nothing until they have erased us from this earth, and you talk of keeping mother and Andras safe. Don't you see what is going on around you? Have you not been listening to Errikos? Look what has happened in other parts of Greece. It's coming here. Don't you get it by now? No. You never have. You were never safe. You are a Jew. You are nothing to them. You are a fly in their web of death.'

'Rosa, you go too far.'

'Listen to you. Even now, after everything that has happened, you are still blind to what is around you.'

'The allies are making gains. They're in Italy. Soon, they will be crossing the Ionian. It will be over soon. I'm sure of it.'

'And until then?'

'We do what we have to do. Everyone at the synagogue is in agreement. It's only a matter of time now; this is why I didn't leave when Lazaros asked me to.'

Rosa shook her head. She couldn't meet his eyes. She inhaled deeply. 'Yes, it's only a matter of time.'

CHAPTER TWENTY-TWO

SAVED BY A COFFEE

The German officer gave Rosa a long appraising stare and then, in Greek, said. 'I've seen you before.'

Her heart jumped in her chest. 'You must be mistaken.' Rosa regretted the words as soon as they left her mouth. She lowered her head, her dark eyes anxious.

'I have. I never forget a face, a name maybe, but not a face. Do you have a sister?'

Rosa's heart raced. 'No.'

'Then it is definitely you. It will come to me sooner rather than later. It always does. It is just a matter of time.' He crossed his leg and the polished leather of his boots creaked. 'Max, have you seen her before?' He asked the officer sitting next to him.

Max glanced briefly at Rosa and then shrugged. 'I can't say I have.'

The officer tapped his finger on the table. 'What is your name?'

Rosa lowered her head, keeping her gaze on the ground

where she saw a cockroach scurry across the cobblestones, and she wished for once in her life to be that insect and escape this inquisition. 'Rosa,' she replied.

He glanced at his watch and sighed. 'Tell the owner to hurry with my coffee. I can't sit here all day.'

She hurried over to Salamo, relieved to escape the officer's attention. 'The officer is getting impatient. He wants his coffee now.'

Salamo placed two cups onto a tray and glanced at the officer. 'I saw him speak to you.'

'He speaks Greek.'

'What was he saying?'

'He thinks he has seen me before, but he can't remember where.'

'Why would that interest him?'

'I don't know.'

'Has he any reason to ask such a question?'

'No. I've no idea why he would ask me. I've never seen him before.' Rosa picked up the tray and turned on her heels.

The officer leaned back in his chair. 'At last. I hope this was worth the wait.'

Rosa placed a cup in front of each officer. 'Enjoy your coffee.'

The officer took a sip and looked at her, slowly nodding his head. 'I remember now. I knew I would. I never forget a face. You were the girl in the square that one of my men took a fancy to. I was having my lunch at the time. Max, you were there too. Anyway, you were sitting with a young man who refused to move when asked, and he ended up on his arse with the imprint of a rifle butt on his face for his insubordination.'

Rosa stepped backwards. She felt nervous when he first spoke to her, but now her nerves were full blown.

The officer turned to Max and spoke in German.

'I remember that. Let's have some fun here, too.' Max grinned enthusiastically while pulling a cigarette from its packet.

The officer drained his coffee. 'Tell the proprietor to come and see me. I want to personally thank him for serving me a coffee that has quenched my craving.'

She turned from them, and as she walked inside the café, the world felt like it was falling away from her feet.

Salamo looked up from the sink and the dish he was scrubbing. 'What is it, Rosa?'

'He wants to see you.'

'About what?'

'He wants to thank you for the coffee.'

Salamo swiped a dish towel from the counter and dried the soapsuds from his hand.

'I see.'

Rosa frowned. 'His Greek is excellent,' she warned.

When Salamo appeared, the officer called him over. Max had fixed a cigarette between his teeth and was lighting it. When Salamo reached them, he greeted the officer.

'Kalispera. How may I be of assistance?'

The officer looked over Salamo's shoulder, ignoring him, and waved Rosa over. She took a deep breath and walked towards them. By now, the few patrons who had not moved off when the Germans arrived were eyeing the proceedings with nervous looks.

Opposite the café, Sophia looked on with worrying glances, pretending to busy herself rearranging the meagre display of fruit and vegetables of her stall in front of her shop.

Rosa stood beside Salamo and clasped her hands together.

'My grandmother made the best coffee I've ever tasted. Since I've been in Greece, your coffee has come the closest to how hers tasted. She made it the Greek way. It was the only way she knew how. She was from a small island called Nisaros, just a few miles from Kos. Do you know it?'

'I've heard of it.' Salamo smiled, deflecting his anxiety.

'Excellent. She emigrated to Germany and met my grandfather, embracing German culture and identity. The only thing she refused to give up from the old country was the way she made coffee and, of course, the language, which she passed on to my mother, who them passed it on to her sons.'

Salamo hesitated. 'I must commend you on your Greek.'

'My grandmother was proud of her Greek identity, but she would have died for Der Fuhrer if asked, even at her age. My only regret is that she never lived to see the Fuhrer's ambitions for our motherland come to fruition.'

The officer got to his feet as Salamo felt a heaviness crawl through him. The officer straightened the jacket of his uniform and brushed his left shoulder with his hand. Eventually, he spoke. 'I'm not in the habit of drinking coffee that a Jew has made, but as I passed, I had an insatiable craving for one. Normally, neither would I thank a Jew, but your coffee reminded me of my grandmother, and I was fond of her.'

From his shoulder, he extended his right arm into the air with a straightened hand and bellowed, 'Heil Hitler!'

He waited. 'Your turn.' He grinned, but there was little humour in his voice.

Rosa shifted on her feet. It was then she noticed the cane in Max's hand.

The officer glanced at his watch. 'I don't have all day. You will do me the honour.'

Salamo took a deep breath, his gaunt pallor draining his face of colour.

Max took a long drag on his cigarette. 'You have disrespected our Fuhrer and Lieutenant Hoffman, which cannot go unpunished.'

The cane sliced the air and whipped across Salamo's shoulder. His legs buckled, and he crumpled to his knees, crying out in alarm and pain. Another blow followed. Horrified, Rosa crouched beside Salamo and wrapped a protective arm around his shoulder. Max raised the cane again.

'Enough. You'll end up killing him,' Hoffman said.

'And that would be a bad thing?' Max scoffed.

'Ordinarily, no. He makes an excellent coffee, like my grandmother did. It brought me comfort when I thought of her and that has saved him.'

Max stared down at Rosa and Salamo and in his eyes, she saw contempt and hatred and it burnt her to her very core. Without taking his eyes from them, Max dropped his cigarette onto the cobblestones and crushed it with the sole of his boot. 'It's a pity I didn't get to stub the life out of you, too.'

In the apartment, Salamo sat at the kitchen table, his shirt unbuttoned and baring his shoulders. 'You have been in the wars, Salamo, that's for sure,' Errikos said, screwing his face in sympathy.

'I've been shot at and whipped. What more can they do to me now?' Salamo winced.

Yvette inspected the wounds on Salamo's shoulder. 'It could have been worse. The skin isn't broken.'

'I know it doesn't feel like it, but you have been lucky. If you were a cat, you'd be running out of lives.' Errikos grinned, trying to make light of the moment.

Yvette frowned. 'Then thank goodness he's not.'

'I just want a quiet life. Is that too much to ask?' Salamo sighed.

Yvette's frown faded to an anxious mask. 'You should have thought about that before you hid that radio of yours. If they find it, they'll surely kill you the next time.'

CHAPTER TWENTY-THREE

THE GAMBLE

Rosa lay on the bed, a sliver of silver moonlight stretched across the sheet. Her skin drenched in a film of cold sweat that clung damp and oppressive.

It was more than a dream; it was a lived experience that visited her again, like countless times before. There would be no reprieve. She would relive each moment like it was her first. The cycle was unrelenting and always it remained vicious in its vividness.

Several months previously, the Italian army had capitulated to the Germans, except for the garrisons on the Ionian islands where Italians resisted the German advancements. On the island of Corfu, on the night of September 13, 1943, the Germans conducted a deadly air assault on Corfu Town that lasted for two consecutive nights.

Rosa had been walking along Avenue Alexandra on her way home from visiting a friend's house when the first bombs struck. Before then, the world around her had been tranquil, the air pleasant and warm. In a second, it would change, and thrust her into a nightmare that even her worse dreams would struggle to conjure as the deathly whistle of indiscriminate bombs plunged from a blackened sky.

In a panic, she cowered under an archway from the crunch and thud of collapsing structures vibrating and quaking the ground all around her. Countless blasts pulverised her ears, and a furnace of heat singed her face. Acrid smoke and raging fires burnt, incinerating and scorching everything in its path. Burning flesh contaminated the air, as did endless wails of sobbing, crying, and hysterical screams.

Her eyes were wide in horror at the gaping holes in masonry and tiled roofs, revealing furniture strewn and tangled in rubble. Around her, homes and possessions disintegrated into a tangled mesh of stone, wood, and rubble where coils of smoke, like apparitions, stretched into the blackened sky.

The hum of aircraft increased with each second that passed. The Germans picked their targets with precision, bringing destruction to the warren of buildings and narrow lanes, trapping the innocent and unleashing their deadly loads to spread maximum carnage and destruction.

People rushed in every direction indiscriminately, as the narrow streets trapped and contained the horror around them. They spilled onto both sidewalks, clutching what luggage they could collect, and scurrying like ants to the outskirts of the town. A petrified woman, not much older than Rosa, clutched a baby to her chest while a man, her husband perhaps, panicking, cried out a child's name that hung in the air, unanswered.

Incendiary casings littered the ground and fell on roofs, crackling with flares that burst into flames spreading destruction. Ancient roofs became engulfed, alight with small fires that rapidly spread, feeding each other, becoming one mass of burning horror that set ablaze everything in its path. Windows shattered, sending blades of glass through the air like hundreds of knives that could slice a body like a melon.

Aircraft continued to drone overhead, depositing another wave of whistling bombs falling like hailstones. The ground quaked and shook violently, throwing Rosa at the cobblestones littered with fallen masonry, shards of glass, and lifeless bodies. She thought she heard another wave falling from the sky, but it was her ears that rang screeching inside her head.

Rosa scrambled to her feet and ran into an alley, the heat unbearable, as if her clothes had suddenly caught fire. She exited at a square littered with fallen beams, shattered tiles, buckled window frames and wooden doors.

People ran in every direction, disorientated and confused, laden with bundles and belongings plucked from the ravages of fires that threatened to burn everything in their path. Everywhere, tremendous explosions rocked the air, turning night into day with blinding flashes and deathly roars.

Suddenly, a man who seemed to have appeared from nowhere grabbed Rosa's arm and pulled her along with him.

'Quickly, follow me. We're heading to the old fortress, it's the only place that will survive this hell,' he bellowed above the clamour.

Rosa's legs could barely move. They were heavy, and her muscles seized. She struggled to breathe the hot air that surrounded the square, her lungs bursting and choking with smoke and dust.

Alarmingly, her arm broke free from his grip, and as the

man continued to run, her eardrums ruptured as a massive blast consumed the square. Rosa found herself blown into a doorway, sheltered from the violent blast and hellish onslaught of death and destruction.

Smoke and debris, stone and glass hurled indiscriminately in every direction, deadly projectiles that thudded and tore into flesh and bone. Screams of terror and dreadful moans punctured the air where bodies lay scattered like broken dolls. People staggered half naked, drenched in blood, their clothes torn and ripped from them. The last thing Rosa remembered was seeing the crumpled and motionless body of the man who, only seconds before, had tried to save her.

Rosa cried out, and Yvette rushed into the bedroom. 'It's all right. I'm here now. Hush, my darling, you're in your bedroom, lying on your bed and I'm with you.' Yvette sat on the bed and cradled Rosa's head into her chest.

Rosa's eyelids fluttered. Her heart thumped. 'It's so real. I experience it all over again, every second in minute detail. It doesn't leave me. It's like a curse. It feels like God is punishing me because I survived and so many perished. I can hear the bombs falling, feel the heat of the fires. People are screaming and running. I can taste the air thick with smoke. It's as real as you are here sitting with me now.'

'I know... I know. I can't imagine how it must have felt being out there in the streets, but God answered my prayers and I'm just thankful you came back to us, and you survived,' Yvette said, trying to comfort her.

Rosa's breath was fast and uneven. 'I can't stop thinking about Nikos. His house is only three houses from ours. Yet it was the only one in our street hit by a bomb. How can someone like Nikos continue to live, when in a few seconds his wife and daughters were taken from him by German bombs? He lives knowing that every day he sees the people responsible for their deaths.' Her face flickered with anger.

Yvette held her tighter. 'They died in their home, a place of safety, of love and precious memories. I can't imagine how he lives each day without them. His sadness must be unbearable.' Yvette took Rosa's hand in hers. 'He has no choice. He still has a son.'

Rosa lifted her head, and with her hand, she took her weight and sat up suddenly. 'His son will be a constant reminder of what he's lost.'

'That may be so, but now, each day, he lives for his son. He has a purpose. His son needs him.'

Rosa rubbed her eyes.

'The headache again?' Yvette's voice was brimming with concern.

Rosa swallowed. 'It will pass soon enough. It always does.'

'You should see the doctor. He might be able to stop these images you keep reliving and give you something for the headaches.'

'It'll take more than a pill. They're stuck in my head. It won't stop until every German has left Corfu, but I think we'll be forced to leave Corfu by then, if what uncle Errikos says is true.' There was a sharp warning to her voice.

'Your father doesn't think it will come to that. Even now, the Germans are not making anything like the gains they were once making. Your father says the allies have the advantage now. The war is turning in their favour. He has heard it on the BBC on that radio that almost got us all killed.'

A chill slid beneath Rosa's skin. 'He's too trusting. It's blinding him to what is in front of him.'

'You shouldn't speak like that. He wants what is best for us. For all of us. He is not the only one who feels this way. Many of the community leaders are also sure the persecutions will stop once it's clear the Germans are losing the war.'

A shadow passed over Rosa's eyes. 'They're gambling with all our lives.'

CHAPTER TWENTY-FOUR

A PROPOSITION

A week later, Rosa and Alvertos were walking along the street Velissariou. Above them, in a violet hued sky, swallows darted between rooftops and terracotta slates where the evening sun caressed the facades of the Venetian tenements, its muted light falling softly across a patchwork of green and red shutters.

It was enough to lift Rosa's spirits, and she held Alvertos' hand as they neared the frontage of the shop and its little alcove where from a small opening ice cream was served.

Rosa smiled widely. 'I haven't tasted ice cream for ages. It's been too long. Do you think there will be strawberry ice cream? What about you? What flavour would you like?'

Alvertos grinned in response. 'Normal ice cream will do me just fine.'

'What do you mean, normal?'

'You know, just ice cream. White ice cream. Vanilla. Normal ice cream.'

Rosa's eyes widened. 'Strawberry is normal ice cream.'

Alvertos' grin widened, and then he laughed. 'I didn't know you felt so strongly about the common ice cream and its array of variety.'

Rosa smiled. 'Here we are and there isn't even a queue, even on a night like this.'

They ordered their ice cream and sat at a table outside the shop. Rosa licked hers and nodded indulgently. She took a mouthful and coughed, covering her mouth with a napkin.

Alvertos laughed. 'I told you. That ice cream is not normal. In fact, by the look of you, it's definitely bad for your health.'

Rosa reached over and pushed him playfully, just as someone approached them.

'Hello Rosa, how are you?' asked a curious voice.

Rosa looked up from her napkin and stared at the newcomer. She hesitated. 'Josefina!'

'It's been a long time.'

'It has.'

'You look good… better than that, in fact.'

'As do you,' Rosa said, forcing a tight smile.

'Don't kid yourself. I never had your looks. How are you?'

'I'm well.'

'And who is this?' Josefina flicked her hair from her face.

'This is Alvertos.'

Alvertos extended his hand. 'Pleased to meet you, Josefina.'

She took his hand in hers. 'Likewise.'

'When did you return to Corfu?' Rosa asked.

'A few weeks ago. I'm staying with my mother.'

'And how is she?'

'She isn't too good on her feet nowadays. She's walking with a stick now and doesn't get out much.'

'Oh! I'm sorry to hear that. Your mum was always an active woman.'

Josefina stared down at her. 'Don't be sorry. She's thriving on all the attention it gets her.'

Rosa was unsure how to respond to this and suddenly felt fragile. 'Please, join us. Take a seat. It's been such a long time since I've seen you.'

'I wouldn't want to intrude.' Josefina said, embarrassingly.

There was something about her that made Alvertos think this was more of an act than a genuine response. 'Have you two been friends long?'

Josefina nodded and tucked her hair behind her ear. 'Since we were children. We went to the same school, that's how long it's been. Although we've not kept in touch for a few years, have we, Rosa? I've been away, you see. But I'm back now.'

Rosa exchanged a guarded look with Alvertos.

Josefina gestured towards Rosa's ice cream. 'Have you tried the chocolate? It's divine.'

'Not yet. This is pretty good too, although some would disagree.' Rosa grinned at Alvertos.

'Apparently, I'm quite restricted in my tastes when it comes to ice cream.'

Josefina studied Rosa intently. Her look was so intense, her face looked of marble. Eventually, she spoke. 'The other day, I saw you coming out of a church of all places. I thought, how peculiar is that Rosa coming out of a church? What is Rosa doing visiting a church, certainly not praying in it, I hoped?'

An uneasiness crept up the nape of her neck. 'No. I was

just looking around. I've never been in a church before, and I was curious.'

'What would your father say if he knew?'

'He could say whatever he liked. We're not children anymore.'

'No. That's true. If I remember correctly, he was very observant when it came to his faith. I suspect he's still the same. That's all I meant.'

'It has nothing to do with him what I choose to do with my time.'

Josefina ignored Rosa's remark. 'I've never been curious about what lies inside a church. I've heard they're full of gold, candles and paintings that the Christians pray to. How absurd is that?'

Alvertos straightened in his chair. 'It was my idea.'

Josefina looked at him curiously. 'Really.'

'Yes. Although I'm lost at what concern it's of yours.'

'I was just taken aback to see Rosa come out of a church. That's all.'

'Then surely you would have seen me too.'

'I did.'

Rosa kicked Alvertos under the table.

He couldn't let it go. 'Why is it of interest to you?'

'It's not every day you see a Jewish girl in a church. I was curious to know, that's all.'

'Well, now you know. And before you ask, I'm not Jewish.'

'I know,' she said coldly. 'Anyway, I need to be going. It was nice to see you, Rosa. Let's not make it as long this time before we see each other again.'

They watched her walk away with a self-assurance about her stride that stuck in Alvertos' throat.

Alvertos sighed. 'Wow! She's a strange one. What was that all about?'

Rosa drew a long breath, and something changed in her face. Her gaze slid sideways.

'What is it, Rosa?'

'She has a loose tongue inside her head.'

'Why does that matter?'

'She'll be spreading rumours about me before the day is out. I can guarantee it.'

'So what if you went inside a church? It doesn't make you any less Jewish, does it?'

'Seeing her again, after all this time, has brought back certain memories that are painful.'

'What do you mean?'

Rosa swallowed. 'When we were younger, just teenagers, something terrible happened.' She bit her lip.

'What happened?'

'There were some kids playing with a ball and Josefina and I were walking with her father when one child kicked the ball and it landed at my feet. I kicked it back, but it went onto the road. Josefina's father ran to get the ball and was hit by a passing truck. I don't know how he didn't see it. One second, he was with us, the next he was lying under the truck. He died instantly. Josefina blamed me for her father's death. If I hadn't kicked the ball, he would never have gone after it.'

'Surely, you don't believe that? It was just a terrible accident. They happen.'

Rosa wrapped her arms around herself. 'I've lived with it ever since. To begin with, I blamed myself. No one else blamed me, except Josefina. She always said one day it would return to haunt me. It wasn't a warning; it was a threat. After her father's funeral, she went to live with relatives in Volos. I never saw her again until now.'

'What did she mean? It would come back to haunt you?'

'I don't know. Now she's back, I might find out.'

'Do you think after all this time, she would still carry out a threat?'

Rosa shrugged. 'Maybe she would. I don't know, but seeing her again, I got the feeling our meeting wasn't just a coincidence.'

'She was a bit strange. Do you think she wanted to provoke you?'

'If she did, you did a good job of that for me. You gladly bit the worm on her hook.'

'I'm sorry.' Alvertos frowned sadly. 'If I'd known, I would have kept my mouth shut. You've never told me any of this.'

Rosa drew a breath. 'It was a long time ago and happened when I was younger. It's not something I think about every day. Not now. To begin with, I blamed myself, but with the support of my family, that feeling gradually got weaker, and I saw it for what it was, just an unfortunate accident. I know now it wasn't my fault. As an adult, I can see it for what it was. But there are still times, it comes back to haunt me. Like just now.'

By now, Rosa's ice cream was melting, long thin rivulets of red staining her fingers. She dropped the ice cream cone into a napkin lying on the table.

'You didn't finish it.'

'I'm not in the mood for ice cream now.'

'That's a shame. You were enjoying it.'

'Can we go now?'

'Would you like to walk? It's a lovely evening.'

She shook her head. 'No. I feel like a snake has crawled over my skin.'

When they returned to the apartment, Melina was out. Rosa wanted to speak to Alvertos about her father. Melina's absence gave her the opportunity to speak freely.

Rosa sat looking out into the street. 'I hate upsetting him, but once he gets something in his mind, it doesn't matter what others say, he won't budge. What more can I do? I've tried to convince him. Even now, he'll have none of it.' She sighed, defeated.

'You have done all you can. I know it's hard, impossible maybe, but you must think of yourself in all of this too, Rosa.'

'It's my family that matters to me, not my safety.'

Alvertos frowned. 'Then you can see it from my point of view because I'm not concerned about myself, but it would feel like every bone in my body was broken if something ever happened to you. If the rumours are true, if God forbid, the Germans are going to send the Jewish community to camps somewhere in Europe, I couldn't live with myself, and I will do anything to keep you safe even if it means…'

She reached out with her hand and with her fingertips lightly brushed his face. 'You don't have to tell me. I know you would, but it would kill me too if it ever came to that.'

'There must be a way.'

'I fear I've lost my family,' she said heavily.

He hesitated and narrowed his eyes. 'Maybe you have, but I don't need to lose you.'

She stared at him speculatively. There was something about the intent look in his eyes. Something had changed.

He took both her hands in his and looked her in the eyes. 'There is only one way out of this, Rosa, and it's something I've been thinking about for a long time. If things were different, the way I'd asked you would have been too. This may seem like we've been forced into necessity, but my intentions are the furthest from it. From the moment I saw you, I knew I wanted to spend the rest of my life with you. Marry me Rosa, become my wife. You'll be safer than you are now. It'll offer you protection if things get worse, which I fear they will.'

This was the last thing she expected, and the colour drained from her face. She had dreamed of this day; it felt a natural consequence of the love they shared for each other. She wanted to spend the rest of her life with Alvertos, and share that life with him, whatever that brought. It was a statement of their commitment to each other and an acknowledgement of how they had grown together as a couple and a union of their love. She also felt in doing so she was abandoning her family, betraying them and their identity, especially now, when they needed each other among the turmoil of uncertainty, the threat of the Nazi retribution and the fear of what the future would bring.

Being married to Alvertos would bring the prospect of safety, removing the threat of daily persecution that her community couldn't escape. It was not a guaranteed insurance, but she could no longer just think about herself.

There was a life growing inside her. It was too early to feel the first signs of a flutter within, but she was pregnant. It had been eight weeks now. She had wanted to be certain before she told Alvertos and then wait until the right time. Being with child and not being married was detriment to both families' beliefs. Now, things had just got a lot more complicated.

The lack of an enthusiastic response made Alvertos sick to his stomach. 'You don't have to answer me right now. I know it shouldn't be like this. I wish with all my heart it was different, but it's not. I know it was presumptuous of me but I've already spoken to the priest, and he's agreed that on the wedding certificate he'll record that you're a Christian. He has even suggested he is prepared to falsify a birth certificate. You will be a Christian only in these documents and, more important, in the eyes of the Germans.' By now, panic had crept into Alvertos' voice. 'This is happening all over Greece. Many priests are falsifying birth certificates and helping Jews.'

Rosa remained silent. Alvertos' eye twitched, and he cursed what now felt a disastrous impulse.

Rosa could feel her eyes nip with tears. When she spoke, she delivered the words so softly, Alvertos strained to hear her. 'Even without this war, the thought of his daughter getting married to a non-Jew would have been impossible for my father to accept. He's put me in a difficult situation, but right now, I've other concerns that are more important than his feelings.' Rosa wiped her eyes. 'I will marry you, Alvertos, not because by doing so, I'll be a Christian which protects me from the Germans. No, I'll marry you because it's what I want. I'll marry you out of love.'

Alvertos released his breath with a sigh of relief. 'Oh Rosa, you have no idea how happy this makes me feel.'

'There's one more reason I'll marry you, Alvertos. I wanted to tell you when I was completely sure, and I am.' Rosa smiled with sudden affection. 'Alvertos, you're going to be a father.'

Her words were sweet and rich in his ears. His mouth fell open. He tried to speak, but words failed him. Instead, he wrapped her in his arms and his tears fell like rain into her hair.

CHAPTER TWENTY-FIVE

EXILED

She told her mother and father the next morning and braced herself for the impending storm. Yvette looked at her with a mixture of despondency, laced with acknowledged delight at the thought of becoming a grandmother, which she curtailed given the circumstances around Rosa's revelation.

Salamo raked his fingers through his hair, then his beard, while simultaneously pacing the floor. His silence was unnerving. It tortured Rosa, who would have much preferred a tirade of words to flow from his tongue.

'It's bad enough that you're talking about getting married to this boy, but a child... my heart has been pierced twice. How could you have done this to your mother and me? Everything we hold sacred you've torn from us. You've disgraced yourself and, worst of all, you've disgraced this family.'

Rosa stood still, like a statue. She thought she was prepared for her father's expected retribution, but hearing his words, seeing the anguished torture on his face, was more than she'd anticipated.

Instinctively, Yvette touched Rosa's arm. It was an unexpectedly small but genuine gesture of support. 'She's our daughter. It doesn't matter what she's done, nothing will change that.'

Salamo spoke sharply. 'She's ruined our lives.'

'You can't possibly mean that? This is nonsense. The Germans have already made a good job of ruining the life we had. We can't change what has happened, but we can be there for Rosa. She'll need us now more than ever.'

'She's thrown away any connection she has ever had with this family. I'll not be seen as an outcast in my own community, because that's what it will come to. We'll be spoken about and treated like we were inflicted with leprosy. It's inconceivable. No. My mind is made up.'

'This is not about you, Salamo. Why does everything have to be about you and your precious standing in the community? Where is your compassion? Your daughter's needs should come first above everything.'

'Even above the laws of God? You ask too much of me, Yvette.'

'What is this called? This is not love. As a mother, my love for my children is unconditional. A mistake can be rectified, even forgiven.'

'You talk of forgiveness at a time like this. She's made a mockery of everything I believe in, of our identity, of who we are.' He stabbed the air with a pointed finger towards Rosa. 'How can she possibly marry a man who is not a Jew, a non-believer?'

'That doesn't make him a bad person. He believes in the same God that we do. The God of the Torah is also the God of their Bible.'

'Married, in a church. This is what it has come to. A baby baptised a Christian. Our first grandchild born a non-Jew.' His face crumpled, and he sank into a chair.

Rosa had never seen her parents talk in this manner before. Their conversations involving their relationship had always been private, hushed words spoken out of reach. Even as an adult, Rosa had never been privy to the details. She had not anticipated this response from her mother. The forthright manner in which she challenged Salamo was a side to her character Rosa had never known. She had never witnessed her mother challenge her father, never in front of her, anyway. Her mother's assertive and empathetic display of support had helped steady Rosa's nerves. It warmed her heart against the turmoil around her.

Rosa bit her lip, her eyes brimming over with tears. 'I never wanted to hurt you. I just hope the pain you feel right now, which I've caused, will lessen with time. I'm responsible for this. I can't change what has happened. I'm not seeking your forgiveness, just your understanding, if you can both find it in yourselves. I love Alvertos and he loves me and this baby inside me testifies to that love, because we both want this. My regret is, I hate how deeply I've hurt both of you, but I've no other choice. I will have this baby and I'll marry Alvertos.' She wiped her eyes. 'I am what I am, and it is what it is. I can't change that.' She had no more to say.

Yvette nodded encouragingly.

Salamo's gaze slid sideways towards the window. 'You are lost to me. I no longer have a daughter.'

CHAPTER TWENTY-SIX

A WARNING

Since the day she told her parents of her pregnancy and her intention to marry Alvertos, Rosa had become an outcast in her father's eyes.

On one occasion, she saw him buying vegetables from the meagre display on offer at one stall in the market. She was standing at the meat stall, only a few feet from him. Her heart jumped inside her chest. She moved forward to greet him and when she opened her mouth to speak to him; he turned his head and glanced in her direction. Her stomach sank as his eyes slid from her, and turning from her, he walked away. She couldn't take her eyes off him. They pored over the figure of her retreating father, as each step carried him away from her, until he rounded a corner and disappeared from her view.

She still saw her mother and little brother, Andras. They would meet occasionally at a prearranged location outside the Jewish quarter. Yvette would tell Rosa of the daily comings and goings, the community news, and about the lives of their neighbours. She enquired about the progress of

Rosa's pregnancy, offering advice on what to eat and drink, so that the baby would be healthy when born. She always asked if Rosa and Alvertos had chosen any boys' and girls' names and how their plans for the wedding were developing. Rosa always asked after her father and if he had asked about her and each time, she knew in her heart what Yvette's response would be, but it never deterred her from asking. Their separations were always difficult affairs, and although both Rosa and Yvette tried to remain strong for Andras, they couldn't help but sob into each other's shoulder.

Rosa stayed with Alvertos and Melina. Their house was now her home. As the weeks passed, her swollen stomach began to show and Alvertos delighted in placing his head to her to stomach and speak to his unborn.

One day, there was a knock at the front door.

Alvertos looked at his mother. 'Are you expecting anyone?'

She turned from the stove where she was preparing a meal for that evening. 'No. Not at this hour.'

Alvertos pulled open a kitchen drawer and took out a knife.

Rosa's eyes flashed with concern.

Alvertos lifted his free hand. 'A precaution.'

'Is this what it's come to? You're not safe in your own home because of me.'

Alvertos held the knife in front of him. 'It's probably nothing. If it was the Germans, they wouldn't bother knocking.'

He bent his ear to the door and felt a knot of fear uncoil inside him. 'Who is it?'

'It's Errikos, Rosa's uncle.'

A palpable relief etched over Rosa's face. She hurried to the door and as Alvertos let Errikos into the apartment, Rosa flung her arms around him. 'Uncle Errikos!'

'And it's good to see you too.' Errikos smiled.

They sat around the table. Melina poured them all a coffee and set a plate with four pieces of cake.

Errikos looked at her in surprise. Melina put a finger to her lips. 'I know the people you need to know to get some of life's little luxuries.'

'I can see that.'

'Don't be shy. Try one,' Melina encouraged, gesturing to the cake.

Errikos didn't need to be asked twice. He picked up a cake and took a generous bite. 'Very nice and moist too.'

'How did you find me?' Rosa's voice was quiet, like the breath of a baby.

'I asked your mother where you were. I wanted to see my favourite niece.'

Rosa smiled. 'You only have one niece.'

Errikos grinned. 'And that's why you're my favourite.'

'Mum tells me you're not around much anymore.'

Errikos nodded. 'I've been putting my experience to good use. I made contact with the resistance, the *andartes*. It feels good to be a thorn in the arse of the Nazis again and be among others who have similar ideologies and who are focused on the struggle. There are still many Italian soldiers that remain here. When the Italian army capitulated, instead of being taken prisoners by the Germans, many of them escaped to the hills and joined the resistance. I've met several Jews who have done the same.'

Rosa smiled as she took in the look of determination on

her uncle's face. 'I'm glad you've found your purpose again, but not so happy with how dangerous it is.'

Errikos shrugged. 'It's dangerous for me to live each day under Nazi occupation, simply because I'm a Jew. What difference does it make?'

'And where are you living? In the mountains?' Alvertos asked.

'Most of the time.'

'That must be difficult,' Alvertos said gravely.

Errikos shrugged modestly. 'It's not that bad. The weather is getting hotter by the day. We move from village to village. So, I always have a roof over my head, well, nearly always.' He took a sip of coffee. 'I know you've been seeing your mother. What about your father?'

'He's made it clear. He never wants to see me again.'

'I'm sorry, Rosa.'

'I made my choice as well.'

Errikos shook his head, a sadness visible in his eyes. 'How have you been keeping? Are you both well?' He nodded towards her stomach.

Rosa instinctively touched her swelling belly. 'We're both well.'

'That's wonderful to hear. At least there's still some happiness left in this world.' Errikos straightened his back and coughed. 'I wish this was just a social visit, but I've also come to warn you. Over the last few weeks, there's been a definite change in the German position concerning the Jewish population of the Ionian islands and elsewhere in other islands, the Dodecanese and Crete. Our intelligence has uncovered the Germans are planning the deportation of Corfu's Jews. The only saving grace at the moment is that there's no transport available, but that will change, mark my words. When I lived in Salonika, every Jew was to remain in their homes from early evening until morning. The number of Jews living in a house had to be posted on the front door with their ages also prominent. Anyone found harbouring, hiding, or helping a Jew was shot. Every male was to report to the authorities. These regulations were to be enforced by the Greek police. In Corfu, every Jewish man has now to report to the authorities.' Errikos' eyes grew dark. 'It's already beginning. The deportations will come soon. I've seen the pattern elsewhere. This is what happens. The Germans are preparing to remove every Jew from Corfu and send them to the camps. Just because the allies are already making headway in Italy and are now in Balli don't think that we've seen the worst of the Nazis' hatred for us. We've seen nothing yet.'

'We're going to get married and I've secured identity papers for Rosa,' Alvertos informed him.

Errikos tilted his head. 'The Germans know there are people who have false identity papers. They've experience of this on the mainland, especially in the populated areas like Athens, Volos and Patras. They're using other means to find Jews, like the Greek police, Greeks of the security battalions, and believe it or not, Jews themselves.'

Rosa held her breath.

'Yes, even among our own, there are traitors and collaborators. They use blackmail. They demand money, jewellery, watches, anything of value. They promise this will buy their silence, but once they're given such ransom, they turn the families over to the Germans, anyway.

'Sometimes, the blackmailers have had disputes with the families in the past. I've known of several interpreters who made a small fortune turning over families to the Germans. In Athens, many Greek Christians helped Jewish families, many of whom were their neighbours. They hid in the attics, spare rooms, anywhere that would be safe. These people were also at risk of informers.'

'And this is happening here in Corfu?' Rosa said incredulously.

Errikos nodded. 'It's possible. That's why you have to be careful, Rosa.'

Alvertos narrowed his eyes. 'I've spoken with the priest. He's agreed to provide Rosa with a birth and baptism certificate along with our marriage certificate. That will prove, if it comes to it, she is a Christian.'

'That may be so, and I hope that will be enough, but the Germans will believe an informer first. I've seen too many sad occasions when this has been the case.' Errikos fixed Rosa with a focused look. 'I'm asking you to be careful. Trust no one.'

'We will.' Albertos answered for her. Rosa nodded her head in agreement.

Errikos rose from his chair and turned towards Melina. 'I must be going. Thank you for the cake. It was delicious.'

Melina smiled. 'You're welcome anytime.'

'When will I see you again?' Rosa's voice quivered.

Errikos fell silent for a moment, and then he reached out and took her hand. 'I don't know. There are things I cannot tell you that are out of my control, but I promise you, I'll be back to see you when I can.'

CHAPTER TWENTY-SEVEN

THE THREAT

Corfu Town felt a profound wind of unease that reflected on the faces of its occupants. The maze of narrow-cobbled streets reverberated with marching boots and the distinct guttural and forceful flow of the German language.

It was becoming increasingly scarce to buy quality food. The Germans had the monopoly of the livestock, vegetables, bread, olives, pulses, everything that before the war the Corfiots took for granted. Even though times were hard, it didn't compare to the stories that circulated among the cafes and streets of Corfu Town about the occupants of entire villages starving to death on the mainland.

It was against this background that the Jewish population of the town were reminded of the brutal attitudes of the Germans towards them and the dangers this placed them in. The Germans looted properties and forcefully took furniture, money, and jewellery. The police station required Jewish males to report once a week. They enforced a curfew from 5pm until 7am and ordered every Jewish household to post the names and ages of the occupants on their front doors. They also declared that anyone found hiding or attempting to help a Jew would be shot on the spot.

The allied armies were pushing and advancing through Italy and rumours spread that Balli would be the next piece of Italian territory to be taken by the allies. Those Jews who still had radios and who listened avidly to the BBC's daily reports confirmed the rumours.

'It might be difficult for us now, but we're safer than those on the mainland, and the war will soon be over. The Germans are being run out of Italy. Greece will be next.' Salamo reminded his customers, their conversations dominated by the daily harsh treatment they faced.

Even when Melina visited the market, there was only one conversation.

'I believe God will help us. We believe in the same God. God wants us to save these people. They're our friends, our neighbours, they're our own, they are Greeks like us.' It was a mantra Melina often repeated to her close friends, but not all were as understanding as she was, and there were some who did not agree with her, either fuelled by their own fear or their own prejudice.

'Only a fool would put their life and that of their family in danger. Why provoke the Germans even more? The Jews are not our problem. We have enough of our own to worry about.'

'How can you say such a thing? It's by the grace of God that we're not subjected to the daily degradation that our Jewish neighbours are forced to endure.'

'Better them than us. That's all I've got to say about it.'

'Shame on you, Theodores. Even their children are not spared the attacks of the Germans. How can you condone such acts perpetrated against innocent children?'

'You sound like you have something to hide, Melina. I've been told that the girl your son is seeing is a Jew as well.'

'Who told you this?'

'It doesn't matter. It would be risky for you as well as him.'

'What are you saying, Theodores? Is that a threat?'

Theodores smirked. 'It would only be a threat if it were true.'

CHAPTER TWENTY-EIGHT

THE CROSS

'Watch, I will show you. With your right hand, join your thumb, your index finger and your middle finger like this, so that the tips of the fingers are touching. See.' Alvertos held up his hand. Rosa, smiling, copied him.

'The reason we join our fingers in this way is because it symbolises the Holy Trinity.'

'What?'

'Here comes the mystery part. The Holy Trinity is what it says, trinity as in three. God the Father, God the Son, and God the Holy Spirit. So, these are not three gods, but one God in Trinity. The Father, the Son of the Father, and the Holy Spirit. They are three in one Godhead. Now extend your index and middle finger towards the base of your palm and slightly bend the middle finger, like this... these represent the two natures of Christ: His Divinity and His Humanity. Now with your right hand, touch your forehead, then down towards your chest and finally, the right shoulder and then the left.'

Rosa made the sign of the cross several times. 'Do I look like a real Christian?' Her sarcasm punctuated the words.

Alvertos was silent for a few moments and then he nodded in recognition and placed his hand on hers. 'I understand. I know it's difficult for you, Rosa. It doesn't stop you being Jewish, but it has a purpose. It's about survival and it might just save your life.'

She swallowed her pride. 'I know, Alvertos. Believe me, I know how serious it is.' Rosa straightened her back. 'So, when do I make this… sign of the cross?'

'When you enter a church, when a priest blesses you, at the beginning and end of a prayer… that reminds me, you'll have to know some prayers. The Lord's Prayer, The Nicene Creed and prayers we say at mealtimes.'

'It will be easier to learn them if they are written down.'

'I have a prayer book somewhere. It was given to me by my mother on my communion day when I was young. I haven't seen it for years, but she keeps everything like that. It won't have been thrown out. I'll find it.'

Rosa narrowed her eyes. 'What's communion?'

'This is what the church calls the Mystery. It's when bread and wine are changed by the Holy Spirit into the body and blood of Christ.'

Rosa looked bewildered.

Alvertos nodded his head. 'I know. It sounds incredible.'

'So, if I'm understanding this, one God changes bread and wine into the body and blood of another God. It's like Greek mythology. I never knew Christianity was so inventive.'

'There's only one God. The same God you believe in.'

'This is so confusing.'

'It's the greatest of all the Mysteries in the Orthodox faith. It's not to be taken figuratively. It's believed that the bread and wine are transformed into the body and blood of Christ and that Christ is present. If you receive holy communion, you receive Christ as well. It's been this way since the beginning of Christianity.'

'And you believe this?'

'It's what I've been taught since I was a child. It's central to the Orthodox faith. It's not a question of do I believe in it, you must know about it and be convincing in your understanding and explanation if you're ever questioned about it. Let's hope that never happens...' he hesitated. 'But you have to be prepared, just in case.'

Rosa nodded her recognition of this. 'How often do people receive this bread and wine?'

'Most people who go to church will take communion every Sunday. That's another important thing to remember. For you, the Jewish Sabbath is a Saturday. For Christians it's on a Sunday. This is very important to remember.'

'I know. Just in case.'

They heard the door open and close, and Melina appeared from the hallway.

'Hello, you two.' Melina dropped her bag on the table and slid out of her coat, sighing heavily as she removed the meagre pickings from her shopping trip.

'Are you okay, Mum?' Alvertos asked.

'I'm afraid it will be soup again. I got bread, some vegetables, but that's all.'

'We'll manage.' Alvertos tried to sound upbeat.

'It will fill our stomachs, I suppose.'

Melina's gaze slid sideways towards the window. Outside, in the narrow street below, a commotion was taking place. Two men were arguing over a frightened boy, his eyes wide with terror. One man held the boy's arm and with his other, he gestured provokingly towards the man in front of him, who lunged forwards, slamming his palms into the other man's chest. The man stumbled backwards. He lost his balance and released his grip on the young boy. Once free, the boy took his opportunity and advantageously ran off, but not before he scooped up a canvas rucksack. Melina hadn't seen the rucksack lying on the ground, and from her advantage point, she noticed several loaves of bread inside that disappeared, along with the boy, who scampered along an alleyway.

'They're fighting over stolen bread now. How has it come to this?' A despondent look flashed across her face.

'Are you sure that's all it is, Mum? There's been food shortages before, and you've always been inventive with your cooking. There's something else troubling you. I can tell. Has something happened?'

Melina nodded. She didn't elaborate. Instead, she stared at her hands as if they belong to someone else.

Alvertos moved towards her. 'Then tell me. What's troubling you?'

There was no point in pretending. Melina didn't have the stomach for it, anyway. She cleared her throat. 'I think it's no longer a secret Rosa is staying with us.'

'But we've been careful. Why do you think this?'

'Theodores.'

'That woman is nothing but a gossip. She thinks she knows everyone's business. Everyone knows this.'

Melina fumbled with the paltry groceries. 'That may be so. With the restrictions in place, all it will take is for Rosa's father not to include her in the list he has to post on his door and for someone to notice she is not on it. Questions will be asked, and you know where that could lead to.'

Rosa reached across the table and took Alvertos' hand. Her stomach fluttered like a swarm of birds inside her.

'What were we thinking? Even with you, I'm not safe, and worst of all, I'm putting you and Melina in danger.'

'What's the alternative? You'd have to go back to your family, to your father who has all but disowned you, and the daily persecutions of the Nazis and their puppet police force. Stay, Rosa. With me. I'll protect you.'

'How can you protect me, Alvertos, when every Jew is a legitimate target and every Greek who shelters a Jew is putting not only their lives but their family's lives in danger? I couldn't have it on my conscience if anything ever happened to you or Melina.'

Melina unclipped the chain around her neck and, taking Rosa's hand, she gently placed it in her palm. Rosa could feel the edges of the cross prick against the soft padding of her skin.

Melina's voice was soft, but insistent. 'My life is not worth more than your life. Under the eyes of God, we are equal, and that's all that matters. This cross will protect you.'

'I can't take it. You have done so much for me already, and now you're giving me your possessions. It's too much. When Alvertos first introduced me to you, it was the first thing I noticed. The cross looked a part of you. It told me who you were and what you believed in.'

'Exactly. That's why it has more worth around your neck than mine. It will not only protect you, but it will also safeguard the child growing inside you. Wear it, Rosa, and make sure it's always visible.'

Rosa enclosed the cross with her fingers and pressed against its metal. Each decision she made wouldn't be for her own self-interest, but from now on, her sole purpose would be to preserve the life of her baby. 'I will. It will become a part of me too.'

CHAPTER TWENTY-NINE

BECOMING A DAUGHTER

Rosa reached out and traced the curve of Alvertos' face. She kissed him softly on the lips, her eyes not leaving his face, and then, smiling, said, 'We need to start thinking about names for this little one.' She patted her swollen stomach.

'Have you any suggestions?' Alvertos asked.

'It's always been a tradition in our family to name a girl after the grandmother and a boy after the grandfather. Do you have any traditions like this?'

Alvertos shook his head. 'Do you want to keep to tradition?'

Rosa thought for a moment. 'I think we should decide what we want to call our child, don't you?'

'From you, I wouldn't have expected anything less. When did you ever stick to convention? I would like that. Have you any thoughts?'

'A few. I've always liked the name Amelia for a girl and Antonis for a boy.' Rosa looked at Alvertos expectantly.

He nodded his approval, and his smile broadened. 'I like them too.'

It felt like a ray of sunshine had fallen on Rosa's face. She reached out and took his hand in hers, threading their fingers. 'Then it's settled. We have our names. Amelia and Antonis.'

Alvertos repeated the names.

Just then, Melina entered the apartment. She slid her arms from her coat and hung it on the coat hanger in the hall. She placed her bag on the kitchen table and removed the items from her shopping trip: a loaf of bread, onions, an aubergine and a bag of pulses.

'No rich pickings, then,' Alvertos said.

'The market stalls are getting barer by the day. There was no fish, and the meat looked like someone had skinned rats. I don't know how we are supposed to feed ourselves. Remember that little boy I saw in the street the other day? I heard the police arrested him for stealing food. It's getting that bad.'

A twitch of guilt crawled up Rosa's back.

'And another thing,' Melina continued as she put away the meagre items from her shopping trip. 'I went to the Bakery on Ioannou Theotokis Street and Theodora, who owns it, told me, in a few weeks, if things continue as they are, there'll not be enough flour to make even the smallest loaf of bread. The Germans are taking most of it for their own. It's the same in the villages, if not worse. At least we have the wedding to look forward to. That's something, at least.'

Alvertos smiled. 'I spoke with the priest, and he's agreed to marry us next Saturday.'

Melina's brow drew together. 'That's only ten days away. There's so much to do.'

'Like what? We're not having a normal wedding; it will only be the three of us in attendance.'

'What about your family, Rosa?'

Rosa's stomach dropped. She shook her head. 'There would be no point in telling them. My father will forbid anyone attending.'

'What about your mother? You still see her. Have you told your mother the day of the wedding?'

'I have. She'll not go against his wishes.'

'The fewer people know, the better. The last thing we want is for the Germans to know. There's to be no fuss. The ceremony will be just us three,' Alvertos said soberly.

Melina wiped her hands on her dress. 'Have you thought of what you'll wear?'

'No. I haven't given it much thought. The shape of my belly is changing by the day.'

A small smile touched Melina's mouth. 'Then we'll have to change that.'

'What do you mean?' Rosa asked, confused.

Melina considered Rosa appraisingly. 'I still have my wedding dress. Believe it or not, I was a lot rounder than I am today. Even with your bump, I can make the dress fit you. That's if you don't mind wearing a second-hand wedding dress?'

Rosa's eyes sparkled. 'It would be an honour.'

'That's settled then. I'll just get some measurements and I'll set to work straight away.'

Once she'd made the measurements, and whenever she'd a spare moment, Melina set to transforming her wedding dress into a garment Rosa would be proud to wear on her special day. Melina worked during the day and at times into the night. The work was intricate, and straining on the eye as Melina's scissors carefully cut and her needle meticulously stitched the delicate fabric.

The work gave her a sense of joy and purpose and she quickly realised just how much she missed this kind of work. It kindled a glow in her stomach she did not want to fade. There was a time, not that long ago, it defined who she was and her standing in the community. Most women in the town had passed through her modest shop and sang the praises of her tailoring skills. She longed for those days to return, but it brought a sadness, for it reminded her of just how much she'd lost.

It was a few days before the wedding and Melina had called Rosa into her bedroom. She was standing with the dress in her hands and Rosa's heart jumped.

'I need you to try it on. There might be some adjustments to make, and I don't want to rush things. It must fit you perfectly.'

'I'm sure it will.' Rosa said excitedly.

Melina tentatively handed Rosa the dress. The fabric felt smooth. The luxurious feel of satin surprising her as its sheen elevated its soft and silky touch between her fingers. She noted the intricate embroidery, the delicate satin stitching, and subtle patterns of raised embroidery and artistry, a unique touch that caught her eye.

Rosa stood in front of a long mirror and stared at her reflection. The dress elegantly and gracefully draped around her, highlighting her figure and, to Rosa's delight, it fitted the curve of her stomach sympathetically.

She bit her lips and closed her eyes.

Melina held her hands to her chest. 'Rosa! What's wrong? Do you like the dress?'

'It's beautiful, Melina, more than I could ever have imagined. It's an honour to wear your dress.'

'It's your dress now. I don't have much to give, but it's my gift for you. It still needs some attention, but nothing that can't be fixed. It will be ready in time. You look just perfect.'

Rosa couldn't contain her tears a second longer. 'My mother won't see me in this dress. It's something every mother should see. Along with everything else, she'll be denied that too.'

'She'll understand.'

'Do you think so?'

'As a mother myself, I know she will. She'll hurt, but she'll sacrifice her happiness for yours.'

'Sometimes, I hate myself for what I've done. I've asked too much of my family.'

'What choice did you have? You have another to think about and the second you hold your baby in your arms, you'll know you've done the right thing. You'll do anything for them. Your life no longer matters, only your child's life and their happiness too. You will understand.'

Rosa looked at the ground. 'I never thought it would be like this. When I was younger, I always pictured my wedding as a big affair, family, friends, the typical Jewish wedding. I'm not disappointed. How could I be? I'm marrying the man I love.' She fell silent. 'We don't have rings. Imagine getting married and not having rings.' Her voice quaked with sadness.

Melina touched Rosa's arm. 'I'll just be a second.'

When she returned, Melina was holding a small box covered in purple velvet. She opened the lid and smiled.

'They were my grandparents' wedding rings. They're the only things I have that belonged to them. When they died, the rings were passed to my mother. I've no idea why. But maybe they have been waiting for a moment like this.'

Rosa glanced at the rings.

'Here, try it on. See if it fits.'

Tentatively, Rosa removed the golden band from its encasement. Melina's eyes urged her to place it on her finger. The ring slid with ease over Rosa's finger.

Melina grinned with satisfaction. 'See. It was meant to be.'

Rosa ran a fingertip over the smooth curve of the ring.

'What was your grandmother's name?'

'Kalliopi.'

'Thank you, Kalliopi.' Rosa took Melina's hands in hers. 'And thank you, Melina. You've given me so much. Not only have you welcomed me into your home.' She gestured towards the dress and ring. 'But all of this, too. You've put yourself in great danger. How can I ever thank you? Words have no currency in such matters.'

Trying to smile through her tears, Melina replied, 'You're now family, Rosa. You're a daughter to me now.'

CHAPTER THIRTY

A WEDDING

It was the most beautiful piece of clothing she'd ever worn. She would never wear the likes of it again. She was sure of it. Next to her, Alvertos's smile felt like the rays of a warm sun caressing her skin. The touch of his fingers entwined in hers bonded their love for each other in their soft embrace. Before them, in the flickering candlelight of the Church of St Nikolas, the priest chanted a prayer, his voice carried on the incense infused air like a kite. It didn't matter to Rosa whether a rabbi or a priest married them, she and Alvertos were demonstrating their love for one another and a commitment to be together no matter what card life dealt them.

Alvertos had explained the significance of the rituals, the prayers, and symbolism of the ceremony. Rosa thought of these as just words that explained a process. But as she stood before the priest, they took on a mystical and personalised quality that affected her to the core.

The exchanging of rings. Two candles lit from the same flame and handed to them both. The crowns that were placed on each of their heads. Prayers recited and the drinking of wine from the same cup. She was transfixed. Caught up in the emotion and sharing the performance of each of the rituals with Alvertos was an intense and moving experience. Rosa couldn't stop smiling, and at other moments in the ceremony, she fought back tears and embraced the oneness and closeness she felt towards Alvertos.

The church was empty apart from the priest, Melina and the silence around them, all witnesses to Rosa and Alvertos joining in marriage.

There was one other. She slid into the church unnoticed and sat still on the chair, her shawl hiding her tears of loss and her tears of joy.

Rosa squinted in the candlelight. 'You came!' she exclaimed, overjoyed and enthralled.

'How could I stay away?'

'How did you know?'

'I told her,' Melina said. 'When the date was set, I went to your family's café and waited. Obviously, I saw your father, and it took all my willpower not to give him a piece of my mind, but I restrained myself and I was patient and finally your mother went to the bakers over the street, so I spoke to her then.'

'Your father knows I'm here. It hurt me more than you could imagine when he found out we were meeting, and he forbade me to see you again,' Yvette said carefully but determined. 'I've come to my senses, Rosa. I told him I was coming and there was nothing he could do or say that would stop me.'

Rosa looked at her mother with a mixture of astonishment and disbelief. 'I didn't think this day could get any better, but here you are.'

'You look beautiful.' Yvette breathed. 'And your dress...' They fell into each other's arms, tears spilling down their faces.

'I have to get changed,' Rosa said, reluctantly easing herself from her mother's embrace.

Her mother, brows set, looked at Rosa.

Rosa answered her mother's confused look. 'I can't walk about looking like this, can I?'

It was then, her mother recognised her meaning. 'Of course not. I will always hold this image of you in my mind. It will live with me forever.'

CHAPTER THIRTY-ONE

MY PRICKLY ROSE

Several weeks after the wedding, Errikos made contact again. As Alvertos walked home, a boy, no more than ten, slipped a note inside Alvertos' pocket. Alvertos turned on his heels, thinking someone had just pickpocketed him. As quickly as the boy was by Alvertos's side, he disappeared. Alvertos called after him and was just about to give chase when he felt his wallet still in his trouser pocket. Alvertos found the piece of paper in his pocket and pulled out the note. He scanned the handwritten message. Alvertos frowned as he ran his eyes over the townsfolk who were going about their normal business. He peered into every corner, every shop and every building. How long had the boy been following him? Worried he had been oblivious to the boy's attention, Alvertos realised how easy it would be for an informer or a plain clothed German to tail his every move and merge into the crowd. It shocked him. His stomach churned. He felt exposed, like an animal being hunted, and for the first time felt the disabling fear that came with not knowing. It flooded him.

Alvertos sat them down at the kitchen table. Rosa and his mother both looked at him with a mix of curiosity and concern.

'What is it that can't wait? The dinner won't make itself,' Melina said.

Alvertos removed the note from his pocket and laid it on the table.

'What's this?' Rosa asked.

'A boy placed it in my pocket as I was passing the market. It was busy, so I didn't see him at first, not until I caught sight of him disappearing toward the Jewish quarter.'

'What does it say?' Melina asked, her agitated frown replaced with a curious look.

Alvertos shook his head. 'I've no idea. It's not written in Greek.'

Rosa lifted the note. 'That's because it's Hebrew.'

'Hebrew!' Melina's eyes blazed with interest. 'Who's it from and what does it say?'

They watched as Rosa's eyes widened, and then a small smile curled her lips. 'It's from Uncle Errikos. He can't visit us this time. It's too dangerous. He wants to meet with us.'

Alvertos scratched his chin. 'Does he say why?'

'He just says it's of the utmost importance.'

'And where does he suggest we meet?'

'Not far. Just along the coast. Kontokali.'

'I know it.'

'Errikos has a friend who lives there. I remember he took me when I was about ten. I know the house. It must be safe, or he would never have suggested it. He'll be there in two days' time.'

'Are you sure it's from him? A boy delivered the note. It could be a trap,' Melina said, worried.

'Who would do such a thing? If the Germans suspected me, they would just knock down the front door.'

Alvertos sighed. 'I'm not sure. I don't like it.'

'It's from Errikos,' Rosa insisted, a trace of annoyance now evident.

Alvertos leaned into her to get a closer look at the note. He grunted. 'How can you be so sure?'

'He referred to me as *"my prickly rose"*. It was what he called me when I was younger. A term of endearment. He knew only I would know this. It's definitely from Errikos.'

Alvertos couldn't help smiling. 'Prickly rose. I like it. It suits you perfectly. Beautiful and sensuous, but beware of the thorns.'

'Then you agree with me. We must meet with him.'

'I don't think we have a choice, do you?'

Melina pushed herself from the table and stood, her face stricken with worry. 'I'll see to the dinner,' she said, her voice wavering as she turned to the stove.

CHAPTER THIRTY-TWO

THE OFFER

They slipped out of the town and walked the coastal road that would take them to Kontokali. It was a risk, but they looked like any other couple taking a stroll beside the sea. Rosa fingered the cross that hung from the chain around her neck, and she found it unimaginable that an object so small and insignificant could shield her from the overwhelming prejudices and intolerance of the Nazis. The thought of being discovered, had at times, frozen her with fear, especially now that the Nazis were ramping up their programme of persecution. Every day brought news of new horrors and hardship for the Jewish community, and she struggled with the thought that she abandoned them, but as Alvertos often reminded her, it was not without its cost to her own personal safety. Every minute of every day was a reminder of the sacrifice and danger those she loved put themselves through. She didn't deserve such heroism and selflessness. Rosa struggled with it more than anyone could know. She even hid it from Alvertos. She couldn't hide from the dreams that continued to plague her, nor could she minimise the effect they had from Alvertos.

At times, she tried to imagine what her world had been like before the war. It was an existence that had removed itself from her reach. She hoped with all her heart that one day she could look back at these long and darkened times and view them also as a thing confined to another world.

Even when Corfu was scarred by the presence of devils, she emanated a beauty that had lasted for thousands of years. Even the Nazis couldn't erase such a thing. It was the incandescent quality of the light, the sparkle of the sun on the Ionian, the lushness of the forests, the depths of colour that flushed the landscape. It seduced Rosa's heart and pacified her mind in a splendid stupor that wrapped around her like the comforting arms of her mother.

'Are you sure you remember the house? It's been a long time since you were there,' Alvertos asked her.

'I remember. Don't worry.'

'It's hard not to.' He couldn't disguise the concern in his voice.

When they reached Kontokali, it was no more than a single street with several houses that stretched for several hundred yards. The only sign of life was a scrawny dog that scratched itself in the middle of the dirt track road.

'Which one is it?' Alvertos asked tightly, his eyes darting from one house to the next.

'The third one along, with the green shutters.'

'You're sure?'

'As you can see, it's the only one that has green shutters. It was something I remembered about the house.'

'And it never crossed your mind that they could have been painted a different colour by now?'

Rosa shrugged. 'Even if they were, it wouldn't have made a difference.'

'Why is that?'

'Because there's an old boat in the garden I played on, and look, it's still there and there's a boy there too.'

'That's the boy who gave me the note.'

The boy turned towards them and, seeing them, he waved them over before running towards the house.

Cautiously, they entered the garden. The boy was standing waiting at the back door, which lay ajar. When he saw Rosa and Alvertos had followed him, he disappeared into the house.

Apprehensively, Rosa held Alvertos arm. 'What now?'

'I think he wants us to follow him.'

'Well, we haven't come all this way for nothing.' Anxiety stalked every footstep as they neared the door of the house.

Errikos was standing by the fireplace when Rosa and Alvertos tentatively entered the room he was in.

He rushed towards them. Arms outstretched. 'Rosa, you came, thank God.' He embraced her and kissed her forehead. Then he backed away, as if pushed by an unseen hand. 'Forgive me. I've not washed in days and must smell like sewage. An occupational hazard.'

'You don't.'

'You were always a terrible liar.'

Errikos wiped his hand on his trousers and extended it towards Alvertos, who shook it enthusiastically.

He smiled at Rosa. 'You're looking beautiful, as always. Married life suits you.'

'How do you know?'

'You've met Spiros?' Errikos tilted his head towards the little boy, who eyed them shyly.

'Yes. This is the second time we've met.' Alvertos smiled at Spiros.

'He is our eyes and ears in Corfu Town. I gave him a message for your mother, just to let her know I was still alive and well. Your mother told Spiros to tell me you were married.' Errikos nodded towards Rosa's swelling stomach. 'How long now?'

'I'm nearly five months.'

'Sit. Take the weight off your feet. You've walked a good distance to get here.'

'I'm pregnant. I'm not ill, Uncle Errikos.'

'I know. I'm just glad to see you... both of you.'

Errikos turned towards a man who sat across from them. 'Do you remember Sokratis? This is his house.'

'I do. It's so good to meet you again.'

Sokratis, although older than Rosa remembered, was still a good-looking man, broad shouldered with wild salt and peppered curled hair that licked at his forehead.

'If only it was under better circumstances.' Sokratis stood and walked over to the stove where food simmered in a pot. 'I hope you're hungry,' he said, stirring the contents with a ladle.

'It smells wonderful.' Alvertos smacked his lips.

'And it tastes good, too. The recipe was handed down through my family. Before my grandparents arrived in Corfu, they lived in Epirus. This was a popular dish in Epirus and handed down to each generation. Gigantes, tomatoes and wild greens, especially dandelions, some onion, garlic, a touch of paprika, and from the garden, mint, parsley, and spinach.'

'It sounds like a feast. We're low on quality food in Corfu Town. It's getting worse by the day. How have you so much choice?'

'It's all from the garden. I've a little patch hidden at the bottom among some olive trees. We don't just hide people from the Germans.'

They settled around the table while Sokratis spooned the food into bowls.

Errikos took a mouthful, then set his spoon next to his bowl. 'Ordinarily, I wouldn't have asked you to come all this way. But these are not ordinary times.'

Rosa looked anxious. 'It must be important.'

'It is. At the moment, I can't risk being in Corfu Town. That's why I asked you to come to me.'

'I knew the note was from you.'

'*My prickly rose*? I wasn't sure if you'd remember.'

'Of course, I remembered.'

'It was a chance worth taking, as was asking you to come here. I know it wasn't without its risk.'

'Whatever it is you had to tell me, I knew it would be important.'

'There's no easy way of saying this, but I'm afraid there's no doubt about it. It's coming, Rosa.'

Rosa detected the hollowness in his voice. 'What do you mean, it's coming?'

'What happened in Salonika is happening in Athens and other parts of Greece, too. Soon, very soon, the Jews of Corfu will be next.'

'How do you know this? How can you be sure?'

'ELAS has eyes and ears in the Greek police, even Greeks who are collaborating with the Nazis. One, in particular is an interpreter. Every day, he puts his life at risk of being discovered. Recently, he reported some troubling news. He was present when a discussion took place among several high-ranking officers. The orders had come from Himmler himself and the Jews on the islands of

Corfu, Zakynthos, the Dodecanese and Crete were to be deported as soon as preparations allowed. The Wehrmacht's intelligence are of the opinion that there would be no political or military opposition to the removal of the Jewish community from Corfu. There was one dissenting voice. A commander by the name of Oberst Emil Jaeger. He was the one who visited your father's cafe and his henchman whipped your father. He was of the opinion that such an extreme act would only incite the population to acts of resistance and violence. He viewed the Italian soldiers, who were still hiding in the hills, as more of a threat than the Jews. Even when he raised the question of how could two thousand people be deported off an island and the fact that a Red Cross Ship was anchored in the harbour and distributing food to the population would witness this, it was to no avail. He was told the German navy would provide the means. It's our understanding that they will use the Old Fort to house everyone before they're deported.'

'Where will they take them?'

'From Corfu they are to dock at Lefkada and then finally they will arrive in Patras. I've heard they will probably be detained in Haidari prison and then by train from Athens to Poland and then, their final destination, Auschwitz.'

'I can't believe this. It's dreadful. What will happen?'

'Most won't even spend a full day in the camp or see the sunset. Their fate will already have been decided and upon arriving they will be murdered: women, men, children, babies, the old, the weak, the sick, the disabled. For those who escape this fate, their time will come later. If anyone survives, they face the prospect of existing in a living hell.'

'How can you be so sure? Even you yourself have told

me the Nazis have tried to keep the camp's existence from the rest of the world.'

'Few have tried to escape, and even fewer have done so. A comrade, now active in my unit, was one such man.'

Alarm flooded Rosa as a heavy silence encased them.

'It's incomprehensible,' Alvertos finally said.

Rosa's throat tightened. 'I need to tell mum and dad.'

Errikos shook his head. 'Don't you think I've tried? He's a stubborn fool. He should have taken his chance when it was presented to him.'

'You know about the offer from his friend, the lawyer who secured a passage to Turkey?'

'Your father told me you found the letter.'

Rosa bowed her head. 'What more is there to say?'

'How has it been for you, Rosa? It can't be easy.'

Rosa took Alvertos' hand in hers. 'I've married the man I love, and that makes me happy.'

'It's come with a tremendous sacrifice.'

'One that I wholly embrace.'

'I don't doubt it, but the community you've left is a close one. It won't have gone unnoticed that you're no longer living with your family and, to be honest, there will be others who know where you live now. Corfu Town is too compact and small for someone to be totally invisible. That's my worry. A Jewish girl living with a non-Jew does not go unnoticed, no matter how diligent you think you are. You might escape the attention of the Nazis for now, but all it takes is for someone to have a grievance against you, or to see an opportunity present itself and you could be arrested.'

'But we've been careful. I have a baptism certificate and a marriage licence. I'm Rosa the Orthodox Christian, not Rosa the Jew.'

'I understand that, but they're just pieces of paper if

there is evidence to the contrary, and which one will the Nazis believe? Knowing what's about to come, you only have one choice. Corfu Town is no longer safe for you, Rosa.'

Alvertos tightened his grip on Rosa's hand. 'What are you suggesting?'

'There's a village inland, up in the hills. The villagers are good people. They're protecting two Jewish families, giving them shelter, a roof over their heads and food. I've secured a place for you, a room in the house of a widow. She would be pleased to have you as her guests.'

'I won't go without Andras. I can't leave him, not after what you've told me,' Rosa said defiantly.

Errikos frowned. 'What are you going to do, walk right up to the house and take him from his parents?'

'I'll convince Mum to do the right thing. She won't leave dad, I know that, but she can save her son.'

Alvertos stiffened. 'How long before the Nazis begin the deportation?'

'According to the intelligence we have, and there's no reason not to believe it, several weeks at the most.'

'Then shouldn't ELAS tell the Jewish leaders what's about to happen?'

'Even if we did, I'm afraid it may just fall on deaf ears. There are some, like Rosa's father, who are convinced the Jews of Corfu have escaped the worst. They're living under a false sense of security. Because the allies are gaining more ground each day in Italy and the Russians are advancing through the Balkans, they're convinced it's only a matter of time before the Germans surrender and the war is won. Believe me, the Nazis' policy towards us Jews is to extinguish our very existence in Corfu.'

Alvertos drew a sharp breath. 'We have to do as Errikos says, with or without your little brother.'

CHAPTER THIRTY-THREE

THE PLEA

'What are you talking about, Rosa? Your father has not mentioned this.'

'Because he doesn't believe it's going to happen. It will. Errikos is certain.'

'Errikos has spent weeks living in the hills. What does he know?'

'That's the point, Mum. He knows because he is with the resistance. The *andartes* are not goat herders, they're the armed resistance, they are organised, disciplined, and they gather intelligence from their sources. Would you let Andras stand in the middle of a busy road and wait to see if he got hit by a vehicle?'

'Why would I do such a thing? It would be irresponsible. Only someone who was mad would allow such a thing.'

'And why is this any different? Will you gamble with Andras' life?

'You have no evidence. You want to take him from his parents and live with strangers?'

'He won't be living with strangers. He will be with me and Alvertos.'

'In a place he has never been, in a house he does not know, and he will be far from me and his father. How can I possibly tell him this is where he is to live?'

'Do you want him to die, Mum?'

'You're not making any sense, Rosa. You're acting strangely, you should see a doctor, you have been through an awful time, you're not thinking normally…'

'Stop it! Just stop! I've never been more serious in my life.'

'Your father listens every night to the BBC. There has been no mention of these places you speak of. The allies are about to enter Rome, and I heard, just last night, a report on the BBC that said they are close to invading Corfu. The war is almost won, Rosa.'

'Oh, Mum. It makes no difference to the Germans. It only makes them more determined to carry out the deportations.'

'Then why has this not been on the radio? The BBC would surely tell people what's happening.'

'They haven't, but they will know, and that is to their shame. Errikos has told you what happened in Salonika. If he hadn't escaped, he wouldn't be alive today. Why would he lie about such things?'

Yvette thought for a moment. 'Errikos is a good man. I remember him as a younger man, good looking, and charming. He was serious even then, but the ladies adored him. Yes, even I. He had a good way with words, too. He could describe things like the words he spoke just fell out of a book and not his mouth. He was adventurous even then. It was obvious this place was too small for him, and the slow pace of life seemed to suffocate him. The world was too big a place for him not to go out into and explore.

'Now, your father, he was completely the opposite. People used to wonder if they both came out of the same womb. They were so different. But I chose your father. He was quiet and gentle, but he could be opinionated too, as well, you know, and when he got something stuck in his mind, not even an earthquake could budge it. Errikos was like the wind and your father was the tree whose roots were nourished by the land he lived on and the community he belongs to. Errikos was the wind that rustled your father's branches and bent them in a storm. They were both the opposite in so many ways. They still are, but they were brothers, and they would do anything for each other.' Yvette smiled at the memories.

'Life seemed simpler back then. Not like now. It has been turned on its head. Look at you, Rosa. Who would have thought it would come to this? This war has changed our lives beyond recognition. It has destroyed families, threatened our way of life. We have lost those we love, and we cling to those we still have, fearing what tomorrow might bring. I'm tired of waking each day into a world of fear and uncertainty. But I have around me walls that are strong and steadfast and your father and Andras are the cement between the stones and bricks. Without them, my wall would topple and crumble to the ground and only death would be my reprieve. My darling Rosa, you were like a bird trapped in a cage and now you're free. Spread your wings and make a life for yourself and your child that is far from this suffering and pain that inflicts us all.' Yvette reached out and gently stroked Rosa's face. 'Make me proud, my beautiful daughter.'

Rosa stared at her mother, defeated and heart torn. 'What will you do?'

'Whatever God has planned for me,' Yvette said simply. 'I will accept his judgement. As long as I am with your father and brother, I have all I need in this world.' Yvette paused and swallowed. 'And knowing you are safe and happy with Alvertos and this little one.' She bent her head and kissed the swell of Rosa's stomach. It was then Rosa's fortitude crumbled. As they embraced, she sobbed into her mother's neck.

CHAPTER THIRTY-FOUR

THEA

Liapades crept up the hillside, the houses like stepping stones, and above them, a crown of trees and thick vegetation stretched towards the green carpeted summit. Rosa and Alertos arrived with one suitcase and the clothes they wore. She stepped from the car and scanned the terracotta roofs and facades of the houses.

Errikos opened the trunk and pulled out the suitcase with a grunt. 'We'll leave the car here. It's a tight squeeze to get where we're going. The lanes were built for mules, not vehicles. It's a long way to reverse if we meet another vehicle head on.'

Alvertos placed a hand on the small of Rosa's back. 'It's not too bad. Maybe the fresh air will do us good, and the sea is only ten minutes' walk away… the best of both worlds.'

Rosa knew Alvertos was doing his best to see the good in a bad situation and he was right. Even the air was different, with its hints of pine and jasmine. Rosa tried to nod encouragingly and gave a resigned smile, but it did not stop the hot fluttering in her stomach.

The narrow lane curved upwards, flanked by an assortment of one and two-storey houses. An opened gate revealed a courtyard with pots and vases of varying sizes that erupted in splendored colour. It took the breath from Rosa. She had come to appreciate that in a world where darkness prevails, glimpses of light should be cherished and savoured.

'Almost there,' Errikos announced, as an old woman sitting on a stool smiled a toothless welcome.

The lane continued to curve at a steep gradient. They went further along it, rounded a corner that flattened out and they stood outside a modest two storey whitewashed house.

'Here we are.'

The weathered wooden door opened and revealed an elderly woman with silver hair that fell in soft waves around her shoulders. She had kind hazel eyes which her advancing years couldn't cloud, and lines fanned from the corner of her lips. She wore the widows' black, her skirt covering her knees. Framed in the doorway, she smiled at the newcomers.

'Thea, I'd like to introduce my niece, Rosa, and her husband, Alvertos.'

Thea gestured for them to enter. 'Yassas. Please come in out of the street.'

They stepped over the threshold and Rosa's eyes peered inquisitively into a shadowy front room simply furnished and clean, with a homely feel. A white embroidered lace cloth covered an oak table, with several wooden chairs positioned around it. In a corner, a bookcase leaned against the wall where paint peeled with age. A worn armchair sat in front of a fire range and Rosa wondered if the old woman sat there at night with a book and read. On the wall, several framed pictures of Christ and another, Rosa presumed to be of a saint, looked down upon them. In the corner, stairs climbed to a landing and three closed doors. Around them, an aroma of coffee wafted towards them, coming from a pot on the stove, where the front room led to a kitchen with a cooker, sink and dresser.

'Welcome. It's not much, but it's home and it has been for fifty years.'

'Thank you for letting us stay,' Rosa said with a composure that contradicted her guilt and embarrassment for imposing upon Thea's generosity.

'It feels good to do something and be of use. I want to play my part. It was bad enough when the Italians were here, but these Germans are ungodly and evil. I can't stand by and do nothing, so it's a pleasure to have you as my guests,' Thea insisted.

Rosa was under no illusion of the enormity of what Thea had agreed to. 'My name is Rosa, and this is my husband, Alvertos.'

Alvertos smiled. 'I'll do any odd job you need me to do.'

Rosa nodded. 'And I can cook, and we have a little money too, so we can buy food…'

Thea raised her hand. 'That's kind of you. I've only had to feed myself these past few years, so I've more than enough vegetables in my little patch in the garden. And I like to cook, although, there are a few things needing repaired around the house that I do need help with. We'll manage, I'm sure.'

'I'll let the both of you settle in. I'll be around and about for the next few days at least, so I'll call round soon.'

No one asked Errikos what he would be doing, and if

they had, they knew he wouldn't have been able to tell them.

'Won't you stay for a coffee?' Thea asked.

'I'd love too, believe me, just smelling that coffee and not being able to taste it is torture. Unfortunately, there are other matters that need my attention.'

'Thank you, Uncle Errikos, for everything.'

'Don't you worry now, you're safe and that's all that matters.' He smiled at her, and nodding in Thea's direction, he slipped out of the door.

'Just leave your bag for now. I'll show you to your room, but for now, I'll get that coffee, and there's some bread and cheese too. You must both be hungry.'

CHAPTER THIRTY-FIVE

DISCOVERED

Rosa could not sleep. The narrow ray of sunlight filtered through the edges of the shutters and she pressed her eyes tightly closed, her mind preoccupied with thoughts that fought for her attention. Frustrated, she opened her eyes.

Alvertos was still sleeping, his hair a ruffled mass across the pillow and his face projected an appearance of contentment, a state of being his wakening hours had lacked for weeks now.

Rosa lay motionless. With light breaths, she indulged herself in considering Alvertos' every pore, contemplating every strand of hair and fine eyelash, extraordinarily long and curved. Not wanting to wake him, she gently slipped from the covers and slid quietly from the bed. She changed into her clothes and wrapped a shawl around her shoulders. Tentatively, she descended each wooden stair that creaked into submission with each cautious step. The house was quiet and still. She crossed the stone flagged floor, deftly turning the key in the lock. She slid through the doorway, out into the morning light. The ground beneath her bare feet was dry and hard. The days were growing warmer by the hour, but there was still a crisp chill to the morning air until the sun had risen over the hills.

Rosa walked to the edge of the garden. It sloped into a mattress of vegetation thick with shrubs and populated with a dense canopy of interlocking branches, mature lemon trees, olive trees, poplar and cypress. Rosa stared at the sky for a long moment. Painted in hues of soft indigo and warm purples, the morning sky was a vibrant canvas where wisps of clouds scorched the sky in brilliant crimson and amber. Around her, the air carried hints of sea salt and jasmine and then a gentle breeze rustled the leaves of the trees below her, infusing the air in citrus and the Earthly aromas of wild herbs. Such splendour filled her heart with wonder and her eyes with amazement.

Rosa heard footsteps approaching and turned, startled. Errikos was smiling, walking towards her with a rifle casually rested on his shoulder and two dead rabbits dangling from his hip. 'You're up early, Rosa.'

'And you've been busy.'

'These two are for the pot. Rabbit stew is on the menu tonight. Where's Alvertos?'

'Still sleeping and missing this beautiful sunrise.'

'It's a beauty, isn't it? In the chaos of war, who would have thought such magnificence could exist to seduce the eye? It's almost as if the world has turned normal again.'

'It's hard to imagine things ever being normal.' Her eyes turned haunted. Her face was ashen.

'I haven't told you, Rosa, but I'm incredibly proud of you. I wouldn't wish what you've endured on anyone, but you've faced it with dignity and a strength of character which can only be but admired.'

'Thank you. It means everything to hear you say those things, although I don't recognise myself in your words.'

'I forgot to mention your humility too.'

'Do you think my father will feel like that?' she said doubtfully. 'I'm not so sure.'

'He's never stopped loving you, Rosa. I know your father better than anyone... well, apart from your mother. He may be hurting and blinded by his convictions and beliefs, but he's never stopped loving you, even if his actions and words say otherwise.'

'And now, I'll never know.'

'You have done the right thing. It may not feel like it right now, but you have.'

'I wish I could share your certainty.'

'You've given your child the chance of a life. You and Alvertos can have a family. You might have more children and in time, they too will have children and so it will continue. Your choices have the potential to give a life to children not even born yet. What a wonderful thing you have done, Rosa.'

Rosa bit her lip, her eyes glossed in tears. 'I never thought about it like that.'

'But it's the truth. You will continue your family's line. Your father will live in your children and the generations to come.'

'How long are you staying with us?' she asked, but feared the answer.

'I can only stay for another day and then I need to join my unit.'

She fought for air. 'So soon.'

'It was always going to be this way. The resistance needs me to do what I do best.'

'Kill Germans.'

'If that is what is called for, but I have other talents too.'

'What does it feel like to know you have taken another's life?'

'It's war, Rosa. If I don't kill them, they'll kill me, and worst of all, they would kill you too, Alvertos and the old couple who have given you their hospitality. Even children are not exempt. I know of terrible things that have taken place. Every German I kill negates the likelihood of that happening again.'

Further below the village and in a clearing just beyond the trees, a large barn stood. 'There are several families sheltering in that barn. They arrived just before dark last night.'

'From Corfu Town?' Rosa asked.

'Yes. Twenty in total. Half of them children. There's even a baby among them, only a few months old.'

'The baby and the parents can stay in our room. Alvertos and I will go to the barn.'

'That's kind of you, Rosa, but they have another two children. They won't leave them.'

'Do you know any of the families' names? If I don't know them, some of them are bound to know my dad.'

'They probably do.' Errikos frowned. 'There're too many of them for the villagers to take in, but they've given them blankets, food and water.'

Just then, two men appeared from the path that flanked the edge of the village and walked towards. Rosa noticed their rifles, and she knew by their worn clothes they weren't villagers.

'Don't worry, Rosa, they're with me… *andartes*. They've been away a few days on a reconnaissance mission. We will leave together tomorrow.'

Errikos raised his hand in welcome, and they returned the gesture.

Suddenly, Errikos tilted his head and listened, staying still, concentrating. His eyes combed the tree line below. Rosa followed his gaze. 'What is it?'

Errikos placed a finger on his lips. 'Something's wrong.'

'What do you mean?'

'The birds have stopped singing.' He turned to her. 'Go back to the house now, and whatever happens, stay inside,' he warned her, as he slung his rifle from his shoulder and held it ready. The two *andartes*, seeing Errikos' change in posture, ran over to him.

A German patrol on foot emerged from the line of trees a hundred yards from the barn. Errikos counted twelve, twelve that he could see. 'There's maybe more in the trees behind them.' He warned as they lay prone on the ground, their rifles trained on the patrol below.

'They seem to be intent on heading for the barn,' one of the *andartes* said.

Errikos tightened his hold on his rifle. 'There are people in there. Jewish families. They've come for them. Someone has betrayed them. There's probably a truck on the main road just beyond the trees. If we do nothing, these people will be taken back to Corfu Town and if they survive the deportation that is to follow, they will certainly not survive what awaits them. If we attack the Germans, more will surely follow.'

The Germans fanned out and moved swiftly towards the barn.

'Or they could kill everyone in the barn right now,' one of the *andartes* reminded Errikos.

The other *andarte* took aim. 'Wait!' Errikos commanded. 'Let them move a little further, so there's nowhere for them to run and we'll cut them down like flies.'

Errikos held the butt of the rifle close to his shoulder, his cheek resting on the stock. He trained his eye on the rear sight. 'Wait... Wait... Fire! Send the bastards to hell!'

An explosion of gunfire rained down on the German soldiers, spreading panic and sending them scattering. Some dropped to the ground for cover, others bolting towards the barn. Three lay dead before the Germans could return fire.

Suddenly, the gunshots to Errikos' left ceased, and when he turned, he witnessed blood obscuring what remained intact of the *andarte's* face.

Another flurry of shots ensued, and the Germans continued to return gunfire. Within less than a minute, Errikos counted eight of them dead, sprawled on the ground. To his horror, two had made it to the barn.

The high ground and the advantage of surprise had worked in their favour, but Errikos knew the sound of gunfire would have alerted those that had remained with the truck, for he was sure there would be at least one to transport the families back to the town.

The air fell eerily silent. And then, from behind Errikos, a cry of despair cracked the stillness around him. It was Alvertos, scampering hysterically towards a figure sitting slumped on the ground, and he was yelling a name - Rosa!

When Errikos reached them, Alvertos was crouched beside Rosa, a pool of deep crimson blood staining the dust around her.

'Rosa!' Alvertos gasped. 'Oh, my God. You've been shot.'

With a choking sob, she stared at the blood that soaked her. 'No, I've not been shot. It's worse than that. I'm losing our baby.'

CHAPTER THIRTY-SIX
A QUESTION OF BLAME

Alvertos carried Rosa cradled in his arms. By the time he got her to the house, she was sweating and fighting waves of nausea. Thea's hand flew to her mouth. She gave out a cry.

'I think she's lost the baby,' Alvertos said helplessly.

'Oh, no,' Thea said, against a mixture of conflicting emotion, relieved Rosa hadn't been shot, but devastated for her loss. 'Take her up to the bed. I'll get towels and a basin of hot water.'

When Thea entered the bedroom, Alvertos was leaning over Rosa and holding her hand.

'I'll see to her now.'

'I'm so sorry.' Rosa sobbed.

'You have nothing to be sorry for,' Thea said, busying herself with the preparation of the towels and water.

'Our baby is gone. Why didn't I know there was something wrong?'

'You're not to blame. There was nothing you could do.'

'I felt a pain in my stomach. I knew there was something wrong, but it came and went.'

'You didn't mention it.'

'I didn't want to worry you. There's enough going on.'

'So, you worried on your own.'

'What would you have done? What could you have done? Go back to Corfu Town to see a doctor? There was nothing you could do.'

'I could have shared your worries.'

'I'm sorry, I should have told you.'

'Don't worry about it. As you said, what could I have done?'

'What if it was my fault? Something I did that made the baby ill.'

'Like what? You've done nothing but be careful.'

'It's God punishing me.'

'Nonsense.'

'I abandoned my family when they needed me most. I should never have renounced being a Jew. What have I done?'

'You have done nothing wrong. You were surviving. You did what you had to do because the alternative was not an option.'

'I did it for our baby.'

'Yes, you did, but you also did it for us.'

'And look at us, hiding with no home to call our own, frightened to be seen, unable to walk freely in the streets we grew up in. What have we got, Alvertos?'

'A future worth fighting for. A future with the promise of a life together. This time will pass.'

Her face crumbled in torment. 'Our baby has gone.'

'You need time to grieve. Let yourself grieve.'

'And what about you? Don't try to be strong for me. We

need to get through this together, not apart. It was our baby, not just mine.'

'I know… I just thought that if I was strong for you, it would make it easier, somehow. I thought I could protect you from your pain.'

'And who was going to protect you? It's your baby too, Alvertos. I'm not the only one who has lost and suffered.'

His breath came in stutters. 'It hurts so much, Rosa.'

'I know. I feel like my heart has been torn from me.'

An urgent look crossed Thea's face. 'Rosa, I need to examine you now. You've lost a lot of blood.'

'I'll go, but I'll just be downstairs if you need me.' Alvertos said, wringing his hands and heading for the door, he glanced at Rosa one last time.

CHAPTER THIRTY-SEVEN

A DECISION MADE

Thea entered the room carrying a vase bursting with orchids and geraniums. 'I thought you would like these. They'll bring much needed colour to the room.'

'They're lovely. Thank you.'

Thea placed them on the bedside table, and standing straight, she studied them for a moment. 'Perfect. There's nothing like flowers to cheer the soul. Nature has the most amazing colours, don't you think, Rosa?'

'I do.'

Thea eased herself onto the side of the bed and sat next to Rosa.

'When I was younger, younger than you, I lost two babies before my son was born, and then I had another three, each year, one after the other. I banned Yorgos from our bed. It didn't matter, we didn't get much sleep, anyway. If two children were sleeping, there was always another one awake crying their lungs out.'

'You have been so kind to us, Thea. I could never thank

you enough. And at such enormous risk to yourselves. Once I'm strong enough, in a day or two, we'll move on. I couldn't put you in harm's way. It's best if we leave.'

'I wouldn't dream of it. What kind of person would that make me? You've been through a terrible ordeal. Your body and your mind need to recover. It's natural to feel the way you're feeling. Give yourself and Alvertos time to grieve. Be there for one another. I can see how close and strong you both are as a couple, and you'll need that strength and togetherness over the coming days.'

'The Germans will come back, and I couldn't live with myself if anything happened to you because you helped us. We'll leave and with us the threat that hangs over you every second we stay will.'

Thea shook her head. 'No. You will stay. Even if you left, we would still fear what the Germans could do to us. I believe God will help us. We believe in the same God, after all. God wants me to help you any way I can. We are Greek, you and I, and that is what binds us. I will not turn my back on my own and that is the last we will talk about it.'

Rosa dared not push the matter further and the truth be told, she did not have it in her. Her emotions felt like a tidal wave crashing over her, and tears filmed her eyes.

Thea reached over and squeezed Rosa's hand. 'Let it all out. It's part of the healing process.'

Rosa struggled for air. 'I don't want to be healed. I want my baby.'

'I know you do. I'll be here for you, but right at this moment, you and Alvertos need to be together. I've taken enough of your time.

'You could never do that, Thea.'

The warm look in Thea's eyes momentarily eased Rosa's angst.

When Thea went downstairs, Errikos and Alvertos were sitting at the table, talking in hushed tones.

Errikos looked up. 'How is she?'

'She's tender in body and mind.'

'It's a dreadful thing, but there are decisions that need to be made. Pressing decisions that need our attention. We've moved the bodies. It wasn't easy, but with a tractor and trailer, we were able to take them further up the hill and concealed them under vegetation and shrubs. There were too many of them to dig a hole deep enough to bury them. With luck, overtime, they'll be eaten by animals.'

Thea shivered.

Errikos continued. 'The Germans will be back. They obviously knew there were Jewish families hiding in the barns. That's why they were here.'

'How could they have known?' Thea asked, alarmed.

'It could have been just a scouting party, but more worryingly, I think they were tipped off and they knew what they were looking for.'

'An informer!'

Errikos raised his hand. 'It doesn't mean it was someone from the village. Unfortunately, there are some of our fellow countrymen who will give information in return for reward. In Corfu Town, the Greek police work closely with the Germans. They're in the Germans' pockets. They too have their way of extracting information, or of gaining information by other means.'

Thea looked at him, shocked. 'I can't believe it.'

'When people are desperate, they'll do anything. I've known people who have held long-standing grudges and now the opportunity has arisen to pay that back. There are many reasons.' Errikos rubbed his chin. 'We're moving the families to another location, higher in the hills. I've asked Alvertos to consider going with them.'

'Rosa is in no fit state to be going anywhere. She needs time to recover. Her body has been through a traumatic experience, and for that matter, her mind too.'

'Thea is right, Errikos. I won't do anything that risks Rosa's health.'

Errikos thought for a moment. 'Then you risk her life. The Germans could have been looking for Rosa as well, and that means they're looking for you too, Alvertos. How do we know they aren't?'

Alvertos bit his lip. 'We don't, but if we go and Rosa gets an infection, I'd be putting her life at risk. If we stay, she's in good hands,' Alvertos smiled at Thea. 'We'll take our chances with Thea.'

'I agree,' Thea said firmly.

Errikos looked at them, concerned, but resigned. 'I'll be honest, it's not what I wanted to hear, but I can see I'm in the minority here. If you feel it's the right thing to do, I accept that. It's settled.'

'It is. We're staying.' For so long, Alvertos felt they had both been walking through life with a blindfold, but there was still a thread of hope, a shaft of light that illuminated the path they shared. The love they had for each other and the potent need to experience all the firsts that their life together had still to offer was a lifeline that sustained him. It was their strength, and Alvertos hoped it would be enough.

CHAPTER THIRTY-EIGHT
A GREATER PURPOSE

The days merged into each other. The expected appearance of more German soldiers failed to materialise. Errikos learnt that a group of *andartes* from his unit fortuitously ambushed the truck in which the soldiers arrived, killing its driver and the remaining soldiers. It would deflect suspicion from the village as it would seem the attack took place several miles from the location. It gave the resistance precious time to relocate the Jewish families to another village higher inland.

With each new day, Rosa eased into the regular pattern of taking walks with Alvertos around the narrow lanes of the village and resting in the square under the shade of a mature oak tree. When Rosa was able, they ventured through olive groves, wild meadows and a winding dirt track, where growing wild rosemary, oregano, thyme and sage sprinkled the earth in a profusion of scents. They ambled under a canopy of branches of ancient oaks and giant elms, where beams of defused sunrays ignited the dry earth in an illumination of silver light. They stumbled upon a foot trodden track, gently descending towards a secluded beach. Perpendicular cliffs clad in shrubs and dense emerald trees slid into the cobalt sea, where beyond, the stretching blue sky fused with the horizon. Every time Rosa and Alvertos visited, it brought a consuming silence, at other times, it produced the occasional smile and words of wonderment from Rosa. Alvertos cherished these moments, as it offered a refuge from the heartbreak at the loss of their baby and hinted at a life that still held promise.

They had decided that if the Germans returned to the village, they would pretend Alvertos was her son, living in his mother's house along with his wife. Thea knew the risks she was taking and accepted it without question. It still troubled Rosa.

Rosa remembered the day the two families left Liapades accompanied by Errikos and other *andartes* who had arrived to assist them. With their meagre collection of belongings, they were moving further away from the comfortable lives they had left behind in Corfu Town. The children, who had witnessed the ambush only a few days earlier, were traumatised and scared, and the sounds and sights of that day reflected upon their innocent faces. One young girl held a doll close to her cheek and Rosa wondered if the girl would ever rediscover her childhood. As they left, Errikos raised a hand in goodbye, and returning the gesture, Rosa prayed she would see him again.

Rosa deliberated whether she'd made the right decision to stay in Liapades. Alvertos had told her Errikos wanted them to move further into the hills. He thought it offered better protection. Rosa wondered if there was anywhere in Corfu that was safe. They couldn't stay in Liapades long. If anything happened to Thea, Rosa would never forgive herself. Could she live with the knowledge that others had sacrificed their lives for her? What right did she have to be the benefactor of such selflessness? Beneath all of this, her frustration with her father and the distress he caused her was beginning to corrode, and she longed to put things right between them for the time neared and the start of the compulsory deportation would soon be upon them.

The thought that she would never see her parents and brother again caused a sadness, so searing, it lodged in her chest. It was more than she could bear.

Could she leave Alvertos and submit to a life of living the last of her days without him? If she went with her family, she knew what the ultimate outcome would eventually be.

Could she make such a momentous decision after all they had been through? Rosa would miss Alvertos desperately, more than life itself. She would worry about him, she would long for him, but if he stayed with her, every second of every day, Alvertos would endure a life of danger. Without her, he would be free. It was a life she couldn't offer him. Such thoughts festered inside her. She kept them locked in her mind. They scared her. A life without Alvertos was unthinkable, but now she considered it necessary.

That night, they made love. Rosa savoured every touch, every stroke and caress. She kissed Alvertos deeply and the pleasures they gave one another aroused such intimate passion it brought her to tears. Alvertos held her close to him and she told him he was her life, and he replied, she was his too, as she dashed away a tear. She hated herself for what she was about to do, but some actions had a greater purpose that only the path of time could reveal. When he fell into a deep sleep, she whispered to him, 'Forgive me, my love.'

CHAPTER THIRTY-NINE
PERMISSION TO LEAVE

The house was dark when she slipped on her clothes and, with lightness in every step; she descended the stairs. At the sink, she sprinkled her face with cold water and, once dried, turned to leave. From the corner of her eye, she glimpsed a figure. Rosa's head spun as the figure moved in the chair and Rosa almost jumped out of her skin. She had been so focused on not making a sound that she did not notice Thea sitting at the table nursing a mug of steaming coffee.

She felt dizzy. 'Thea! You scared me to death.'

'Being light on your feet and preoccupied, I could have been an elephant sitting here and I don't think you would have seen me.' Thea smiled. 'There's enough coffee left for another, if you'd care to join me.' Thea continued, 'You can't sleep either? But wait, you're already dressed, and the hour is still late, its dark outside. In fact, it's still the middle of the night.'

Rosa's hair fell loose around her ashen face, and she tucked a strand behind her ear. She tried not to, but she knew she looked uncomfortable. She didn't know what to do. Thea was playing with her. Her plan foiled before it had a chance to unfurl.

Thea replaced her playful tone with a serious look. 'Talk with me for a while. I've been watching you closely, Rosa. I can see your torment, the pain of leaving your family and your daily anguish of staying with Alvertos and the unthinkable prospect of being discovered and what that would bring for him.'

'You speak as if it was written on my face.'

'It is, Rosa. If life has taught me anything, it's how to be an observer and not judge the actions of others until I can walk in their shoes.'

'I don't know if by leaving I'm doing the right thing.'

'You'll only know once you get there.'

'I can't just let my family go without me. My mum thinks I'm still pregnant.'

'Will you tell her?'

'If she knew the truth, it might do more harm than good. I know that with or without knowing what had happened, she would certainly want me to stay with Alvertos. There's no way she would want me to go with them. The thought of Alvertos and I being a family would be her strength and courage in the days to come.'

'And you're prepared to take that from her. Can you imagine what that would do to her?'

'Believe me, I've thought of nothing else.'

'What about Alvertos? Either way, Rosa, whatever you decide, there's not going to be a good outcome.'

Rosa's eyes filled with tears. 'I haven't told Alvertos I'm leaving. How could I? What would you do, Thea?'

'Oh, child. It's not what I think that matters. Although hard as it is, you're leaving Alvertos because you love him.

You want to protect him. He won't see it like that. When he wakes and you're gone... well, you can imagine his reaction. I don't need to explain how that will be. I won't lie for you, so don't ask me to. If Alvertos asks me if I know where you have gone, I'll tell him.'

'Should I have told him? I've never lied to Alvertos.'

'Do you think he would have let you go if you did?'

Rosa shook her head slowly and Thea's mouth softened, and her shoulders dropped in agreement. 'How are you going to get to Corfu Town?'

'I've secured a lift as far as Gouvia.'

'Who's taking you?'

'Spiros.'

'The schoolteacher? At this late hour.'

'He has... a woman friend,' Rosa said bluntly.

'In Gouvia?'

'I'm presuming she's married.'

Thea gazed at her. 'How do you know this?'

'You know that sometimes I have trouble sleeping, especially when I've had one of my dreams.'

'Yes. The nightmares.'

'Sometimes, I would sit where you're sitting by the window and a few times I heard a vehicle pass the house. Then, on one occasion, I noticed it was Spiros. I knew he could help me, so the other day, when he'd finished his lessons, I confronted him. I wasn't expecting to hear what he told me. I was just as surprised as you are. I think it was a relief for him, but then he got worried, regretting what the consequences would mean. I assured him I wouldn't tell anyone.'

'And he agreed to take you with him tonight.'

Rosa wiped her tears with the back of her hand, her

heart coiling inside her. She covered her mouth and tried to muffle her sobs. 'Why does it have to be like this?'

'I wish I had the answer.' Thea stood and walked towards her with outstretched arms. Rosa fell into them, and they embraced, Rosa welcoming Thea's sweet scent and the ardour of the hug.

Thea's emotions welled inside her. She searched Rosa's eyes. 'I've never known anyone as brave as you, Rosa,' her voice shook. 'You've already made your mind up, that's why you're standing here at this time of night. Go now, before Alvertos wakes.' She kissed Rosa's forehead, giving her permission to leave.

CHAPTER FORTY

THE BEGINNING

Rosa rested by a stream as the haze lifted, and the sun rose above the horizon. She sat with her eyes on the smooth rocks carved and shaped by decades of flowing water, where light twinkling like gold coins on its surface. Around her, the gentle cadence of birdsong carried a soothing quality that gently pulsed the air. She bit her lip. Alvertos' absence in such a moment lodged a disconsolate rock in her throat that tightened and burnt. Not long ago, the thought that she would never see Alvertos again would have been inconceivable to her, but now she'd made that choice and such a thing constantly prowled at the edge of her consciousness. Her only consolation being her anguish and torment would be short-lived if Errikos' descriptions of the Nazis' deportations and their outcome were true.

It wasn't just *knowing* that she made the right choice; she had to *feel* she'd made the right choice. Rosa felt sick, but there was nothing in her stomach, so she retched, her eyes instantaneously watering. She wiped her mouth.

Who was she? Nothing in her life made sense to her anymore. She was returning to the family her father disowned her from. She was returning to the prospect of the immediate deportation from the only place she knew as home. She believed she would be sent to a foreign country where she, along with her family, would face imminent death. If this was not her fate, she faced an existence where she would be treated as subhuman, caged like an animal, with the daily threat that each day could be her last. She had left the man she would willingly die for, who she loved with her whole being, and who would wake that morning to find her inexplicably gone. And if she stayed with him, what then? They faced the unimaginable prospect that if the Nazis found them and discovered she was a Jew, they would shoot him. Most things in life she couldn't be sure about, but these were her impending future.

When Rosa entered the environs of the Jewish quarter, she was aghast to see posters plastered to walls instructing all the Jews to remain in their homes. As she neared her parents' home, the commotion she encountered was deafening. German soldiers moved from door to door, ordering everyone inside to make their way to the Spianada, the large square in front of the Old Fortress. The narrow lanes of the Jewish quarter choked with people spilling from their apartments and houses with the few possessions they gathered and carried.

Rosa knew many of the terrified faces, neighbours and friends, people she'd known all her life. She glimpsed Sophia, who owned the bakers opposite her father's café and called out her name, only for her voice to be swallowed by the clamour around her.

When she reached her home, outside, her father carried a suitcase. He had lost weight and his shoulders seemed lost inside his coat. His other arm protectively draped around Rosa's mother's shoulder, and Andras huddled close to her thigh like a petrified puppy.

Rosa's heart felt clawed from her chest.

Yvette looked up and, astonished, saw Rosa hurrying towards them. Yvette's hand shot to her mouth, and she cried out, 'Rosa! What are you doing here?' Immediate alarm contradicted her joy.

'Rosa, you've come back,' Andras' face lit up.

Rosa flung herself at her mother, almost toppling Andras.

'I had to come. I can't let you go without me.'

Yvette tenderly touched Rosa's cheek. 'What are you thinking? Errikos told me you were safe.'

'I'm going with you.'

'You can't. What about the baby?'

A look passed between them.

'Move! Keep moving.' A Greek police officer glared at them.

'Rosa! What has happened?'

'I've lost the baby.'

'I'm so sorry.'

'Where's Alvertos?'

'He's not here.'

'What do you mean? Why is he not with you?'

'I didn't tell him I was coming back. He's better without me. What life does he have? With me, he has a gun to his head.'

'You're not making sense, Rosa. Look around you. Look at what is happening.'

'I know. I told you this was going to happen. We're a

family. We should be together. I cannot let this happen without not being here. I'm going with you.'

'Alvertos is your family now. With Alvertos, you still have a future.'

'I won't leave you.'

'You're young. You'll have children. You and Alvertos will have a life together. Think about what you're giving up, Rosa.'

'I have, it's all I've done since… I lost my baby.'

'Go now, while you can. We've to assemble in the square. Once we're there, it will be more difficult to escape.'

'Dad, are you going to look at me?'

Salamo ignored his daughter's request, his eyes still bitter towards her betrayal.

'It doesn't matter to me if you won't speak. I'm with you and that's all that matters.'

CHAPTER FORTY-ONE

RECONCILIATION AND FORGIVENESS

They were being driven, shoved, and funnelled into the square. A line of German soldiers and Greek police circled the outskirts, rifles raised and threatening.

Yvette pleaded, 'Salamo, speak to Rosa. Speak to your daughter. What's done is done. It's in the past. Please, find it in you. She has found forgiveness. You are a good man. Be the father I know you are.'

Salamo turned to Rosa and took her hand. He drew in a breath. He was shaking, and she thought of the times when she was a child, and he would walk with her holding her hand, how strong his hand felt and how protected she felt, and with it, her world was a safer place.

He looked into her eyes. 'The allies have entered Rome. I heard it on the radio last night. Look around you, Rosa. Everyone is being forced from their homes. I can't deny what is happening now. Our house is on fire, and we have no water to put it out. They're taking everyone to the camps, even now, with the allies advancing they still want to wipe us from the earth. I should have listened to you. I should have accepted Lazaros' offer and followed him and taken us all to Turkey. I'm responsible for this. Look how I treated you. When you needed us most, I abandoned you. I should have been there for you, and your mother should have been there for you when you lost your baby. Because of me, your mother has cried every night you were gone, and I denied her what would have been her need to comfort you and be there for you when you when you needed her most. I cannot ask for your forgiveness, Rosa. The shame I have caused is too much. I don't deserve it.'

'There is nothing to forgive. I should be asking for your forgiveness. I'm the one who has shamed my family.'

'I hurt you because I put my beliefs and standing in the community before your needs. It was an unthinkable thing to do. If you had been home, you would have seen a doctor, and we would have saved the baby.'

'No. There was nothing anyone could have done.'

'Go, Rosa. Leave the square. You and Alvertos will have a life together. And, when my time comes, just knowing this, I will die a happy and contented Pateras.'

A dread filled her. 'No, I'm staying with you, with Mum and Andras. We will be together. We will leave as a family.'

Salamo leaned close to Rosa, his face exhausted, drawn, and grey. 'I didn't give the authorities your name. I didn't register you. There will be a roll call and you're not on their list. They have no knowledge of you. They will not look for you. You must go now, Rosa. You cannot be with us. We will be together again, I promise, either in this world or the next.'

Tears ran down Rosa's face, and she gasped for breath between sobs.

'Listen to your father,' Yvette pleaded. 'Just knowing

you're safe, and you have your whole life in front of you will make whatever we are about to face, so much easier to endure...' Yvette paused. She gazed into Rosa's eyes, mustering strength. 'I loved you the second I looked into your eyes when you were born, and I've never stopped loving you. You have grown into the most thoughtful, beautiful woman, inside and out, and my heart bursts with joy. My love for you is unconditional and immeasurable. We will die for you, my daughter. Let us do this. Let us protect you.'

As the reality of what her mother was saying began to sink in, Rosa cried, 'What will become of me?'

Salamo squeezed Rosa's arm. 'Whatever you decide, that's the wonder of life. It's a precious gift. Take it with both hands and go with your mother's and my blessing. Go now and don't look back. You have a lifetime in front of you.'

Andras' eyes were big and wide as he gazed up at Rosa. She bent towards him and ruffled his hair. 'Look after mama and baba for me.'

'Aren't you coming with us?'

'Not just now. You need to be brave. Promise me you will be.'

Andras nodded. 'I will. I promise.'

Rosa embraced Yvette and Salamo, tears sliding down all their faces, and when she pulled herself from them, her voice broke. 'I love you both.' She wiped her tears with the back of her hand and, finding the courage from deep inside her, she tore her gaze from them, and distraught, disappeared into the crowd.

CHAPTER FORTY-TWO

AN INQUISITION IN THE SQUARE AND OTHER TORMENTS

His gaze settled on her. 'You! Stop right there.' The German officer demanded in fluent Greek.

Rosa stood still and waited, blood rushing to her ears.

The officer approached her, eyeing her suspiciously. Beside him, a young German soldier raised his rifle.

'Where are you going?' The officer demanded. 'You seem to be in a hurry, running and going in the wrong direction.'

'I'm going home.'

'And where is home?'

I need to make him believe I'm not a Jew. 'My house is next to St Nicholas church.'

'Then if you're not a Jew, why are you among them, especially here, today?'

A chill steeled across her neck. 'I have some friends I wanted to say goodbye to. I didn't get the chance earlier. This has all happened so quickly.'

'And not before time. Friends you say?'

'Yes.'

'Did you speak with these… friends?'

'No. There're so many people. It's too crowded. I couldn't find them.'

'Corfu has seen the last of the Jew. Today is a glorious day.'

Rosa remained silent, unable to speak. Suddenly, she recalled where she'd met this officer. It was the one who had whipped her father outside the cafe.

'Your papers, now!' the officer demanded.

Rosa fished her identification from her pocket and handed it over. She lowered her head, staring at the ground.

'I may speak your language, but I never had the inclination to learn to read it.' The officer called over a woman who was standing with a group of soldiers and Greek police.

When the woman reached them, Rosa's head remained bowed. 'Verify these papers,' he demanded.

The woman took them and narrowed her eyes as she read. There was a long pause.

'Well then, I haven't got all day.'

'They're genuine.'

A spike thrust into Rosa's heart. It couldn't be, but it was her. Josefina. Her onetime close friend. A collaborator. An informer. It was unthinkable. Yet, she said nothing. Why was she protecting her?

Rosa couldn't stop shaking, struck with fear, she clasped her hands together.

'It's not uncommon for papers to be falsified, the black market's thriving with such activities. If you are who you say you are, then you are a lover of Jews. Of course you are. You were looking for your Jewish friends.'

Her hatred for this man and his kind boiled inside her.

'Maybe you too are a Jew.' He sniffed the air. 'I can always tell. They have a certain smell about them. Rancid and putrid.' His nostrils flared as he sniffed again, this time longer and deeper.

His eyes slid to the cross around her neck. The officer stepped forward. Raising his cane, he gently tapped the cross. 'Ah! Although this would say otherwise,' he said, staring at her undecidedly, assessing her for a moment.

Around them, a tide of humanity filled the square. Men, women, old and young, mothers pulling their children towards them and cradling babies. The entire Jewish population had assembled to wait for their fate.

'You puzzle me. You see, I have the faintest recollection that I've met you before. Am I correct in this matter?'

Rosa shook her head. 'I've never seen you before.'

'Ah, you've found your tongue. Are you sure?'

'I would have remembered if I did.'

'So, you're an orthodox Christian, or a Jew masquerading as one?'

'I told you. I'm just trying to see my friends.'

'You did, but the thing is, I'm having trouble believing you.' He pressed his finger to his lips and commanded, 'Recite the Lord's Prayer.'

She tried to swallow the panic tightening her throat. Unable to raise her eyes, Rosa narrated the words just as Alvertos had taught her. When she finished, her mouth was uncomfortably dry, and she drew a sharp breath. The officer smiled and took pleasure in her discomfort.

'A prayer for all prayers. Be careful who you make friends with. Associating with Jews is nothing short of an abomination.' He flicked his hand. 'You may go.' The officer turned his back and walked away. Rosa stole a glance at Josefina, who briefly nodded before moving on.

Rosa gasped for air and instantly wanted to cry. She turned once over her shoulder and glimpsed Josefina following the Germans, and then Rosa merged with the crowd.

Rosa felt an indiscernible force had hit her. Josefina was collaborating with the Nazis. She was betraying her own people. How could she have fallen to such depths? Yet she did not speak the truth. Instead, she saved Rosa's life.

Rosa picked her way through the mass of people, rubbing against shoulders, sidestepping suitcases and piles of belongings. The voices around her were fearful, driven with uncertainty, terrified and anxious. These were her people, the heart that gave life to her community now herded like animals to the slaughterhouse. An old woman stumbled forward and fell in Rosa's path. Rosa bent towards her, and tears stung her eyes as she eased the old woman to her feet.

'Thank you, my dear,' the old woman gasped through a confused and tired smile. In that instance, Rosa knew the woman's face and the fear in her eyes would forever brand her memory.

She quickened her pace, but the crowded bodies jostled her off balance as they pressed against her.

The air sagged heavy with groans and weeping. Protective mothers clutched tightly and pulled close wide-eyed children. Desperate voices, laced with alarm, spilled into the air, stifling with fear. It was now muggy and clammy, the sun's fierce heat unrelenting and oppressive around her.

A rumble of thunder groaned in the sky. The unmistakable drone of planes grew ever closer, spreading panic and fear as shockwaves rippled through the throng of Jews. To quell the alarm, gunfire erupted as the German soldiers fired into the air and over heads. Instinctively, everyone dropped to the ground as a formation of allied planes bellowed above them, heading for the mainland.

In desperation, Rosa continued to pick her way through every gap in the crowd that opened to her. The German officer turned, running his eyes along the lines of faces, scanning the mass of bodies. Eventually, he found her, his expression registering his newfound recollection, and she caught his gaze, his eyes ablaze with fury.

The officer turned to a group of soldiers and screamed. 'You two. That Jew is trying to escape. Bring her to me. Do not return empty-handed. I will make an example of her.'

Rosa's heart leaped into her throat as she heard his command barked like a savage dog. Everywhere she turned, fear-stricken faces stared back at her, their eyes awash with the palpable dread of the menacing fate that awaited them.

Their faces etched with grim resolve; the soldiers wove a path through the parting crowd with menacing purpose.

Awash in the chaotic maze of bodies, panic grabbed Rosa and with a surge of determination, she pushed through the crowd and then once in the openness of the square, and spurred by instinct, she broke into a run. She had an advantage over her pursuer; she knew the labyrinth of alleys like the back of her hand.

Her heart pounded as she darted through the narrow and winding lanes, her breath coming in ragged gasps as behind her, not too far, the German soldiers' boots thudded against the cobblestones, echoing with methodical precision.

She had underestimated them. Panic surged through her, and her mind raced. Being caught was not an option. Every fibre of her being screamed at her to survive.

Her hands trembled, and she steeled herself, her breath coming in shallow gasps. There was nowhere to hide from the soldiers' relentless pursuit.

Suddenly, from the shadows, a figure emerged. Startled, the soldier spun around, his eyes widening in alarm as Errikos hands closed around the soldier's throat with a vice-like grip. Desperation clawed at the soldier as he struggled against the hold, but it was futile. Errikos' knife sliced through the soldier's throat like butter. Errikos' sudden assault surprised the other soldier, causing a delay in his reactions. Stumbling backwards, he raised his rifle only to see a silver blade cut through the air with deadly precision and thud into his chest.

Rosa watched in horror as the soldier fell, his body crumpling to the ground and she stood frozen, her breath caught in her throat as she stared at the two lifeless bodies.

'Errikos!' Rosa whispered his name, dumbfounded.

'Thea told us where you had gone. We came straight away. I knew where you'd be and as luck would have it, I saw you being chased by these two.'

'You said *we*.'

'Alvertos is waiting for you. I persuaded him to stay in the van. It's parked in the old harbour.'

'Alvertos is here.'

Just then, they heard the footfall of heavy boots.

'Quickly Rosa, get out of here.'

'I'm not going without you.'

'Go!' Errikos scooped up one of the dead German soldier's rifles. 'I'll join you as soon as I can.' He gave a half smile and Rosa knew it was a last goodbye.

'How can I thank you? You have done so much for me.'

'By surviving.'

'I love you, Uncle Errikos.' Rosa turned and ran, as a volley of gunfire echoed through the narrow lane.

CHAPTER FORTY-THREE

THE CAMERA

Rosa made her way to her family's apartment above the cafe. To her dismay, the doors to the café hung from their hinges, and smashed crockery, overturned tables and toppled chairs littered the floor.

Desperately, she ran up the stairs. The door to the apartment was at an angle and she had to force it open as her mother's china cabinet lay against it, the contents either stolen or lying in fragments and shreds. She pressed her shoulder to the door and when the opening was large enough; she slid into the apartment, her worse fears realised.

The German soldiers had taken everything of value and stamped to pieces what was not. They had emptied every drawer in the house. Around her lay an orgy of destruction. In the bedrooms, after pulling back the sheets, they had searched mattresses and strewn the contents of wardrobes over beds. Her mother's treasured embroidered linen ripped and trampled on. Every piece of furniture smashed or damaged, picture frames thrown from walls, and the pages torn and scattered from her father's books.

The radio her father had hidden when the Nazis raided each house months before lay in pieces.

It was then, Rosa remembered the hidden space behind the wall panelling. She glanced over the room; the panel was still intact. She crouched beside the wall and with a little effort removed a section of the panelling. Rosa peered into the hollow space and felt a surge of relief. She reached out her hand and took hold of the tin container. She extracted it from its hiding place and opened the lid. Neatly stacked rolls of money still lay inside. There was more money than Rosa had thought, a lot more, enough to last for months. Something else caught her eye. She reached into the darkened space and wrapped her hand around a solid object. It was a case no bigger than a handbag. She opened it, and to her astonishment, found a movie camera 185 with an assortment of lenses. The camera was small and compact, and her initial reaction was, why did her father have a camera? She had never seen him with it. And why was it hidden? And then it came to her. The camera didn't belong to her father at all; it was his older brother's camera, the one who emigrated to America in the 30s and returned to visit the family in Corfu. It was the year before the war broke out. She recalled him taking films of the neighbourhood and the locals. Rosa's heart lifted with the sudden realisation, there would be images of her father and mother on the reel. There could have only been one reel as there were no others stored in the hiding space. With haste, she placed the camera in its case and the tin container with the money into a bag she found in the kitchen. Scarcely breathing, she turned to take in the rooms that had been her home all her life, and with anger and fear, she tore her despairing eyes from them and left.

CHAPTER FORTY-FOUR
REASONS TO SURVIVE

He saw her round the corner, clutching a bag to her chest. He felt a twinge of fear and relief encase him as he threw open the car and ran towards her. The elation of finding Rosa among the confusion and turmoil of the deportation matched the nervousness that pressed against Alvertos.

'Thank God you're alive. Come quickly. We need to get away from here. I have a car.' He glanced in the direction she came from. 'Where's Errikos?'

Her face looked grim. 'He told me where to find you. He saved my life. If I hadn't left you, he would still be alive.' She burrowed into Alvertos' chest and sobbed through her pain and loss.

Rosa's pain echoed his own. 'And he would have died for you another time. He would have had it no other way, Rosa. He saved you.'

'But it's come at a terrible price. We can't just leave him lying in the street.'

'We have no choice. Quickly, we need to go, Rosa. We can't stay a minute longer.'

He turned his eyes to the bag 'What's in there?'

She pulled it tight towards her. 'Precious memories.'

The journey along the costal road was arduous and worrisome. They passed the turning that led to Kontokali, and it spurred memories of the house where they secretly met Errikos. 'Uncle Errikos,' Rosa murmured his name and dug her fingernails into her forearm.

Alvertos peeled his eyes from the road ahead and glanced at Rosa. 'Errikos arrived at Theas this morning, just as I was about to leave for Corfu Town. Thea told me where you'd gone and why. He insisted on coming with me.'

Rosa fingered the cross resting in the dip of her clavicle. The morning felt like a lifetime ago.

Alvertos turned and concentrated on the road. 'I don't understand why you left.'

'To save you.'

'From what?'

'From me.'

He frowned. 'I don't need saving from you.'

'I pose a threat to your life every day.'

'Don't you think I know that? I love you, Rosa, and if that love means I put myself in harm's way, then so be it. It's what I've been doing since we got married. I knew what it meant. Keeping us together is all that matters to me. I thought you felt the same.'

Rosa scanned the countryside that flashed past her. She needed him to understand. She would make him understand.

Rosa turned to Alvertos. 'Do you have any idea how it

makes me feel? To know that because of me, I could be responsible for your death. I chose you over my family, who I'll never see again. You can't imagine what it's been like.'

'How can I if you've never told me?'

'I'm not accusing you, Alvertos. You're not responsible for any of this. I accepted this situation, or at least, I thought I did.'

'You left me to return to your family, even though you knew it was a death sentence. Yet, you were willing to do it.'

'If that was my fate for falling in love with you. Yes.'

'How do you think that makes me feel? Did you think about that?'

'I was doing it for you.' She buried her face in her hands. 'Losing our baby made it easier.'

'And if you were still pregnant, what then, Rosa?'

Rosa heard a jagged edge of anger in his voice. She looked at him then, and her hands shook so much she could hardly keep them still. 'Losing our baby changed me. It consumed me. I thought if I left with my family, it would serve two purposes. It was comforting knowing that without me, there would be no threat to your life, and so I could give myself freely to the fate that awaited me.'

He raked his fingers through his hair. 'You were prepared to die.'

'If I was with my family, yes. I thought I could make amends and repair the pain I'd put them through.'

'Did you see them, your mum and dad?'

Rosa nodded and turned from him.

'And yet, you came back to find me.'

'It was the most difficult thing I've ever done. I don't regret seeing them. It's given me a peace I wouldn't have had. I would have found it unbearable otherwise. It would have haunted me for the rest of my life. Now, in my heart, I know I've repaired what I thought I'd broken forever.

'My dad forgave me, and he saved me. I couldn't break his or my mother's heart again. They were insistent that if they were to face what lay ahead of them, they could only do so knowing I'd returned to you and, in doing so, my life would continue. Life would be embraced, and a part of them would always be alive and live through me and our children. It gave them comfort. Even in death, a part of them would still be alive, their family would survive. I found what I was looking for, forgiveness and a reason to live, but it hasn't stopped my heart from breaking.'

Alvertos remained silent. Eventually, he turned to her, his eyes fixed on hers. 'I feel I've woken from a nightmare. What you've said makes perfect sense to me now.'

She took a deep breath. 'I tried to tell you how I was feeling, but I couldn't. The weight of it was too much to share.'

With one hand on the wheel, he reached out with the other and took her hand in his. He had set his mind to it. 'We both have a reason to survive this war.'

'Do you remember Josefina? We met her that day we were eating ice cream.'

Startled by the abrupt change in subject, Alvertos answered. 'The not very friendly Josefina. I remember her. Why?'

She kept her eyes forward. 'I saw her today. She's an informer for the Nazis and I owe her my life.'

CHAPTER FORTY-FIVE

THE END

The Germans, assisted by interpreters, took a roll call of every family's surname and then the full name of every member of that family. Rosa's name was not on their list, her father having not registered her.

Then, like cattle, the Germans, assisted by the Greek police, herded everyone into the Old Fortress, stripped them of anything of value: jewellery, money, watches, even the keys to their homes. They remained interred in the Old Fortress without food or blankets.

Several days later, from the harbour below the fortress, ships took them to a makeshift detention camp on the island of Lefkada. From there, the Jews of Corfu were moved to the infamous Haidari prison camp in Athens for a week and then loaded onto sealed cattle trucks without food, water or sanitation, and transported from Athens to Auschwitz – Birkenau.

On arrival, many did not survive their last ordeal. The young, and elderly, newborn and the disabled perished in the claustrophobic, unsanitary and toxic conditions and lay where they died in the cattle trucks among the living.

Those that remained glimpsed at the wooden huts, the barbed wire fences and guard towers before walking in lines to the promise of hot showers and clean clothes towards number two crematorium.

CHAPTER FORTY-SIX

SOMETHING GOOD

Thea welcomed Rosa like a daughter lost and found. She cried tears of relief and stood in front of the icon of St Spyridon that hung from her wall, blessed herself three times and thanked the saint for answering her prayers.

They sat round the table and ate soup made from vegetables picked that morning from the garden that Thea had cut and sliced on her chopping board while every bone in her body ached with worry.

Rosa's head hung low, and her dark eyes glistening with a film of tears, as she described what unfolded that morning in Corfu Town. Thea listened in dumbfounded disbelief. Occasionally, Thea made a sound of disgust, but tempered her reaction so not to disturb Rosa's flow of words that needed to be exorcised.

As Thea and Alvertos listened with tight and bleak looks, it seemed time slowed down and stretched out over the table.

Around them, silence prevailed for a while; finally, Thea said, 'Your father did a beautiful thing.'

Rosa thought it a strange choice of words, but as their meaning percolated inside her, a faint smile crossed her lips. Thea was right, her father had given her permission to live. It was a gift given to quell the heartache, and from it, the possibility of love, family, and a new life could emerge. Even among the horror and devastation that had transformed their world, these were things that still mattered. Although her loss was unbearable, there was still a comfort to be found knowing that through her and the possibility of having children, her mother and father, in a way, would continue to live on.

Rosa took her father's camera out of its case and lay it on the table.

'I haven't seen a camera before. Where did you get it?' Thea asked.

'After I left Errikos, I went back to my home. It was awful. The Germans had already ransacked every single room. Everything that had value was taken. What was left was ruined and broken into pieces. I remembered my father had a secret hiding space behind the wall panelling. It hadn't been discovered. I found his savings and this camera. It belonged to his brother who had emigrated to America. He visited just before the war. Tragically, he died unexpectedly, but not before taking some film of the family, our neighbours, the town and footage of his favourite places. I hope the film hasn't been damaged.'

'That's amazing, Rosa. Something good has come out of all this.'

Alvertos held the camera in his hand, inspecting it as he turned it over. 'I wonder if it still works?' He put his eye to the viewfinder.

'Do you know how to use it?' Rosa asked hopefully.

Alvertos shrugged. 'It can't be that difficult. How hard can it be?' He inspected the camera further. 'And here.' He pointed out the lens. 'You need to make sure it's focussed and this lever here winds the motor.' He removed the film door. 'That's a good sign. There's a film already loaded.'

'Will it work?' Rosa asked.

'I can't see why not.'

'How do we see what's been filmed?'

'You need to use a projector.'

Rosa bit her lip. 'So, we can't see what might already be recorded.'

Alvertos raised a brow. 'Not without a projector, but we can still record. I just need to work out how to do that.'

It didn't take Alvertos long to work out what mechanisms did what, and the functions of the dials, switches and numbers. It was a distraction he welcomed, but also, he hoped it would offer Rosa the chance to film around the village, not to escape her grief, he knew she couldn't do that, but to sit alongside it and reduce its impact from time to time.

And so, Alvertos and Rosa took it upon themselves to record the villagers going about their daily business, cats, lazing in the afternoon sun, a medley of old women congregating outside the church after a Sunday service, a mule almost buckling under the weight of sacks filled with vegetables picked from the fields that the Germans had not already plundered. Rosa also filmed Thea, cooking at the stove, sweeping the floor, and resting in her armchair, smiling contentedly as she read a book. It was not only people she filmed. Rosa delighted in capturing the dawn's breaking with a panoramic sweep, where the cockerel's crow interrupted the birdsong – a chorus that melodiously ascended above the surrendering dew. Higher still, a mist dispersed into ghostly figures as the sun spilled over the crests of rolling hills in tender beams of gilded light, bathing the treetops and the expansive fields below. It was times like these, Rosa was at her happiest.

CHAPTER FORTY-SEVEN

AN UNSETTLING TRUTH

Several weeks later, a group of *andartes* entered the village. Rosa recognised one of them. Christos had been involved in relocating the Jewish families who had hidden in the barns.

As the *andartes* rested in the village square, eating a meal prepared for them by the villagers, Rosa approached them, and Christos raised his head from his bowl and smiled at her. He pulled his cap from his matted hair.

'I remember you from a few weeks ago. You helped get the families to safety.'

Christos nodded. 'I did. Have you heard how they're doing?'

'They're alive. It's all they can ask for.'

'I'm glad.' He tilted his head. 'It's Rosa, isn't it? I remember you. Errikos is your uncle.'

The mention of his name wrenched at her heart. 'He is, or was.'

'I know. I'm so sorry. He's a tremendous loss to the resistance, and as a friend.'

'You knew him well?'

'When I became an *andarte*, Errikos took me under his wing. I'm alive today because of him.'

'As am I.'

'We retrieved his body. It had lain in the alleyway for a few days. We received a message through our usual channels informing us what had happened, so we moved in at night and brought him back. We have a few Jewish comrades who have joined our ranks. They gave him a burial according to their customs.'

Such news gladdened her heart.

'I was told by my commander. He'd tried to get a message to Errikos' woman by the usual channels but could not.'

Rosa's brow clouded. 'Errikos' woman?'

Christos could see by her face he had startled her.

'Her name is Josefina. She's a lot younger, but when you saw them together, you could tell they were close.'

Rosa couldn't disguise the shock in her voice. 'That's impossible. Josefina and Errikos were lovers!' Even just saying the words out load was a contradiction. 'She's an informer. She's betrayed her own people. Why would Errikos have anything to do with her? She is his enemy. There's no difference between her and the Germans.'

'Well. I don't know anything about that. All I can tell you is they were together and by all accounts Errikos had feelings for her.'

Rosa rubbed her temple, as if trying to erase his words.

'Errikos never mentioned this. If anyone had won his affections, anyone special to him, I'm sure he would have said. But Josefina, no, it's unthinkable. I saw her in Spianada Square. Even then, she knew what was about to happen to the people she'd known all her life. She was complicit in the deportations. Why would Errikos be involved with anyone like that? It's unthinkable.'

Christos scratched his head. 'I've no idea, but whatever the reason, Errikos has taken it to the grave.'

CHAPTER FORTY-EIGHT

THE HAUNTED RETURN TO WHERE NOTHING REMAINS THE SAME

The boy ran like a deer being chased by a pack of dogs.

From the rooftop of his house, in the distance, he had seen the truck and the soldiers it transported. In his haste, he turned and tangled himself in the washing his mother had hung to dry in the afternoon sun. He blurted out to his father what he had seen, who instructed him to run along every lane and cobbled street in the village and warn everyone.

'They're coming, the Germans are coming,' he yelled at every corner, panting for breath between every word.

Alvertos heard the boy's voice and hurried out into the street. 'How do you know this?'

'I saw them with my own eyes. I saw their guns.'

Alvertos turned on his heels, and heart pounding, rushed back into the house. 'German soldiers are coming.' He jerked his head towards the stairs. 'Rosa, we need to hide upstairs.'

Thea put down the knife she was using to cut onions for

the soup that dinnertime and walked over to the window. She glanced down the narrow street and then turned to face them.

'It would be best if you left the house. Staying here is too dangerous. If they searched the house, they would find you. It's too small. You must go now, out of the village and into the woods.'

'What if they find our clothes?'

'I'll tell them my son and his wife live with me. Now go, they could be here any minute.'

'I don't want to leave you, Thea.'

'You don't have a choice. Now quickly, you must go.'

Rosa sank into Thea's embrace.

'It's not as if this is goodbye. I'll see you when they've gone. Now hurry.'

As they left, Thea ensured the door was tightly closed and then sank into her chair and waited.

With a heavy heart, Rosa left the house, and both she and Alvertos moved as quickly as they could. They sped through the village and followed the path that led to the camouflage of the trees. Once they found themselves some distance from the village, Rosa pulled at Alvertos to stop. She stood still and listened. It had already begun.

A look of apprehension crossed Alvertos' face. 'What are you doing?'

'Listening,' she replied without hesitation. 'Can't you hear it?'

The sound of wrathful German voices, and a volley of threatening footfall, struck fear in Rosa. 'It's already beginning.'

'We need to keep moving. We need to get further away.'

They ran along a dirt track that passed an olive grove, the sun's rays speckling the dry earth in patches of silver light. Rosa's breath came in rasps, her lungs burnt, and her stomach felt as if it had turned inside out. Through the trees, to their right, she caught the tantalising sight of the Ionian shimmering in turquoise and aqua blue, in sheer contrast to the panicked thoughts that occupied her mind.

'We'll stop here for a while,' Alvertos suggested, and Rosa welcomed the rest as they sat with their backs against a thick tree trunk. Alvertos sighed. They weren't prepared for a night outside and although the nights were becoming warmer, they had no water or a place to shelter.

'She'll be okay, won't she?' Rosa felt her stomach tighten.

'She can give as good as she gets, and anyway, the Germans are not going to suspect an old woman, are they?' Alvertos gestured with his hand as if it were evident.

The fearful look on Rosa's face was enough to let Alvertos know she didn't share his optimism.

Later, they moved on. They had not been walking long when they came across a small building made of breeze blocks topped with a corrugated roof that had collapsed on one side.

They huddled together in a corner and late afternoon turned to evening and hundreds of pin-pricked stars lit up the night sky in the opened space above them.

'What is it?' Alvertos asked, as Rosa stared at the night sky.

'I think about them all the time, my parents and Andras.'

Despite their predicament, Alvertos couldn't help a small smile of acknowledgment. 'I know you do.'

'I hope they're still together. I couldn't bear it if they've been separated. I couldn't imagine such a thing, especially for Andras. He needs them. He's still a child.' She sobbed into Alvertos' chest. 'I'm tired of running and hiding and pretending to be someone I'm not.' Alvertos held her close to him, and her breathing became deeper and eventually, she succumbed to sleep.

The sun was bathing the walls of their shelter when they awoke and debated if it was safe to return to Liapades. They decided they would return.

Rosa shook her hair with her hands and combed them through it. 'Did you sleep well?' she asked.

Alvertos rubbed the knot in his neck. 'Not exactly. Did you?'

'When you stopped snoring.'

'I don't snore,' he faked being affronted.

Rosa smiled. 'How would you know? You're the only one sleeping.'

Even though Rosa's eyes were strained, it brought a warmth to his chest to see her smile again.

Alvertos relieved himself in a corner of the shelter. 'I'm starving,' he announced

'How can you think of food at a time like this?'

'It's easy. My groaning stomach keeps reminding me.'

'Well, hopefully Thea will have made some breakfast for you.'

Alvertos sensed the apprehension in her voice.

With cautious footsteps, they returned to Liapades. Nothing stirred as they entered the environs of the village. Most shutters were tightly closed, and a scrawny cat sat beside a cracked clay vase licking its fur. As they moved further into the lanes, Rosa reached out and took Alvertos' hand.

They turned a corner and the village square opened up to them. The few cafes that still plied a meagre trade were devoid of customers, and opposite the church, whose doors were always wide open and welcoming to the small band of daily worshipers, was ominously silent and still.

Rosa's heart leaped from her chest when she glanced towards the centre of the square and saw a huddle of men around the old tree that dominated the square. Alvertos' hand tightened around hers when he realised what they were doing.

Two bodies were lying motionless on the ground. Alvertos saw the rope dangling limply from a sturdy branch and one man removing a noose from a body.

Rosa stared at the group of men and Alvertos felt her body go limp as he suddenly realised the magnitude of horror they had stumbled upon.

A cry escaped Rosa's mouth, startling the men in front of her. Tears streamed down her face. She paced backwards and forwards and then slumped to her knees as her legs buckled from beneath her.

Thea's eyes bulged from their sockets, and her mouth had fallen open. A gruesome purple and red ligature mark curved around her neck as her body lay lifeless, cut from the tree. It was difficult to watch, but Alvertos could not turn away.

One man stepped forward.

Alvertos hunched beside Rosa and pulled her towards him. She was inconsolable. She screamed then, and her cries and choking sobs muffled against his chest.

As the man neared them, out of the corner of his eye, Alvertos saw the man's hand move to the inside of his jacket and curl around a pistol. Instantly, Alvertos thought it was a trap.

He felt the warmth of Rosa's body against his and if this

was where he was going to die, his last vestige of life would be with Rosa beside him.

The man pulled out the pistol and stood expressionless. Alvertos pulled Rosa close to him, who continued to sob uncontrollably.

Alvertos sat motionless in dread.

'Stand down.' A deep, hoarse voice emanated around the square.

Alvertos glanced towards an older man in a white shirt and blue waistcoat. His thinning silver hair swept back from his forehead, one eye closed and scarred. As he moved towards them, Alvertos noticed how the others sunk in stature around him in an air of reverence.

'It's a dreadful thing that's happened. I only wish I could have stopped it, but by doing so, many others may have died needlessly. It was necessary, but regretful all the same. I've known Thea most of my life, and Mitsia, he tried to intervene, and he, too, paid with his life.'

'What happened?'

'The Germans knew where they were going. Someone informed them. Thea said nothing and knew the consequences her silence would bring. My name is Georgios. I'm the owner of that café over there, but more importantly, I'm a *kapetan*, an officer for ELAS. I coordinate the resistance against the Nazis in Corfu.'

'And these are your men.'

Georgios nodded. 'I was sorry to hear about Errikos. He was a good man, and a tremendous loss. He was one of our own... a brother.'

'You knew we were in Liapades, staying with Thea.'

'I did. Errikos and I arranged it.'

'What happens now?'

'First of all, we have two friends to say goodbye to. We

bury our dead in Oditria. It is the village cemetery. There are no relatives to dig Thea's grave, so I was wondering since you received her charity and hospitality...'

Alvertos glanced at Thea's body. 'It would be an honour.'

Georgios nodded approvingly. 'Thank you. We will take Thea to the church where her body will rest.'

Rosa looked up at Georgios and rubbed the tears from her eyes. 'I'll also help to dig the grave.'

Thea's body rested in the church of St Anastasia in the village square for two days before her coffin was paraded through the village towards the cemetery. A solemn procession of villagers followed behind it. Alvertos and Rosa walked with them. Both knew the danger they placed themselves in if the German soldiers returned, but Rosa insisted on being present to say her goodbyes.

As was the custom, after the funeral, they ate dishes of cod washed down with locally made wine with Thea's neighbours and friends. Everyone made Alvertos and Rosa feel welcomed and encouraged them to stay in Liapades, as Thea would have wanted.

As a precaution, they slept in the room above Georgios' café. A new manner of apprehension wormed through Alvertos. Before Thea's death, there was the possibility they would be hunted, but now they knew the Nazis were actively searching for them. Georgios had received word from his men the Germans had increased their patrols. Even though the allies continued to advance through the Balkans and Italy, threatening to isolate the German army in Greece, the Nazis continued their murderous intent to carry out the final solution and eliminate every Jew in Greece.

Alvertos returned to Thea's house. The Germans had

ransacked it and taken everything of value. He retrieved what remained of their possessions and was relieved to find the camera and Rosa's father's savings still intact underneath the floorboards in the bedroom. When he informed Rosa of this, she looked at him with deep-set eyes that revealed immense joy and relief.

CHAPTER FORTY-NINE

THE RIGHT THING TO DO

A few days after Thea's funeral, and once the café was empty, Georgios sat with Alvertos over a coffee. He handed Alvertos a cigarette and lit one for himself. He inhaled deeply and considered Alvertos. 'Have you any thoughts about what you will do?'

Alvertos shook his head. 'Not really. Rosa and I haven't approached the subject yet. I was waiting until she'd recovered from the events of the last few days.'

'It's been hard for her, that's for sure, and for you, too. But what I've seen of her, Rosa, is a woman with a strong constitution.'

'It's just as well. The last few months have been tough. I don't know how she's got through it, but she has. She has her own demons to face, but she is good at hiding them well, in public at least.'

'I heard what happened to her family, and she was there when Errikos was killed, and then, seeing what the Nazis did to Thea would be enough to send even the hardest of men over the edge. You're lucky to have a woman such as she.'

'I know. I remind myself of that fact every day.'

'You know you can't stay. They'll come for you. If not today or tomorrow, they will come.'

'It's something that's continually on my mind. Where can we go? This is an island. There's only one way off.'

Georgios exchanged a look with one of his men, who entered the café. He smiled and took another deep draw on his cigarette. He cocked his head towards the man who had just entered the café. 'I've been waiting for confirmation of a solution to your problem, and I've just been given good news.'

'It can be arranged for tomorrow,' the man confirmed.

'What can be arranged?' Alvertos asked, puzzled.

'Leaving Corfu and going to Erikoussa,' Georgios replied.

'Erikoussa! Why there? It's a small island and hardly anyone lives there.'

'Precisely. There's not a single German soldier based on the island. They must approach by boat and when they do, they're usually seen. The islanders are very vigilant in that regard. Rosa would not be the first Jew they have helped, but that's all I will say. If the sailing is fair, you could be there in under three hours. There's a fishing boat leaving tomorrow morning.'

Alvertos looked into Georgios' scarred face. 'So soon.'

'The boat is taking a family to Erikoussa, a Jewish family who escaped the deportations. You can be on that boat or take your chances fearing each new day could be your last if you were caught by the Nazis, who we know, are right now actively looking for Jews who have fled Corfu Town.' Georgios jabbed at the map with a finger. 'From here, it's only a day's journey to Italy if the weather is favourable. It can be precarious if the weather changes. You could charter a boat. There are fishermen who will welcome your money if you have the funds?'

Alvertos' eyes narrowed. 'We do.'

'Then you need to seriously consider this. It's your only option of evading the Germans. You know what will happen if you're caught.'

That night, as they lay in bed, Alvertos felt the warmth of Rosa against him and he fought the familiar urge to touch her softly, inch by inch, and cover her in light kisses and satisfy his desire. Reluctantly, he pushed the craving from his mind, and instead, explained to her what Georgios had told him. He emphasised it could be their only chance of having a life together without having to look over their shoulders and scrutinise every stranger they met in the fear they could be an informer. What kind of life would that be? It wouldn't be living; it would be just existing. His words were gentle in their delivery, in the hope they would reinforce the importance of their meaning, and not viewed as an ultimatum.

At first, Rosa didn't want to entertain the notion. She was against it, but Alvertos had given it much thought, and he was determined to change her mind. He could see the sense in it. He eased his way into convincing her it was the right course of action.

Rosa thought of her family and felt a sudden yearning to be with them. 'My last memory of my mother and father is them telling me of their hope that at least we would survive, and them knowing, our children and their children too, would be testament to the Nazis' failure and defeat. I cannot dishonour the faith they put in me.' Her throat constricted. 'It's the right thing to do.'

Alvertos leaned towards Rosa and kissed her forehead. 'It will be so, I promise you. We'll honour that memory,' he said, determined to make it so.

CHAPTER FIFTY

A CHOICE MADE

A rooster welcomed the morning as Rosa wiped the sleep from her eyes. Alvertos was still sleeping as she eased herself from the sheets and, trying not to wake him, dressed in a hushed manner. Rosa caught her reflection in the mirror. She looked drained. The skin under her eyes shadowed. She slipped out of the room.

Downstairs, in the taverna, she smelt coffee brewing on the stove and, feeling disappointed that she was not alone as she'd hoped, she stepped around the tables and chairs and headed outside.

The puff of smoke rose above his head, dissipating in twists and twirls. Rosa noticed the cup of coffee on the table. Sensing she was behind him, Georgios turned and studied her for a moment.

'Good morning, Rosa. I think it's going to be another fine day.'

She couldn't argue with that. There wasn't a single cloud to view as the sun etched its light across the sky.

'Would you like some coffee?'

'I'm fine, thank you.'

Georgios looked at his watch. 'You're up early. It's only six thirty. I hope you slept well?'

'I did, thank you,' she lied.

'I'm glad one of us did. I've suffered from insomnia for years. Yiannis, the doctor, tells me I smoke too much and drink too much coffee, that's why I can't sleep.'

'You don't believe him?'

'He may have a point, but I like to smoke and drink strong coffee. Life has few pleasures as it is.'

'You should take his advice; you might like sleeping longer.'

Georgios raised his brows, and with a hand, directed Rosa's attention towards the empty chair opposite him. 'Please, take a seat.'

Rosa settled into the chair and ran her hand through her hair. She hadn't been alone with Georgios before, and the emptiness of the square unsettled her. 'I didn't realise how hard this was going to be.'

'War is a dirty business. It has no regard for the young, the old, the strong, or the weak. It has no feelings, no empathy, no right or wrong. It is unnatural, inhumane and demonic, but where there is pain and suffering, there is also hope. I must believe that the unjust will be brought to account, and the oppressed will throw off their shackles and grind the bones of their enemies into dust.'

'That's very biblical.'

'You hadn't considered me as a religious man, a man of faith.'

'I take people at face value, as I find them, rightly or wrongly. I know of no other way. It makes no difference to me if you're religious or not. It's what's in a person's heart that interests me, that's more important.'

'We're very similar, you and I.'

'How do you come to that conclusion? You don't know who I am.'

'We've both lost loved ones in horrific circumstances and because of it, we've had to make hard decisions, life-changing ones. We're pragmatic and realistic and we're both survivors. Alvertos has your back. He is your rock, and he would do anything for you as he has demonstrated by being here with you, and I… I have my men. They have my back and I have theirs and we would willingly die for each other as you would for Alvertos and he for you.'

Her face and heart softened towards him. 'How did you get involved in the resistance?'

'Now, that's a long story.'

'It's still early. There's only you, me and that cockerel awake.'

Georgios was silent for a moment. 'Very well. Although I was born and raised in Liapades, unlike most of the men in the village, I've travelled and experienced the world. When I was twenty, I joined the merchant navy. It gave me the taste for experiencing different places and cultures. Eventually, after five years, I settled in Malta, married and lived a happy life. Then, one night, my wife was attacked and robbed. She died two days later from her injuries. The authorities never caught the man responsible, but I swore I would find him and carry out my own justice, an eye for an eye. After many setbacks, I eventually found him and tracked him down. He drank in the same bar most nights, so I waited for an opportunity. I cut his throat in an alleyway, but not before reminding him of why he was about to die. I took my revenge, but it didn't bring my wife back. Nothing changed, except it was too dangerous for me to stay in Malta.

'I left Malta and went to Athens. My life was quiet and uneventful until I had the notion of joining the army. I'd been in the army for ten years, was promoted through the ranks and then Italy began their manoeuvres to invade Greece. My unit held the Italians in the Pindos mountains and sent them back into Albania, but when Germany came to Mussolini's aid, we were up against a different kind of enemy. I took a German bullet and spent several months in hospital. During this time, I met like-minded soldiers who shared my political affiliations and during our convalescence, we would discuss the popularity in Greek politics of political organisations such as the *National Liberation Front* (EAM) but more importantly, their military wing, the *Greek People's Liberation Army* (ELAS). I submerged myself in their manifesto, *What is EAM and What does it Want*. I'd finally found people who shared my political convictions. I joined ELAS, and I was soon active in their operations. It remained so for a year and because of my military experience, I rose through the ranks to a *kapetan* and was put in charge of operations in Corfu because of my knowledge of the island and because I was raised here. This was my father's taverna. When I returned to Corfu, it was the perfect cover from where to run our operations.

'Every man who has joined us has done so voluntarily because they believed it was the right thing to do. Some had no jobs, while others heard about us through word of mouth. A lot of them are just young boys, while others are men who have their own reasons for joining our ranks. Many have relatives who were killed by the Germans, wives raped, parents and brothers and sisters killed, or starved to death in the cities, like Salonika and Athens. When the Italians were removed from Corfu by the Germans, we seized many of their weapons.'

'So, they have joined the *andartes* for revenge. How does that make a disciplined organisation?' Rosa asked.

'Not all are nursing grief, but if they were, like the others, they embrace the struggle, with the pulse of a free Greece pounding in their hearts. Allegiance, commitment, and steadfastness to the cause. It is a holy struggle; we are always one. We are fighting to rid Greece of Nazis, but we are also fighting for the people, the working class, the hungry, national liberation and social reform.'

'You're talking about the ideology of socialism.'

'If that is what it takes for social justice and social freedom to exist in a free Greece. What have we got to look forward to? We are a country under occupation. The basic needs of a decent life have been denied to us. The country is hungry, crippled by inflation and a disintegrated government that is blind to the needs of the people and their suffering. At least, we speak the language of the people.

'We have a few radios, and in the villages, telephones are a luxury, and most don't have adequate connections. It can take days for news to travel, especially when the medium of that news is on foot, trekking through mountains and inhospitable countryside.

'The men you see around you are loyal not only to me but to the idea of a liberated Greece, free of German occupation, a liberation that will transform Greece. Every Greek will be one, man and woman, rich or poor, and we will live by the people's will.

'You're not the first who has passed through Liapades and needed to make themselves invisible. His name was Frank. He was Scottish and an artist. I liked him. He had principles, and he was loyal to those who had put their trust in him. At great risk to his own life, he undoubtedly saved the lives of people he didn't know by his unselfish actions and courage. He was very likeable, but also very stubborn.'

'What happened to him?'

'I told him it was too dangerous for him to stay in Corfu. We would need a few days, but it was possible we could get him off the island.'

'And did you?'

'His stubborn side won that argument. He was in love with the woman who had sheltered him from the Germans. He would not leave her. One more day with her was of more value to him than his own life.'

'Did he return to her?'

Georgios nodded. 'He did. An incident happened that meant they were no longer safe in Lakones, the village they stayed in. Ironically, they went to Corfu Town and stayed with someone they knew. The Germans caught him, and he was deported the same day your family was. He probably ended up in Haidari prison camp.'

A chill ran through Rosa. She had heard of this prison camp and the stories of cruelty and torture were synonymous with it.

'His chances of surviving such a place as a prisoner are slim. I hope his death is quick and painless, but that is just wishful thinking on my part because I liked him. The truth is, everyone who enters that place is as good as dead.'

Rosa knew what Georgios was insinuating.

'Sometimes, we make choices that have good intentions, that are guided by love, or a noble commitment and such choices, although admirable, can turn out to be fatal and catastrophic.'

Rosa was silent.

'Has Alvertos spoken to you about leaving for Erikoussa?'

She nodded.

Georgios regarded her closely. 'Rosa, you know you have to leave here, don't you? This is your only chance to get out of Corfu. Have you made a decision?'

She held her head high, emphasising the decision she'd already made the night before. She looked into his eyes. 'I feel like an abandoned boat at the mercy of the sea's currents, but it has been decided. I have agreed. We will go to Erikoussa.' She couldn't fail to notice her decision pleased him.

'Then I hope that the sea is calm for you, Rosa.'

CHAPTER FIFTY-ONE

A JOURNEY BY BOAT TO HEAVEN

When they boarded the caique, the fishing boat that would take them to Erikoussa, Alvertos' greatest fear was that he couldn't protect Rosa if they were discovered. It played heavily on his mind. He could see only one course of action to avoid such a thing happening. They would have to leave Greece, but go where? Georgios' voice rang in his head, like a continuous loop — take a boat to Italy. Could they leave behind the only life they knew? They would be refugees in a country ravaged by years of war and economic ruin. They would be leaving one shell of a country for another but also the persecution and constant daily threat of being exposed as a Jew. Rosa still wore the cross around her neck, and Italy was a Christian country.

Alvertos was moving further from his mother, leaving her on her own. He hadn't seen her for many weeks and the day he went to retrieve Rosa from Corfu Town with Errikos; it nagged at him to go and see her. He desperately wanted to, but it would have deflected him from his purpose, with the unpredictability of the situation and the limited time available. He wondered if he would ever see her again. His heart ached and his stomach churned.

What mattered most, he was with Rosa, and she filled his world with a love he never thought possible. As long as he was with her, he could face anything that was thrown at him.

They watched as Erikoussa grew closer. Rosa took Alvertos' hand in hers and looked at the land ahead, the hills carpeted in thick forest. The family that accompanied them, three girls and a husband and wife, sat huddled in a corner of the boat. The father stood, and shielding his eyes from the sun; he peered at the island that was to be his family's new home.

'We're all in the hands of God now.'

They sat in silence as the sugar cubed buildings grew, and soon, they could make out the intricate details of each building. Rosa's stomach lurched into her throat as the small port gradually came into view.

'It doesn't look too bad,' Alvertos said, trying to sound convincing as he reached for Rosa's hand. The breeze caught her hair loose about her face and she flicked the wisps from her eyes.

Rosa winced. 'I've lived in Corfu all my life and never once had any inclination to come here, and now these people are risking everything for me. Thea did the same, and it cost her life. It has to stop.' Her grip tightened around Alvertos' hand.

'It can stop.'

She turned to him curiously. 'What do you mean?'

Alvertos paused. 'We don't have to stay.'

'And where would we go?'

'Georgios told me we could charter a boat to Italy. It

would cost a lot of money, it would be dangerous, but if we made it to Italy, no one would care that you were a Jew. The British and the allies have almost driven the Germans out of Italy. In Italy, the war has already been won.'

A small reception party met them. One man, tall and thin with kind eyes, introduced himself as Sokratis Karagounis. He welcomed them to Erikoussa and invited them to taste his island's hospitality in one of the few tavernas on the small island.

They ate a chicken stew infused with basil and mopped it up with bread and wine. It was the best meal both Rosa and Alvertos had enjoyed since Thea's passing.

Sokratis explained the island from the southernmost part to the northernmost part was only three kilometres in size and covered in cypress forests and olive trees with a network of unpathed tracks that connected remote houses and dwellings. He informed them that one had been chosen for Rosa and Alvertos. It was a small one storey stone building concealed in a cove just a mile from where they were. It would offer them privacy and was still not too far from the small port which they could walk to for provisions and food which would be given to them without cost. Rosa remonstrated that such a gesture wouldn't be necessary as they had the means to pay, but Sokratis insisted it had been decided; they were guests, and as such, what they needed would be provided for by the islanders free of charge.

They ventured down a steep track that took them to a cluster of cypress and olive trees and a crescent-shaped beach that gently sloped into a sapphire surf. The track ended at a stone building, atop with fading terracotta tiles with two windows framed by dilapidated shutters and a wooden door half eaten by woodworm.

'It has character,' Alvertos announced optimistically. Rosa, casting her eyes over the dwelling, suddenly warmed to its diminutive proportions and imperfections 'Looks can be deceiving. All it needs is some attention and care.' She stood with her hands on her hips. 'Let's see what awaits us inside.'

Unlocking the door, Alvertos feared it was about to topple from its hinges before fully opened. Inside, a shadowy light obscured the interior, only a slit of light visible from under the shutters propelling Rosa into action. Hastily, she threw open the shutters and met a sight that caught her breath.

A table sat in the centre of the room, on top of which sat a glass vase with a profusion of geraniums sprouting outwards. She moved closer into the room and traced a finger along the grain of the table. She inspected the tip of her finger and smiled to herself. Not a trace of dust. The stone floor, clean and dirt free, felt like a carpet under her feet and she noticed every work surface was spotlessly scrubbed. The iron kitchen range caught her eye, appearing as clean as the day it was made.

In a corner stood a bed atop with pillows and sheets arranged with care and crease free. Despite their situation, Rosa couldn't help smiling.

Rosa opened a cupboard door, expecting it to be bare, but was taken aback. She inspected its contents and gasped at the array before her: goats' cheese, ham, bread, an abundance of herbs, a variety of vegetables, oranges, rice, beans, flour, and oils.

She took Alvertos' hand and pulled him to her. Her eyes welled with tears. 'Look what they have done for us.'

Alvertos' eyes widened. 'I haven't seen as much food for... well, I don't know how long.'

'It's a banquet. You would never think there was a war.'

'They're self-sufficient. There're no Germans to steal their food.'

'And look.' Rosa pulled out a bottle of wine. 'I'm in heaven.'

CHAPTER FIFTY-TWO

A FISHERMAN AND FARMER AND ALL THE TIME IN THE WORLD

The days passed effortlessly. They went for walks in the forest and followed the coastline, hand in hand, with the warm sun on their backs. They ate lunch, chunks of bread and cheese, while sitting on the beach that was so close to the house, Rosa described it as their garden.

At night, she lit an oil lamp. 'I could be happy here, Alvertos. The house is small, but perfect. I've never lived so far from other people. It's so quiet, but not in an unsettling kind of way. It feels normal.'

'I know what you mean. I've never heard so many birds and the constant sound of the waves is like a soft melody played daily on the beach. Nature's symphony.'

'Instead of rushing to leave, let's stay awhile. In the morning, I don't wake with the constant fear that today could be the day. I'd forgotten how that feels, to be normal without the threat of discovery. My body and mind were exhausted, but every day we spend here, I can feel that negativity physically drain from me, replaced by a feeling of hope that maybe soon we can have a normal life. I'm tired of feeling broken. At last, I feel complete, and I don't want to lose that feeling. My mind and body no longer feel shattered. I feel whole, and I like it. I don't want that to change.'

'I can see the effect this place has had on you and it's truly wonderful. It really is,' Alvertos said. 'I haven't seen you this happy for a long time and I don't want that to end. My heart yearns for the day when the war is over. It's easy to think it's ended, but I saw something today that unsettled me greatly.'

'What do you mean?' Rosa said.

'This morning, when I went to get provisions.'

'You didn't mention this.'

'I didn't want to worry you.'

'Well, you're worrying me now, so tell me.'

'I saw German soldiers.'

A chill steeled across Rosa's neck. 'Where!'

'They arrived on a patrol boat. I met Sokratis. He told me the patrol boats normally pass by the island but occasionally they'll land and come ashore. Not for long and they've never left the port. Normally, they'll have a coffee or something stronger and be on their way. This time was different. They stayed longer than normal and ventured further than usual. They were definitely more aware of the comings and goings, and they asked several questions.'

'Like what?'

'If any new people had arrived recently. They didn't mention the word "*Jew*" but Sokratis detected a change in their demeanour. They were on edge, almost nervous even. It didn't stop them accepting the bottle of wine he gave them, and they left soon after.'

'Just when I thought life was changing for us.'

'It doesn't mean they are looking for us or the family

that came with us in the boat. It could just be coincidental. Sokratis visited a relative in Corfu a few days ago and was told the BBC predict the Germans will evacuate Greece within days. They've already started to move out of Athens.'

'Can it really be true?'

'Why would he lie about such a thing?'

'I suppose he wouldn't.' Rosa thought for a moment. 'Then we wouldn't need to think of going to Italy, or anywhere else, for that matter. We could stay here.'

'And not go back to Corfu?'

'Look around you, Alvertos. It's perfect. Our cup is full. We go to bed with the sound of the house creaking, like old houses should do. I've never slept better and my dreams are no longer haunted by those dreadful images and terrifying sounds. We wake up every morning to the sound and sight of the sea. There's space all around us. We're not hemmed in by buildings and apartments and the constant sounds of a town.'

'What's wrong with Corfu Town? It's been your home all your life.'

'And what would I go back to? My family's house that is empty and trashed. That would remind me every second that my mother and father and Andras are gone. I don't even know if they are alive or dead. What would you have me do, Alvertos? I can't even think about it without my heart breaking.'

Alvertos narrowed his eyes. His mouth opened, but words failed him. He took a breath and cleared his throat. 'I wouldn't ask you to do anything you didn't want to do. If we stayed, how would we live?' He held out his upturned palms. 'I don't have a job. How would I provide for you... for us?'

'We have my father's money. We won't starve. You could buy a boat.'

'A boat?'

'You could be a fisherman. You would be a good fisherman.'

Alvertos laughed. 'I don't know the first thing about catching fish.'

'How hard could it be? Fish are stupid creatures. Hundreds of them will swim into your net.' She was smiling now. 'If you don't want to catch fish, we could buy goats and grow lots of vegetables.'

'A farmer!'

'Why not?'

'You're that desperate to stay here?'

'Not a farmer, then?'

Alvertos reached out and gently touched her cheek. He smiled. 'There's no rush to leave.'

She could feel the knots in her stomach unravel. 'I think you would make a good farmer.'

He smiled. 'I know nothing about growing vegetables and keeping goats.'

'You would have all the time in the world to learn.'

CHAPTER FIFTY-THREE

A LESSON ON STARS

Rosa and Alvertos sat outside the house, watching the sun melt into the horizon and polarise the sky with hues of indigo and amethyst. A warm glow stretched over the beach and brushed over the stone of the house.

A tepid breeze, soft like whispers, stroked their skin as the words they spoke to each other carried the promise of possibilities and contentment. They sat awhile longer until the concealing cloak of evening consumed the landscape and sky in black and the only light around was the enduring moon glistening liquid silver on the glasslike surface of the sea.

Rosa stared at the night sky for a long time.

'I never knew there were so many stars in the sky. The more I look, the more stars are revealed.'

'Stars are fascinating. They're little miracles that light up the night sky.'

'I've never thought of them like that.'

'A star's brightness depends on its size, its temperature, and the distance it is from Earth.'

Rosa looked at Alvertos as if he had spoken another language. 'How do you know that? And when did you become interested in stars?'

'I've always had an interest in astronomy. It started when I was at school. I must have been about ten. The teacher gave us a project to learn about our solar system and my love affair with the universe began. I've just never told you.'

'I can't believe I never knew that.'

Alvertos shrugged. 'It just never came up in conversation, I suppose.'

'No. It never has.'

He studied her for a moment. 'Is there anything about you I don't know?'

Rosa blinked. She wasn't sure if there was, and then she smiled. 'Not unless it hasn't come up in conversation.'

Alvertos chuckled to himself, appreciating her humour.

Rosa considered his question again. 'Would it matter if there was?'

He raised an eyebrow. 'Not really. And if there was, I'd like to think I'd find out sooner or later, since I expect to spend the rest of my life with you.'

Rosa leaned her head against his shoulder. 'That's a comforting thought.'

Alvertos wrapped an arm around her. 'Intriguingly, some stars are brighter in the sky because they're hotter or bigger than others.'

'Really.' Her voice was monotone as she pulled a face.

'The stars that don't shine as bright do so because they're usually smaller, or distance wise, they're further from the earth. This used to fascinate me when I was younger, and it still does.'

'I can tell it does.' The corners of her mouth turned into a grin.

'Did you know the light we see when we look at a star isn't actually there?'

That piqued her attention, and Rosa looked at him as if he had gone mad. 'But I can see it.' She pointed to the night sky. 'Look! Look at all the stars, they're all shining.'

Pleased with himself, Alvertos smiled. 'I know. The light we see when we look at the stars takes a lot of time to travel through space and reach us. In fact, it can take thousands, millions, or even, in some cases billions of years to reach us. How amazing is that? It blows my mind.'

'So, you mean, that star up there in the sky, the one I can see right now, is actually in the past?'

'Yep, it is. Or it might not even be there.'

'That's impossible.'

'Stars have a life cycle. They come into existence and eventually, like all things, they die. It's natural. The star you see right now might have exploded and died thousands or even millions of years ago, depending on how long it took the star's light to reach us.'

Rosa sighed contentedly, her eyes fixed on the sky above her. 'That's amazing.'

Alvertos stroked her hair. 'It's not the only thing that's amazing.'

Alvertos placed his hand on her chin and turned her head towards him. He gazed softly at her, and Rosa raised her face to his. He traced the tip of his finger along her lips, not taking his eyes off her.

His finger paused. 'I love you, Rosa Koumeris.' Even

though his voice was soft, it resonated with an ache. 'From the very first moment I laid eyes on you, I'd never wanted someone so much in my life. You altered it forever. My life before that moment suddenly had no meaning. All that mattered to me was you. You consumed me, my every thought, my every yearning. It didn't matter to me what others thought, or what others said, what I felt in my heart transcended community and religion.' His voice grew fervent with each word. 'All I wanted was to be with you, to hear your voice, the sound of it when you spoke, to feel the touch of your lips against mine...' He took a breath. 'And now I have these things. It scares me because what we have is sacred, but it's fragile at the same time. If you were ever taken from me, I would spend every second of my life finding you again. I would kill every Nazi with my bare hands.'

Rosa raised her finger to his mouth. 'That will never happen,' she announced with joy and trepidation.

Her words settled on him decisively and steadily. She pressed her lips to his, and she felt the tension in him melt away.

They lay naked on the bed; the dark shielding their eyes apart from a silver beam of moonlight that illuminated one wall. He cupped his hand under her breast, and bending forward, he kissed their swell. His hands travelled the curve of her waist and then folded around her. Rosa rested her head against his chest and soaked in the scent that rose from his skin. She breathed him in as if her life depended upon it.

She closed her eyes, her breath coming quickly. 'I want you to touch every inch of me,' she whispered in the dark.

CHAPTER FIFTY-FOUR

INTRUDERS

Rosa woke to bright sunshine illuminating the house. Alvertos had already dressed and was staring out of the window towards the beach. She could detect a tension in the way he stood, his back stiffened, and his head shook.

'Alvertos, what is it?'

He turned on his heels. 'There're two Germans down by the beach. They've come by boat. I think it might be the ones I saw the other day.'

Her stomach lurched inside her. 'Why are they here?'

'I don't know, but I'm going to find out.'

She threw the sheet from herself and briskly dressed. 'Wait, I'll come with you.'

He shook his head, rebuffing her request. 'No. Get dressed, quickly. Leave the house through the back window. The grass is long enough to hide you. Keep running until you get to the trees. They won't see you. Once they've gone, I'll come and get you.'

'I'm not leaving you. Let me stay,' she pleaded.

He turned his head to the window and then whirled around again to face her. His eyes bore into her, tortured and alarmed. 'I'll come and get you,' he repeated insistently.

He crossed the room in four strides and reached the door. Now dressed, Rosa reached for him, clasped her hands around him and raised her face to his. 'Don't go outside. Stay here.'

He took her face in his hands, and she felt his breath warm on her mouth. 'I can't. If they came to the house, I'd never forgive myself if anything happened to you. It's better this way.'

Her hair tousled around her face as she pressed her lips to his and he encircled her with his arms. As he tightened his embrace, she willed the moment to last forever, but he let her go and stepped to the door. His eyes fixed on her as he placed his hand on the door handle. 'Make sure you get as far away as you can.'

She nodded immediately as her fear swelled. He opened the door and slipped from her. He was gone.

She stood as if fixed to the ground, as silence filled the house. The air around her felt thick and charged. A trembling ran through her chest. Hardly breathing, she whirled around with only one thought on her mind.

She scrambled blindly through the long grass as it whipped at her face and legs. It felt like trying to wade through water, her arms and legs constricted and heavy. Rosa could see the line of trees ahead, temptingly close. She willed her legs, burning with the exertion, to work faster. She turned her head to see how far she'd gone and possibly glimpse Alvertos. Rosa could see the back of the house and further, the white of the sand and the boat that seemed to float above the sapphire water.

She glimpsed Alvertos then, and the two German soldiers standing in front of him. Her foot struck a rock and to Rosa's alarm she stumbled, grabbing at air, free-falling and buckling inevitably towards the stationary ground. Her skull smacked the solid earth, the pain instantly piercing, as a fog clouded her dazed mind. She heard a gunshot crack in the air, and immediately her shock turned to fear and the dreadful possibilities such a sound evoked. A shudder ran through her, and a weightlessness dragged her further from the smells and sounds she desperately needed to be among. The more she attempted to focus, she teetered on the edge of consciousness before finally succumbing to the inevitable pull of blackness. The last thing she felt was a warm sensation running down her legs.

Rosa limped and staggered towards the house. *How long had she lain unconscious?* She winced with each step from

the pain in her foot and the throbbing in her head. Her eyes, still bleary, darted from the beach to the sea, the sea to the house and everything else in between.

When Rosa reached the house, she stood in the doorway. She knew he wasn't there, but something inside her still made her call his name. If anyone apart from Alvertos had been here, there was no sign that it had been so. Apart from one detail. Someone had moved the suitcase from under the bed and left it open. She could feel the anger pulse in her veins. Rosa took a deep breath and, with a shaking hand, she lifted the flap where the envelope was. She let out an exhausted groan. It was gone.

Rosa rushed from the house, down the track that led to the beach, her heart pounding like a sledgehammer in her chest.

She saw him lying on the sand. 'Alvertos!' Rosa screamed, his name burning in her chest. She trampled through the sand to reach him, the pain in her foot no longer a concern. She fell to her knees and turned him over, and gasped at the dark stain in the middle of his chest.

Her soaring scream reached the sky, and she howled his name over and over. Rosa pulled his limp body close to hers. His eyes were closed, and she pleaded with him to open them. She stroked his hair, her tears staining her cheeks, her throat burning with sobs. She couldn't breathe. She didn't want to breathe. She didn't want to continue living when her entire world lay still and silent in her arms. Rosa pressed Alvertos' head to her chest and, rocking backwards and forwards, she moaned, no longer able to speak. Her body shook, and she pressed her forehead against his, her face wet with tears and blood.

They found her still cradling him and carefully prised his dead body from her arms. Numb with grief, Rosa shuffled behind the two men as they carried Alvertos' body from the beach and placed him in the cart they had been travelling in.

From the house, they covered his body in the bed linen and collecting Rosa's belongings; they turned the mules toward the small port, where only a few weeks earlier, Rosa and Alvertos had arrived.

. . .

By the end of the summer, the rapid fall of Romania and the Russians' inevitable advancement through the Balkans saw the German army begin its withdrawal from Athens and then the rest of the Greek mainland and its islands. By October 1944, British troops had already entered the capital and liberated Athens.

CHAPTER FIFTY-FIVE

RETURNING

Her heart pounding, Rosa dropped the suitcase next to her feet and knocked on the door, softly at first and then with more force. When the door opened, and Melina gazed at Rosa, she didn't have to ask. In that moment, she knew. She took a sharp intake of breath, her face crumbling. She swayed and then regaining her composure, she said, 'You'd better come in,' her voice barely rising above a whisper.

Rosa could see Alvertos in every space and every corner of the apartment. She couldn't contain herself any longer, her emotions were too raw, and she was fraught with grief. Rosa covered her mouth with a hand and as she gulped for air, her grief boiled over.

'Melina, he is gone. Alvertos is dead.' It was the first time she had to acknowledge this to anyone, and the reality slammed into her. Her legs buckled, and she crumpled to her knees, her sobs rasping her throat.

Melina crouched beside her and cradled Rosa in her arms.

'I knew the second I opened the door and saw you standing there, alone. I've dreaded this moment since the day the Germans arrived.' Her tears fell onto Rosa's hair.

Rosa raised her head, her eyes lined with anguish. 'I'm so sorry, Melina. You've lost a son, and I'm to blame.'

With angst, Melina tightened her embrace. 'Don't you ever think like that, do you hear me? He would have done anything for you, and not because you asked him to, but because he wanted to. Alvertos loved you. Yes, I've lost a son, and a parent should never experience such a thing, but you had your whole life together.

'I'm so sorry about your mother and father and your little brother. How much more pain can you take? Have you heard of them?'

Rosa shook her head. 'Nothing. I'm not expecting to. I don't know if they're alive, but I fear the worst. The stories I've heard about such places...' Her heart wrenched. Rosa looked into Melina's face. 'My life is over.' She pressed her face into Melina's chest, capitulating into another wave of sobs.

Melina let her cry, and then, with a hand, she gently combed away strands of hair that stuck to Rosa's wet face.

'You're exhausted. You need to sleep.'

They both rose to their feet and Melina guided her to the bedroom Rosa had shared with Alvertos. Melina pulled back the sheets and Rosa sunk into the mattress. She removed Rosa's shoes and laid the sheet over her and already Rosa had succumbed to sleep.

The next morning, when Rosa awoke, Melina had already made breakfast and set the table.

Melina mustered a smile. 'Would you like two eggs? There's some bread, and the coffee is on the stove.'

Rosa cut two slices of bread and placed one on Melina's plate. She poured two cups of coffee and set them on the table. She sat down; her face was ashen and her eyes dark. She left the food untouched.

'You must eat,' Melina encouraged her. 'You're dressed. That's good. Did you sleep well?'

'I did, thank you. It was the first time I've slept all night since...'

'You should still talk about him, Rosa. It will help you. Alvertos might not be here, but he is still in our thoughts and in our hearts. In time, you will be able to mention his name with a smile on your face.'

'I don't think I could ever do that.'

'Not just yet, no, but you will. My husband was taken from me suddenly and it took me a long time to come to terms with that. It's normal, but one day you'll be able to accept what has happened. It doesn't mean you will have stopped loving Alvertos or miss him with your whole being. You will.'

It was hard for Rosa to imagine ever feeling that way. They sat and ate their simple breakfast in silence, lost in their own thoughts. And then Melina raised her head and looked at Rosa. 'I need to know what happened to Alvertos. I know it's hard for you. Don't spare me the details, I must know.'

Rosa had been expecting this request, even though her heart felt it had been torn from her body, she owed Melina this.

It was difficult for Melina to hear Alvertos' last moments. Once finished, Rosa said, 'He's buried in the small cemetery in Erikoussa. The entire island attended the funeral.'

'That's a comfort to me. I will visit him.'

'He sacrificed himself for me. He knew exactly what he was doing. How can I live knowing this?'

'You must, for Alvertos.'

Reluctantly, Rosa nodded an acknowledgment.

'What will you do now?' Melina asked.

Rosa shrugged. 'The Germans have ransacked most of our homes and now strangers are living in them.'

'How can people do such things? It's shameful. These are our neighbours' homes. I don't know what to say, Rosa.'

'Not everyone thinks like you, Melina. The occupation has brought out the worst in people, but it's also shown the humanity in others. I wouldn't be here today if it wasn't for people like you.'

Melina, calm and thoughtful, placed her fork on the plate in front of her. She raised her head and her face set, she insisted, 'You will stay with me. It would be what Alvertos would have wanted, and most importantly, expected. It's also what I want too.'

This took Rosa aback; it was not why she'd returned to Corfu Town; she had done so to tell a mother of her son's death.

Nothing was clear to her anymore. Where was her life heading? What would the future hold? There were so many uncertainties.

Rosa could see in Melina's brown eyes she would not break her word. She was a woman of principle, and her word was her bond. She was also Alvertos' mother and given Rosa was now family; Melina loved her as her own and Rosa loved her as well.

Under the bed in the small room she'd shared with

Alvertos, her suitcase sat emptied of her clothes, but for one item. Enclosed in its case, the camera still captured and stored the images of the men, women and children systematically erased from the streets, the cobbled stone lanes, the houses and apartments, the synagogues, the cafes and shops of Corfu Town. Generations of Jewish families, Greek by birth, language, culture and blood, wiped from the very fabric of the town, that for centuries had been their home, their identity, their birthright.

CHAPTER FIFTY-SIX

FACING HER DEMONS

Corfu 2002

'Oh, my word.' Rosa checks her watch. 'Look at the time. I didn't think it would take that long. It's almost morning. I'm sorry for keeping you from your bed. You should have stopped me.'

Elly is sitting opposite Rosa, her arms wrapped around her legs that are tucked close to her chest. 'I can't believe what you have just told me. I could never have done what you did or survived such loss, such pain. It's incredible.'

'I was about the age you are now.'

'To have gone through so much in such a short time, I don't know how you did it.'

'There was no other choice. There were many such stories. I wasn't the only one. During that time, everyone suffered, lost those they loved and witnessed human depravity on a scale that was unimaginable, unprecedented.'

'When you spoke, it sounded like another world. I've only seen films about the Second World War, and it has always felt like such a long time ago.'

'Not for me.'

'No, and not for me now. You're a living connection to that time, and I feel privileged. I now know your story, my family's story. Being in Corfu, where it all happened, is a privilege. I'll cherish this time with you, Grandma. Alvertos was a special man. I can't imagine what you both went through. It's a true love story.'

'Yes, I suppose it is.'

'Did you tell grandad about the war, about Alvertos?'

'Eventually. I had to. It is part of me. It is who I was, and because of it, who I am. It was his right to know.' She grins. 'He needed to know what he was getting himself into.'

'I wish I'd met Alvertos.'

'But you can. I still have the film reel that I took when we found the camera. He is on there, as large as life itself.'

'I can't wait to see it, especially now.'

'It's the first thing we'll do when we get home.'

Elly yawns and covers her mouth.

'You should try to get some sleep.'

'And you too,' Elly says. She considers Rosa. 'I hope you've not regretted coming back to Corfu?'

'Not at all. I'm glad I did, for many reasons.'

'Good. You need to have closure.'

Rosa sighs heavily. 'I'm not sure I'll ever have, as you put it, closure, but what I need to do is to face my demons. At my age, there won't be many opportunities to do so. Quite unexpectedly, I've been given the chance to do just that.' Rosa remembers the uncomfortable encounter with Josefina the day before.

'What do you mean?'

'Yesterday, do you remember the woman I spoke with, just briefly? I need to meet with her again,' Rosa explains.

'If she was a guest at the ceremony, I could ask Marianna, she'll be able to get in touch with her. Would you like me to do that?'

'I would, if you don't mind?'

'It would be no trouble at all, Grandma. Who shall I say you want to see?'

CHAPTER FIFTY-SEVEN

THE TRUTH

They meet in the hotel lounge. Josefina appears dressed in a sky-blue jacket and skirt, her hair tied back from her face where she has applied minimal make-up. It is mid-morning with only a few people sitting at tables conversing in hushed voices.

Rosa feels awkward when Josefina walks towards her. She braces herself, takes a deep breath and raises herself from her seat when Josefina lifts her hand. 'Don't get up on my account.'

Rosa sinks back into her chair.

There are no pleasantries on Josefina's part.

Rosa wills herself to smile. 'Thank you for coming, especially with it being such short notice.'

'It was a surprise.'

'But you came anyway.'

'My flight home is not until tomorrow. I wasn't expecting to see you again. Especially after yesterday. It wasn't one of my, let's say, best moments. The words that came out of my mouth could have been expressed... more subtly. It's a wonder you wanted to see me again. Although, seeing you after all these years did come as a shock. I wasn't prepared for that, hence my reaction.'

'I've spent all these years believing you were dead. It came as a shock to me as well.'

'There're not many of us left now. We're getting rarer by the year. There'll come a time, no one will be left alive who lived through that time. There's only you and I left; it would seem.'

Rosa wonders how different their lives would have been if they had both experienced the war living in Edinburgh instead of Corfu.

'I like your necklace. Pearls?'

Rosa is not sure if it's a question or simply an observation. 'They were a present from my husband for our fiftieth wedding anniversary.'

'I never did marry. I had plenty of offers, but the truth be told, I prefer my own company too much.'

Josefina has an elegance about her that defies her years, and it forces Rosa to straighten her back and shoulders. She can feel the dull ache of a headache beginning and she reaches to lift the glass of water she ordered before Josefina arrived. It reminds her she hasn't offered Josefina anything to drink.

'Would you like a drink, tea or coffee? A water perhaps? They have a nice selection of cakes.'

'Oh. It's too early for me to be eating anything like that. Too sweet. I could never understand how people eat so many sugary items for breakfast. In my hotel, the morning buffet is full of muffins and croissants, and syrups of every variety. It's no wonder we're going through an obesity epidemic. People have no willpower these days.'

A silence sits between.

'I owe you my life, Josefina. Because of you, I had a life after the war. I had children and grandchildren. Your actions are the reason a further two generations of my family continue to exist.'

Something changes in Josefina's face. 'And life has a sick side to it, too. Because of you, Rosa, I lost the two most precious loves of my life, my father and Errikos. I have lived my life regretting what I did. If only I had said your papers were false. Every day of my life has been a torment because I too am to blame for what happened to Errikos. I just as well signed his death certificate. You see, Rosa, if I had turned you over to Lieutenant Hoffman, the officer in the square, Errikos would not have died trying to save you. You took my happiness. You took the life I could have had with Errikos. Your life is a reflection of what was lost to me that day. My heart has wrenched throughout all these years with such despair. I've spent a lifetime hating you for that.'

Rosa shrinks from Josefina, apprehension bubbling inside her with the weight of this knowledge. She shifts in her seat. How can she answer such a devastating accusation? She is stunned to silence.

Josefina continues. 'The war shaped our lives. We both suffered, as did most, some more than others, depending on their inner strength, and their fortitude, their ability to endure the circumstances they found themselves in. We didn't ask for what happened to us. We certainly didn't welcome it. We faced it with dignity, with a determination to do what had to be done, no matter the personal consequences. In our different ways, we've both sacrificed so much. We suffered and lived each day with a fear that clung to our skin. We didn't know it at the time, but you and I were the same, Rosa. We had so much in common, but at the time, we couldn't see that our personal circumstances blinded us to it. In a way, we were kindred spirits. I've had a long time, a lifetime, in fact, to think about what happened and how it affected me. You have occupied a lot of my thoughts. I knew when I saw you yesterday I'd been given the chance to fill this hole inside me, to heal once and for all. I struggled with that, as you know, but I knew, even as I walked away from you, it was the right thing to do.' She turns her palms to the ceiling. 'So, here I am.'

Josefina crosses her legs and taps her fingers on her lap. She clears her throat. 'I know it sounds unlikely, but we met through a mutual acquaintance. The age difference didn't matter to us. God, nowadays, no one would raise an eyebrow. It was twenty years a difference. I was twenty, he was forty. There was a connection between us. It was immediate. We saw each other after that for several weeks. We both felt the same about one another. Errikos was the most passionate man I ever knew. He confided in me, as I did him. I knew what he did. I knew the kind of man he was. He was like the others, but different. There was a belief in him that he was not only fighting for Greece, but he was also fighting for humanity against the evil he had seen the Nazis capable of.

'The leaders of the resistance were looking for a way to have eyes and ears in the German headquarters. My brief was simple: gather information that would be of value to the resistance.

'Errikos was against it. He said it was too dangerous, and I was a Jew. A lamb sent to the lion's lair. I convinced him it was the right thing to do. Who else had my credentials? I was born in Berlin. I could speak perfect German and I was brought up a Greek. My family returned to Corfu when the Nazis took power in Germany and began the persecutions.

'I started off doing administration tasks, transcribing German into Greek and vice versa. Then, as my skills became apparent, I was used in other ways. My role quickly evolved into becoming an interpreter. I was present at meetings with the Greek police and Gestapo, the major and officials, and the German hierarchy on Corfu. I was able to siphon information and get it to the resistance. I saved lives, Greek lives. What I was doing was just as important as those that took up arms.'

'I had no idea.'

'Why would you? It came at a cost. And it was that cost that worried Errikos. You see, Rosa, like others, you thought of me as a traitor to my country and fellow Greeks, fellow Jews. It was a coat I was prepared to wear. It was necessary, but underneath that coat, my true intentions were hidden.

'There were times I was vilified, spat on, punched and kicked in the street, but my suffering was necessary, my work too important to let such things sway me from my purpose. I was the lamb whose claws wounded the lion, and I hoped one day would kill it.

'I was present at the talks the Germans had concerning the deportations and the preparations. I wasn't privy to all the information. I was sent from the room. Later, knowing the filing cabinet where the transcript notes would be, I managed to read them. There had been no objections from either the military or the island's politicians, but a most extraordinary turn of events took place. A German commander, Jaeger was his name, objected to the plans and claimed it would do nothing but breed disorder and trouble among the population who viewed the Jews as Greeks just like them. It was his opinion that the Italians that remained on the island were more of a threat to security than the Jews. He was convinced that such numbers could not be moved off Corfu, and it troubled him that a Red Cross ship that recently arrived to deliver food would witness the deportations. His superiors didn't share his concerns.

'I managed to get this information to those that mattered, but they felt it was an impossible task to stop the inevitable. Most Jews still believed they were safer staying than trying to leave. Even I thought I was invincible, but I too was sent to Auschwitz.'

Rosa feels the familiar sting of guilt. 'You were in Auschwitz? I didn't know that. I thought…'

'A Jew is a Jew, even if they had their worth. The Nazis had only one solution, of all people, you should know that, Rosa.'

To that, Rosa has no reply. She is sweating, and she sways slightly. Josefina gazes at her for what seems a long and uncomfortable time.

Eventually, Josefina speaks. 'When we left on the boats, it took a day and a half to get to the island of Lefkada. They were still constructing the detention centre when we arrived. Greek collaborators guarded us. A priest approached a young man in his early twenties and offered him a cigarette. He had only taken a few puffs when an enraged officer put a pistol to his head and shot him. He took delight in informing us the dead man was the luckiest Jew among us all.

'We were given scraps to eat. If it wasn't for the town's people slipping bread and vegetables through the barbed wire, we would have been in a worse state. Then, from there, we were taken to Athens. We spent a week in Haidari prison. Then, after a dreadful train journey from Athens, crammed in putrid cattle trucks, we eventually arrived.

'Immediately, they took everyone's belongings, separating the men from the women and children. Some of us, the younger men and women, were yanked into another file of people. It was pandemonium. I know it now as Auschwitz. My mother and my sister never saw the first nightfall on their arrival, they were among the first to be murdered. I didn't know until later they were immediately gassed, as were the mentally ill and the disabled. All were burnt in the incinerators. I'm not sure why, among all those poor souls, I was spared. Maybe it was because I was young and healthy, and they could put me to work.'

Rosa's jaw falls loose. 'I had no idea, after all these years. I'm so sorry, Josefina.'

There is a silence between them that stretches a lifetime.

'Did you see my mother and father?' Rosa's voice quakes.

Josefina nods. 'They were in the same line as my mother and sister. I was moved to another, much smaller line.'

'And Andras?'

She shakes her head. 'I too, am sorry.'

Rosa had known her family had not survived. She'd lived each day with this truth, but hearing it being confirmed by Josefina, who was in the place they were and who had seen them, made it feel she was hearing about her parents' and brother's fate for the first time. She presses a fist to her chest.

Josefina's jaw hardens. 'Most of the others who arrived from Corfu died, eventually. At one point, I was weak and sick. I had a bad chest infection, but I managed to hide my frailties, others didn't, and many died. I heard of the dreadful things that the Nazis were doing. They called it research. They experimented on people as if they weren't human. They sterilised and castrated many before being gassed. Others went mad as they were forced to work in the gas chambers, burning the bodies of their fellow Jews before they too followed them.' She sighs. 'Many were ill with madness. At least they escaped into the darkness of their minds. I awoke each day into light that brought nothing but suffering and death.' She sucks back a breath. 'When we were liberated, I never returned to Corfu. I couldn't. I was the traitor, an informer. The worst of the worst. There were too many memories, anyway. It crushed me. I tried to make a life for myself. Months after the war ended, I embraced the loving arms of Israel.'

Rosa's throat constricts. She has no words. They are redundant. She is stunned to silence.

Josefina slows her pace. 'Sometimes, I think I've found what it is to be happy, but then, my bitterness burns me like a hot poker and whatever that feeling was deserts me, like most of the men in my life. It's just as well, none of them have ever lived up to Errikos, only he made me truly understand what it meant to love another with all your heart and soul.'

Rosa takes a long drink of water, her thoughts rushing, one on top of the other. Everything she'd thought Josefina was just disintegrated before her. She tries to compose herself and then she asks, 'Is this your first time back?'

'Yes, and you?'

'The same.'

Josefina folds her hands in her lap. 'I was never ready. Just the thought of returning and evoking the memories, the pain... I've been traumatised most of my life because of what happened. There'll no doubt be a name for it, a diagnosis of some sort.'

'I was lucky. I found love.' The words strengthen Rosa's resolve. 'I'd moved to Edinburgh by then. Albert was my lifesaver. I dealt with what happened in my own way, the only way I knew how. I'm sure at times I put him through hell. We had each other and when the family came along, life became busy. I became a mother and there were always flickers of joy…' Rosa stops in mid-sentence and averts her eyes.

Josefina smiles. 'It's okay. You don't have to watch what you're saying on my account. It was my choice to live this life on my own. Now that you're back in Corfu, how does it feel?' Josefina enquires.

'It's different, but the same. That doesn't make sense.'

'It does. I know what you mean.'

For the first time since they met again, Josefina's eyes are warm and understanding, but Rosa can detect something else. There is a change in her.

Josefina exhales a breath. 'Maybe I should have had that drink. It has suddenly got warm in here.'

'I could get you water?'

'I think it's the fresh air I need. Do you mind?'

'I'll come with you if you want?'

'Yes. I would like that.'

The light outside outlines every line on Josefina's face and Rosa is aware the brightness will carve hers, too.

They walk side by side, as they did when they were young girls before the war. This startles Rosa. She is aware how astonishing it is; how bewildering life can turn out.

She turns to Josefina. 'That day in the square, we could never have imagined this would be possible, seeing each other again over fifty years later and walking in the same streets.' It is something she would never have imagined possible even if she'd thought about it, but she never has. 'Out of all those people, there must have been hundreds, over a thousand even, when I think about it, there is only you and I left that have witnessed that time.'

Josefina thinks. 'Why us, Rosa?'

Not for the first time that day, Rosa has no words.

Josefina shakes her head. 'So few survived and returned to Corfu. And what did they come back to? A decimated community. Our culture and heritage, once distinct and part of the fabric of life in this town, was lost forever. There was no footprint that we had ever raised families or worked and lived for generations in the town. It saddens me more than words can say.'

They find themselves walking around the perimeter of Spianada square under the shade of trees. There is a vast area of grass and paths, beddings and a profusion of vibrant flowers that sprinkles the greenery in adoring colour. In front of them, the Old Fortress looms, as if carved from the very rock it sits upon.

Josefina gives out a long sigh. 'This is a fitting place as any.'

'For what?' Rosa asks.

Emotion pulses in her throat. 'It's something I should have told myself a long time ago.' Josefina stops walking and turns to face Rosa. She lifts her chin and searches Rosa's eyes. 'I was wrong.'

Rosa steps back, not sure how to answer.

Josefina continues. 'I've spent my life regretting what I did that day. I let you go, but I've spent every day since regretting I didn't tell that officer you were a Jew. I did it for Errikos because I knew what you meant to him. You were his family and I couldn't break his heart, not my dear Errikos. Since then, I've been consumed with hatred and rage. I thought I deserved more than life gave me and it's only now I can see what a fool I've been.

'You see, Rosa, I needed someone to blame for what happened to my father and Errikos, so I blamed you. You had what I didn't have. All these years, I was wrong about you. You weren't responsible for what happened. I can see that now. The truth is, no one was. We were all surviving the best we could.'

She reaches out, and with a gentle touch, places her hand on Rosa's forearm. 'Please forgive me.'

Rosa looks into Josefina's eyes and sees genuine regret. She can feel herself soften towards her.

'It was a long time ago, another life,' Rosa says. 'People did things because of circumstance. We were all forced to become different people, to do things against our nature, our better judgement, things we would never normally do. There has never been a time like it. It was extraordinary and unprecedented. I did and said things back then that I'm not proud of, that still give me sleepless nights.'

'There's something else I need to tell you.' Josefina moves awkwardly closer. 'When everyone was in the Old Fortress awaiting the deportation, the Nazis were intent on capturing and rounding up every Jew who had evaded them, at all costs. My usefulness to the Nazis had expended itself, they no longer needed me, and I too was to be deported. I knew what lay ahead. Most of us were going to die and since I was seen as a traitor by my own people, I would be lucky to survive a night among my fellow Jews in the Old Fortress. It mattered nothing to the Nazis that throwing me among my kind could lead to my death. I was nothing to them. I knew if I spoke the truth, I was working for the resistance, it would only look like I was trying to save my skin. To every Jew, I was an informer who worked for the Nazis.

'My heart ached for Errikos and the life I thought we would have, the life we spoke about once the war was over, but someone had torn it away from me. And in my mind that someone was you. In that moment, all I wanted was to be with him and that was never going to happen… ever. So, I did a terrible thing, Rosa, something that I'm now dreadfully ashamed of.

'I thought I'd struck a bargain with Lieutenant Hoffman. I agreed to tell him where the rest of the island's Jews were, where they were hiding and who was protecting them in return for not being deported. Obviously, he agreed, and to my shame, I told him where you and Alvertos were. He didn't honour his end of the bargain. As soon as I gave him the information, I was sent to the Old Fortress.'

Rosa steps backwards. Her hands shake and a pain constricts her chest. It is unbearable and she can see her horror reflect in Josefina's eyes. 'Have you any idea what you did?' Rosa balls her fists. She wants to hit her.

'I know I did a terrible thing.'

'The Nazis murdered the woman who took Alvertos and I into her home, the very ones you sent. They hung her from a tree. Her name was Thea. She was brave and had a beautiful soul. Errikos trusted her. He trusted her with my life. You're as much to blame as they were.' Rosa covers her mouth with her hand. 'You killed her.'

CHAPTER FIFTY-EIGHT

THE NEED TO VISIT AN OLD FRIEND

Rosa doesn't allow herself to dwell on Josefina's revelation. What good would it do her now, nearly half a century later? She couldn't change what had happened, and she'd lived most of her life without such knowledge. Living in ignorance had its merits.

She is nursing a glass of lemonade in the hotel lounge when she glances up and sees Elly scanning the lounge, looking flustered and concerned. Rosa waves her hand and a palpable relief fans over Elly's face.

Elly sinks into the chair opposite Rosa. 'I was beginning to wonder where you had got to.'

'You really mean you were concerned that I was on my own with another old lady and something untoward might have happened to us.'

'There's no use pretending otherwise. Yes, you're right, I was beginning to worry.'

'I get around Edinburgh just fine and it's bigger and busier than Corfu Town.'

'I know you do, but you're used to Edinburgh. It's your home.'

'As was Corfu once.'

'I'm sorry.'

'Don't be. It's nice to know you care, and it's reassuring.'

Elly looks at the empty seat next to Rosa. 'Where is Josefina?'

Rosa lets out a long breath. 'She's gone.'

'Do I detect a falling out?'

Rosa tilts her head. 'Let's just say we weren't compatible after all.'

'You seemed to be getting on all right. Did I miss something?'

Rosa smiled at her. 'Nothing to concern yourself about. We were just two old ladies reminiscing.'

'Are you going to keep me in the dark? I know you, Grandma. I know when you're hiding something.'

'I'd prefer not to talk about it, Elly.'

Elly knew when to back down with her grandma.

'Did grandad know about what happened during the war? Did you tell him about Alvertos?'

'Your grandad was the most kind and gentle man. He would do anything for anyone. He wouldn't see anyone stuck. Nothing was too much trouble. He was one of life's gentlemen. There aren't many of them left now. If you're asking if I kept any secrets from him, the answer is no. He knew everything there was to know about me, just as I knew everything about him. Your grandad and I were a good match. I was the glove that fitted his hand perfectly, and I loved him dearly and miss him dreadfully every day of my life.'

'After the war, when I met your grandad, we watched

the films Alvertos and I took with my uncle's camera. It helped him understand what I went through.'

'That must have been difficult for you both.'

'It brought us closer. He could see my mother and father, my home in Corfu and the town, as well as the film Alvertos and I took in Liapades. I could show you the film when we get back. Would you like that?'

'That would be amazing. I'd love to see it.'

'Then that's what we'll do, a night at the movies.'

Elly smiles. 'And I'll bring the popcorn.'

'It's a date, then.' She considers the saying and then asks, 'Do you still say that these days?'

Elly laughs. 'It's a bit old-fashioned, but sometimes the old ways are the best ways.'

Rosa grins at this. 'Yes, I would tend to agree with that.'

Elly scratches her head. 'I was wondering, is there anything else you want to do or see before we go home?'

Rosa takes a sip of her lemonade and carefully places the glass on the table in front of her. 'There's one more thing I need to do.'

'And what's that?' Elly asks.

'I need to visit an old friend.'

CHAPTER FIFTY-NINE

FINDING HERSELF

The cemetery has changed since she was last there, but a path still meanders through a canopy of ancient trees just as she remembers it.

In her mind, it has always looked the same as it did all those years ago, but now, she can see, over time, it has grown, the graves numerous, more lavish in their appearance and populated atop with white crosses. The church remains relatively unchanged, its walls echoing the memories of generations as the bell tower stretches towards the limitless blue ocean of the sky.

Rosa shields her eyes and peers at the bells, the very same bells that rang out when she and Alvertos and the rest of the villagers escorted Thea's coffin to her resting place. The decades strip bare and she remembers it like it's yesterday, her chest tightening just as it did then. She straightens herself and takes in a deep sigh. Almost there, she tells herself. Elly gently touches Rosa's arm. 'I'll let you go ahead on your own.'

Rosa nods. 'I won't be too long.'

'Take all the time you need,' Elly says.

She knows exactly where she is going. The memory of that day has not faded. It is crystal clear. Finally, she stops in front of a grave, less opulent than those around it and neglected in its appearance.

Rosa stands in silence, not sure what to say. She tries to summon an image of Thea in her mind and as she does, the curtain of time draws back and floods her with memories. She tells Thea of her life since the war and how if it wasn't for her generosity, there wouldn't have been a life at all for her to live.

Then she speaks to her in Greek. 'So, you see, you are the reason I am standing here today, an old woman. You welcomed me into your home, you treated me as if I was your own daughter, you gave me advice that only a mother could give and at the end of it all, you protected me, you gave the ultimate sacrifice that only a mother would endure willingly. Your courage astounds me, and although the trauma of what happened to you scarred me for years to come, without your sacrifice, I wouldn't be standing here today. You gave me a future. And what you did for me will be told and passed down to each new generation. You've given life to them, too. They owe you their lives, just as my mother and father had hoped would happen. You have sown that hope, and what is life if there is no hope? The darkness did not prevail, it was the light that did so.

'I remember you once told me I was the daughter you never had but always longed for. I never got the chance to tell you, but even though I knew you only for a short time, you were like a mother to me, and I loved you as such and loved you for it. Soon, our paths will cross again. Until then, my beautiful Thea.'

Rosa wanders back to where Elly is waiting. She thought

her heart would be heavy, yet something has lifted from her. She can feel it in her bones and taste it in the air around her.

Rosa gazes over the rooftops and the houses of Liapades that stretch up the hill towards the small square where a lifetime ago, everything changed forever.

She is glad she came back. At first, the decision to do so was a torment to her, but she understands now, it was the right thing to do. Even in old age, life has taught her a lesson on living. Her heart fills with the understanding, returning to Corfu has helped to heal her, and that sharing her story with Elly has instigated a reconciliation with her past and helped her discover a purpose for the present.

CHAPTER SIXTY

COMING HOME

Edinburgh 2002

She has only been gone a few days, but the moment she opens the front door and steps into the hallway, she feels like someone has wrapped a soft blanket around her shoulders. She remembers it all as if it was yesterday, but it's a comfort to be back among familiar surroundings, possessions collected over a lifetime, and the warm cosiness of her home.

Rosa hears the front door open. Elly has visited her every day since they returned from Corfu over a week ago.

When she enters the living room, Rosa is sitting in her armchair, rubbing the sleep from her eyes, an unopened book lying in her lap.

Elly's eyes scan her grandma. 'Everything all right?'

'Fine, my dear. I must have nodded off.' Rosa glances at the clock on the mantelpiece. 'Is that the time already?' She rises stiffly. 'I should have had the table set for you coming.'

'I'm not coming for dinner, just a cuppa and a biscuit.'

'I know, but I like to be prepared. It's difficult to forgo a lifetime's habit, and anyway, there's something I want to show you. I've been meaning to do it since we got back, but with one thing and the other and that hospital appointment, I've no idea where the time has gone.'

'I told you I'd take you to the hospital.'

'I know. It was kind of you to offer, but I don't want you feeling obliged that you must chaperone me every time I leave the house.'

'I get it. You value your independence, and long may that last, but the hospital's two bus rides away.'

'Well, as you can see, I got there, and I got back in one piece. And before you ask, everything is fine, all in working order, and I've got at least another ten years left in me.'

'Is that what they said?'

'A slight exaggeration, if you ask me. I think it was more of a figure of speech.'

'It's positive, and that's a good thing.'

Rosa tilts her head. 'Especially at my age?'

'You're doing great, Grandma. Age is just a number. Anyway, I'm glad it's nothing. What exactly did they say it was?'

'Oh, it was one of those Latin sounding names.'

'So, you don't remember the exact details then?'

'They're going to send a letter to my GP. It's routine, seemingly.'

She knows full well what the consultant said and the implications, but she cannot bear the thought of telling Elly.

The previous night, she found what she'd been looking

for; it had sat in a drawer waiting for this day to come, and now, in light of recent events, its significance was profound and known to Elly.

Rosa looks over at the kitchen. 'As I said, there's something I want to show you.'

CHAPTER SIXTY-ONE
THE KEEPER OF HER STORY

Elly dips her biscuit in her coffee as Rosa slides a velvet lined wooden jewellery box across the kitchen table. The lid opens with a click.

'This is the cross that was given to me by Melina, Alvertos' mother. I haven't worn it since the day I left Corfu. I was too scared to. I didn't want anything to happen to it. It's too precious to me.'

Elly gasps. 'Wow! You kept it all this time.'

'It's the only tangible object I have that connects me with Alvertos. His eyes fell upon this cross countless times whenever he looked at me. It's the only thing I have that he physically touched. There are no photographs of us together, no letters... nothing.'

'What about the camera? You must have filmed him?'

Rosa sighs. 'There's some but not much, a few seconds of him getting in the way of the lens, and me complaining he was ruining the shot. At that time, we didn't think about filming one another, or even to ask Thea to film us together. It just didn't occur to us. Having a camera was a novelty. I filmed Thea, the village, the countryside, the sea… but not Alvertos. I've beaten myself up about it all these years. It's the only regret I have of our time together.'

'Oh, Grandma! You have your memories, and you can recall them anytime you want. That's a deeper connection, don't you think?'

Rosa smiles. 'Yes, I do. There are things I will never forget. And that reminds me, we have still to have our film night.'

'Yes, I'm definitely keeping you to that,' Elly insists.

Rosa takes the cross from the box and gently unfolds the chain. She rests the cross in her palm.

'It's beautiful and much more than just a cross,' Elly whispers.

'It is, and I'm glad you see it that way. You see Elly, what this cross represents is priceless. No materialistic or monetary value can be placed upon it. In real terms, it's not worth much, but it's the most precious object I own, more than life itself. It's my connection to my past, a past I cannot forget, even if I wanted to, because it's with me every second of every day and with each breath I continue to take. I hope what I'm about to ask of you is received gratefully and not seen as a burden?'

Elly glances at the cross, still sitting in Rosa's palm. 'I'd never view anything you ask of me as a burden; you should know that.'

'I do, but I needed to ask, all the same. It's too important to me not to. I want you to have this cross and be its keeper for me. You know its story, and there is no other person I trust to ensure its story will continue to be told and be remembered. It's my story, but most importantly, it's your story too, and your children's story, they need to know where they have come from, there must be meaning to the suffering and loss, it can't have all been for nothing.'

Elly leans a little closer and smiles. 'It would be my honour. I now know where I've come from. My heart will now be forever connected to my great grandma and my great grandfather and to Andras. I will always remember Errikos with a fondness, he is now my favourite great uncle.' Elly reaches over and gently squeezes Rosas' hand, 'And, of course, Alvertos, my other grandfather who I never met, but now, I feel I know, and the man he was and how much you loved each other. It's incredible to think what you both went through together and I can't believe you were the age I am now. I could never have had your courage, your hope, and your strength. What you experienced was beyond my comprehension. For all of my life, I didn't know who you really were. You have always been grandma and I love you for it. I saw a version of you that you wanted us all to see. I feel privileged to know the truth, to have been given the opportunity to appreciate where I've come from. I'm indebted to you. Even after all you went through, the suffering and the loss, you have carried yourself with a humility and a grace that defies the hatred you faced, the fear you bore, and the suffering you endured in such dreadful times. We think because we have known someone all our lives, we know all there is to know about them. Well, you have just blown that out of the water.'

'I wasn't alone in what I did. All over Greece, there were young men and women just like me, who faced the threat of death every day. Even under the shadow of grief, of all the loss, the suffering and sorrow, to this day, I still don't know where my strength and determination came from. I only know that the Nazis' vile and hateful ideology could never win over love, and when there was love, there was hope, and where there was hope, there was a reason to live and to survive. That was my armour. Without Alvertos, it would have been different. He is the reason you're here today. I've learnt a great lesson on my visit back to Corfu. Life can only be lived forwards when it's understood backwards, and that's my gift to you.'

Elly can no longer hold back her tears. Her face creases with emotion as she embraces Rosa in a tight hug that she never wants to end.

Elly lifts her head from the warmth of Rosa's shoulder, black smudges under her eyes and cheeks wet with tears. 'It has just occurred to me, Grandma.'

'What has?'

'You've never told me how you came to Edinburgh and met grandad.'

'Ah!' Rosa threads her hand through Elly's hair. 'Now that's a different story altogether, and one for another day.'

CHAPTER SIXTY-TWO

UNDER THE STARS

It is a warm and still night as Rosa leaves the house and carefully makes her way to her favourite chair in the garden. She sinks into it, heartsore and exhausted. A globe moon immerses the garden in a silver glow and bathes everything it touches. She lifts her eyes to the vast expanse of the night sky and, as always, she takes in a breath of awe, as one by one, stars emerge as her eyes adjust to the darkness and like scattered glitter they twinkle softly and shimmer in an enthralling spectacle of light.

'*Stars are fascinating. They're miracles that light up the night sky.*'

She remembers Alvertos' words as clear as the day he spoke them.

'Do you remember Alvertos? No one really believed the Germans would do what they did. Not after the Italians. All they were interested in was women and wine. They didn't see us as an inferior race. Not one Jew was deported during the time the Italians were in Corfu. And now, many years later, I've heard stories of how the Italian army and diplomats helped many Jews to flee. As long as the Italians remained in control, we were safe. How little did we know how things would change?

'Even to this day, I can't understand how so many people could be swept up in such an ideology of hatred for their fellow human beings. It's beyond comprehension, but sadly, that was our reality. So much suffering, so much hatred and…vileness. There're no words that come close to portraying the Nazi mindset.

'Remember when I told you my family was Romaniote Jews? You'd never heard of the word before, but you soon knew what it meant.

'Greek was our first language. I told you of the many Romaniote Jews that lived in the Ionian islands, Athens and central Greece, and how we were one of the oldest Jewish settlements in Europe. Even before the Byzantine period, that's how Greek we were. That's how much Greek blood ran in our veins.

'After the war, I learnt that throughout Greece, the Nazis raided our homes, our schools, our banks, hospitals, newspapers and synagogues. They stole priceless artifacts and manuscripts, they desecrated and reduced our cemeteries to rubble.

'As you would have expected, I followed the Nuremburg trials with a keen interest. Of course, I would. The Nazis thought they were invincible, but the one lesson we can learn from history is nothing is permanent.

'At Nuremberg, Dieter Wilsliceny who oversaw the deportations and confessed at the trials to seeing a document with an order from Himmler that Hitler ordered the final solution of the Jewish question. The Jewish Question? Three words meaning the extinction of the Jewish race from Europe. Wilsliceny was well aware he was complicit in the murder of millions of innocent people. As were they all.

Such a horrendous act is mind blowing. I will never understand it.

'Since the war ended, it's now known that from nearly fifty-four thousand Jews that were deported to Auschwitz Birkenau from Greece, the majority were immediately sent to the gas chambers. Can you image such horror?

'I know now over two thousand Jews were deported from Corfu and sent to their deaths. It decimated our community. Only sixty people returned home to Corfu from Auschwitz and in the rest of Greece ninety percent of Greek Jews were killed. Can you believe that, Alvertos?' Rosa sighs. 'It was such a long time ago, but when I returned to Corfu with Elly, it felt hardly any time at all had passed. How strange that feeling was. I half expected you to appear from around every corner.

'I was dubious if going back after all this time was the right thing to do, but now, I can tell you without hesitation, I'm glad I did. It's had a profound effect on me, for various reasons, some made me confront the demons I'd been haunted by all these years, while others gave me an opportunity to say a final goodbye, and there were some revelations I didn't expect, and to be honest, they floored me. I have no regrets.

'In Edinburgh, I've had a good life, a loving marriage, a family and grandchildren. What more could an old Greek woman ask for? I've had a life, and that's the point, isn't it? So many never got that chance.

'Oh, my dear Alvertos, we were so young, weren't we? In my mind's eye, you still are. While I've grown old, and my body's no longer capable of doing the things I took for granted, my mind's still sharp, and my memories have never faded. That's a blessing. I don't know what I would've done if I could no longer remember our life together. It would be unbearable.'

Her eyes scan the night sky one more time. 'I've been visiting the hospital recently, having tests and speaking to a consultant. I've got what is called an aneurysm. It's a word that rolls off the tongue quite effortlessly. Apparently, the wall of my aorta, which is the body's major artery carrying blood from my heart to the rest of my body, has a large bulge in it. I never knew such a thing existed. The only symptom I seem to have is back pain, would you believe? How that happens, I'm not quite sure, but according to the very nice consultant, who is a woman by the way, which I was pleased about, I was born with a condition called, now let me get this right, coarctation of the aorta, which basically means, I've a narrowing in a part of my aorta. It's amazing the things you learn about yourself. I've lived all this time in blissful ignorance. My high cholesterol hasn't helped. At least I've known about that for years.

'Anyway, what does this all mean? I can almost hear you getting exasperated with me. So, if I remember correctly, the nice consultant explained, once an aneurysm reaches a certain size, 5.5cm, the risk of it rupturing is high and the only option is to have it repaired with surgery. Well, my one is 6.5cm, which means it could burst at any time. Seemingly, I wouldn't know much about it. I've thought about that, and I've always wanted to die with the least bit of fuss. It's kinder that way to the family. So, I've decided I'll take my chances with the little time I've left. No surgery for me. I haven't told anyone, only you, my darling. It's our secret.

'If I'm to be honest, I felt guilty for not telling Elly when we went to Corfu, but she would only have worried. It was a risk. I could have put her in a dreadful situation, I know, but apart from the emotional trauma that my demise might have brought, I made sure the insurance would pay out to get my body flown home. It cost an arm and a leg, though.

'I've made all the arrangements. The Co-op funeral care was very helpful in that regard. They will see to everything. This will be the last time I'll speak to you like this. I'm saying goodnight for the last time, my sweet Alvertos.'

CHAPTER SIXTY-THREE

REMEMBER

It is a bright sunny morning when Charlie opens the gate at the side of the house that leads to the garden. He can see Rosa sitting in her favourite chair, which is not unusual, as she often drinks her morning coffee in the garden if the weather is clement.

'Morning Rosa. I'll just get the hoe from the shed. There's some weeding needing doing in the plant beds.'

She doesn't answer, but he's aware her hearing has deteriorated these last few months, and she seldom wears the hearing aids she bought, at great cost, after her audiology assessment at Specsavers.

Once he has finished pottering in the shed and returns with the hoe, Charlie sets about weeding the garden. Now and then he looks up in Rosa's direction. It's her habit to read a copy of The Times, which is unusually delivered at a reasonable time by the young paper boy from the local newsagents, but not this morning, Charlie observes.

'It's fine weather we're having for a change, and it's expected to last for the rest of the week. You probably saw a lot of the sun in Corfu. You'll have to tell me all about it once I'm finished.'

Something isn't quite right. 'Rosa, are you all right?' Charlie calls with a frown.

He drops the hoe and walks stiffly but purposefully towards her. Rosa's back is facing him and when he approaches her, he can see the hearing aid behind her ear.

'It only works if it's turned on,' he reminds her and then his eyes fall upon her face. Rosa's chin rests on her clavicle, just above a cross that hangs from a chain around her neck. Charlie has never seen the cross before, and knowing Rosa is Jewish, it's the last thing he expects to see. Charlie bends forwards, and glances at her face, unexpectedly, her eyes are closed. He gently places his hand on the bare skin of her forearm. Her skin is cold to the touch, and he shudders in shock.

'Oh, Rosa!'

The funeral takes place in the local crematorium attended by family, neighbours and a few close friends that had survived Rosa. In her will, Rosa stipulated her wish that the service was to be a humanist celebration of her life. She had attended many over the years, as each friend gradually passed. The celebratory nature of the service always impressed Rosa and how the humanist gave a detailed but often light-hearted oration of the life of the deceased.

There was one exception to the non-religious service, one Jewish prayer.

In the rising of the sun, and its going down, we remember them. From the moment I wake till I fall asleep, all that I do is remember them. In the blowing of the wind and the chill of winter, I remember them. On the frigid days of winter and the moments I breathe the cold air, I warm myself with their embrace and remember them. In the opening of buds and the rebirth of spring, I remember them. As the days grow longer and the outside becomes warmer, I am more awake, and I remember them.

ALSO IN THE HELLENIC COLLECTION

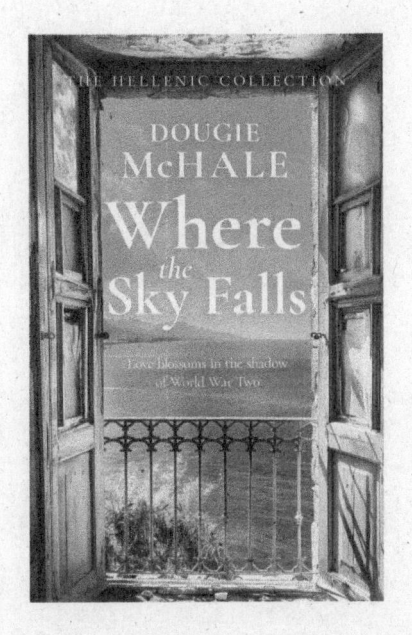

vinci-books.com/skyfalls

In the shadow of World War Two, love blossoms—but at a devastating cost.

Turn the page for a free preview…

WHERE THE SKY FALLS PREVIEW

Chapter 1

Edinburgh 2010

Calton Hill

He feels it instantly, plummeting through him, a surge of regret, a spasm of unfaithfulness. In the slanting light, her sapphire eyes sparkle, like the gliding seawater of the River Forth that carves the shoreline behind them. It was an immediate reaction; he felt it the moment Zoe looked at him, a definite attraction. Admitting his desire felt a betrayal to his past.

'We were on holiday in St Monans, staying at a caravan park,' Rob tells Zoe, whose gaze is fastened to her shoes as they stroll.

'I was fishing with my dad on the pier and caught a flounder, or a plaice. I'm not sure which. It was a flat fish, anyway. Mum gutted it in the sink, cooked it and we ate it for dinner. Before that, I had my photograph taken with it. It was the late 70s, and I had on these jeans with massive flares, so wide they looked like sails. I couldn't tell you what my shoes looked like. And my haircut, God, it was a typical bowl cut. Horrendous now, but back then, it was your mum that cut your hair and there wasn't a menu of styles on offer.'

Zoe laughs and lifts her head. She glances at Rob. 'I'd love to see that photograph.'

'I'll need to dig it out. It's still at Mum's, in the cupboard under the stairs. She's got hundreds of photographs. Not that long ago, she said she was going to throw most of them out. There were too many of them, she said. Luckily, I persuaded her not to. I told her it would be like throwing away your history. They're not just photographs, they're time capsules, captured moments of family and friends, past generations who live forever in images that are precious, that tell the story of where we've come from and who we are. She said she'd never thought about it like that.' Rob smiles. 'A few weeks later, when I visited Mum again, she couldn't wait to show me what she'd done.'

'And what was that?'

'She'd put them in albums, catalogued them, recorded who was in a particular photograph, where it had been taken, and all in chronological order. I couldn't believe it.'

'You must have made a big impression on her. She went from one extreme to the other.'

'She did, but that was her nature.' He smiles at the memory. 'There was never any middle ground with Mum.'

'How is she?' Zoe asks.

Rob thinks for a second. He scratches his head. 'She looks like Mum, but Mum has gone. The person she was no longer exists. She's been erased. I don't know how else to describe it.'

'It's a terrible disease… devastating.'

'I try to visit as often as I can. I know she's in the best place. The staff are amazing. I can't fault them. It doesn't make it any easier, though.'

'You had no choice. She was a danger to herself, wandering outside in the middle of the night.'

'I know. I just thought I'd have more time with her. I didn't expect the dementia to take her from us as quickly as it did. It's not just that. I feel like her whole life has disappeared. The house is going on the market, the furniture is being sold or going to charity shops. I'm sifting through everything just now. It's going to take a while. She never threw anything out. I've found receipts from years ago.'

'What about Sue? Is she helping you?'

'She keeps promising to come up from London, but there's always an excuse, usually work related.'

'She's her mother, too. Has she visited her?'

'Not much. The last time was about two months ago.'

'That's bad. You'd think she'd want to spend time with her.'

'She hardly visited Mum at the best of times. Mum would never hear a bad word against her, always made excuses for her. She'd say, *"A job like that comes with a lot of responsibility."* It was her default for Sue's constant absence. It came with a big salary. It would be nothing for her to jump on a plane and be up here within an hour.'

'I don't understand that. Why wouldn't she want to visit her mum, especially now? And what about her children? It's their gran. When did she last see them?'

'It must be about a year ago.'

'That's dreadful,' Zoe snorts incredulously.

'I know. The thing is, Mum never did get on with Gary, Sue's husband, and the feeling was mutual. Sue was oblivious to it. I'm sure half the time she wasn't even in the room. It was like her head was in a bubble.'

'Maybe that was intentional. Easier to just ignore it.'

'The things Gary used to say to Mum were dreadful at times. He treated Mum like she was beneath him. I'm sure that's what he thought, anyway. You could tell he hated having to visit. He made no attempt to hide his disdain. *"The house was too small, the neighbours were too noisy, and why did Mum still live in a council estate?"* He seems to forget that's where Sue grew up, too. I'd hate to think about what he used to tell his kids; it would be all lies. It's a shame. They have never really got to know their gran. Gary made sure of that.'

'And it's too late now.'

There is a silence as Zoe's words seep into him.

'They think Mum won't last the month.'

'That's just two weeks.'

A resigned smile crosses his face. They look out over the panoramic cityscape. A slight breeze licks at their clothes; Zoe's hair blows over her face and she flicks the strands from her eyes. The light is fading as a bank of clouds rolls above the River Forth and silver pin prick lights twinkle over the coastline of Fife.

'How did your mum end up living in Elie?'

'My mum's sister, auntie Betty, moved there when she got married to my uncle Max. He was a lawyer and had just become a partner in a practice in St Andrews. Mum loved to visit them in their little mansion, as she called it. It wasn't, it was just a big house, but I suppose it felt like a mansion to Mum back then. Anyway, Betty and Max never had children and when Max died, Mum stayed every weekend. She even went to the church on a Sunday with Betty and, as a result, met a lot of people who became friends. When Betty died, to Mum's disbelief, Betty had gifted the house to her. By then, Dad had passed away, so Mum left her little council house and moved into her little mansion, where she lived for several years blissfully.'

'That's so lovely and I bet it stuck in Gary's throat. I'd have loved to have seen his face.'

'Oh, he never visited Mum. Sue came a few times with the kids, but always had an excuse about why Gary wasn't with her.'

'God, I hate that man and I haven't even met him.'

Rob laughs. 'I wouldn't worry about it. He has that effect on most people.'

They strolled for several minutes until the imposing clock tower of The Balmoral Hotel came into view and the Gothic spires of Scott Monument and St Mary's Cathedral rose above Princes Street towards the early evening sky.

'There's something empowering and calming at the same time when you see Edinburgh on this hill. Don't you think?' Zoe asks.

'She's full of contradictions, but isn't that her charm?'

Zoe's eyes fasten on him. 'Your eyes seem to brighten when you speak about this place. Your face lights up. If Edinburgh were a woman, you'd be madly in love with her.'

'There's only one woman I've ever been madly in love with.'

'Oh, Rob. I'm sorry. I still miss Soph every day.' Zoe touches Rob's arm. 'I can't imagine how it must be for you.'

'If I said it gets easier as time passes, I'd be lying. I think I've just got used to living this way, but there isn't a day that goes by that the loss of Soph doesn't stab my heart.'

They walk a little further and then Rob turns to Zoe.

'I'm going to Mum's tomorrow. There're a few documents I need to pick up for the solicitor. Would you like to come?'

'I've nothing planned. I'd like that.'

'I'll show you that photograph if you promise not to laugh.'

She smiles. 'I'll try.'

Rob was married to Sophie for two years when a routine trip to the doctor changed their lives. Sophie had been feeling tired and lost weight and thought she might be iron deficient. Being vegetarian, and ironically, not liking many vegetables, she thought the supplement tablets she took were enough to balance what she otherwise lacked.

The resulting blood test highlighted something more sinister. Sophie was referred to a specialist and after further investigations involving an ultrasound scan and CT scan, they diagnosed her with ovarian cancer. She underwent surgery to remove the cancer, but they discovered the cancer had spread.

Zoe was Sophia's best friend, and they both enjoyed the same social group. They went to the same university, and trained as primary teachers, securing their first job, and starting on the same day in the same primary school. Zoe was the chief bridesmaid at Rob and Sophie's wedding.

Rob had been married for 857 days when his wife was taken from him, and for the next six months, he too felt like he was dead.

Chapter 2

Elie

The Photograph

'I've never been to this part of Fife,' Zoe says as she scans the fields that gently descend into a thicket of trees and the wide River Forth and in the distance, she can make out the familiar shape of The Bass Rock.

He turns to look at her, his hands set flat against the steering wheel. 'Really!'

'Yeah. I wasn't expecting it to be...' she pauses, searching for the word.

'So nice.' It is a weak attempt to hide his sarcasm.

'I can't think of the word, but sometimes the simplest expression is best... just beautiful.'

He smiles. 'We're almost there.'

Soon, the flat fields, farm buildings and narrow road are left behind as the wider road and stone and brick houses of Elie engulf Zoe's view. She catches site of a church with a dominant steeple and when they turn into the High Street with its quaint shop fronts; she notices a small deli and café and imagines Rob's mum shopping and meeting friends for lunch. To her surprise, around them, the sky fills with large black birds, gliding, and landing in several small trees that populate the ground amongst picnic tables. She cranes her neck to get a better look.

'They're crows. Look up into the trees. You'll see their nests.'

Zoe sucks in her breath. 'My God! I've never seen so many nests. They're huge and so close to people.'

'I know. I had the same reaction when I first saw them. Here we are, just in here.'

Rob turns right, and the car enters a gate between a garden wall draped with foliage. They stop in front of a red brick house where the bricks around the windows are painted white, as is the prodigious entrance door. They step out of the car and Zoe is delighted to see an apple orchard.

'Mum was famous for her apple pies. She had an endless supply of apples here,' Rob says, smiling at the memory.

'I can't believe you're selling this place.' Zoe takes in the house and garden.

'Sue wants to sell it.'

'And you don't?'

Rob manages a smile. 'What do you think?'

'I think I know who's behind it.'

He puts the key in the lock and opens the door. They step into a black and white tiled mosaic hallway with a dark wooden staircase.

'Wow! This is incredible.'

'It's all original features.'

His expression is hard to read, but she can hear a sadness in his voice.

After a tour of the house, they sit in the kitchen. Rob hands Zoe a coffee and settles into a chair opposite her.

Zoe cradles her cup in both hands and looks around the kitchen. 'There's no way I'd sell this house. It has far too much potential.'

'House prices have gone through the roof, especially for property like this. There's a high demand for this area.

There's a lot of city types who'd pay well over the price to have a house in the East Neuk.'

'A holiday home, you mean?'

'It would make an ideal family home.'

'It would.'

'Mum was happy here. She loved it. I'd hate for it to be empty half of the year.'

'It doesn't have to be.'

Rob tilts his head. 'What do you mean?'

'Buy her out.'

'Sue?' His voice rises.

'Yeah.'

'I couldn't afford to. You're talking about four hundred and fifty thousand pounds, maybe half a million.'

He gazes out of the window at the sunshine shafting through the branches of the trees in the orchard.

'I thought you were going to show me that photograph,' she says, attempting to lift his mood.

'They're stored in the cupboard under the stairs. I'll just be a sec.'

He returns with a large box and places it on the kitchen table. The dates 1980 to 1985 written in a felt-tip pen on the lid.

'There're hundreds of photographs in here. Luckily, since Mum catalogued them, it should be easy to find.'

'I love looking at old photos. There's just something special about holding one in your hand. It's handy being able to store them on your phone, but I just feel you're closer to the subject, the person... that sounds weird,' she says dismissively.

'I don't think it does. I'd agree with you.'

Rob opens the box and peers inside. He runs his finger

along the spines of the photo albums where specific dates are written. 'This is the one.'

He pulls out a photo album and sits down, grinning to himself. 'Promise you won't laugh.'

'I'll try not to.' Zoe smiles and shuffles to the edge of her chair.

He locates the photo and turns the album so that Zoe can get a better look.

She leans in. 'You look so cute, and your hair is blonde... Wow! Now that's what I call flares and that must be Sue standing next to you.'

'She must be about six.'

'And you. How old were you?'

'I'd be ten.'

Zoe raises her eyebrows. 'The fish isn't the biggest I've seen.'

'No, it's not. It looked big to me at the time. It was probably the first fish I caught.'

'And were there more... fish?'

'I can't remember ever enjoying fishing. It was the only thing Dad and I did together. I was playing football for the school team by then, so the fishing took a back step.'

Zoe flicks through the photographs that sit smugly in their protective sheets. 'Here's one of your mum and dad. He was a handsome man, and your mum looks so young.'

'Let me see.' Rob thinks for a second. 'That was Sue's First Holy Communion. There's a photo of her on the next page looking saintly.'

Zoe moves on to the next page and tilts her head to the side in mild bemusement. Sue is wearing a white top and skirt and a blue sash with a silver pendant pinned to it. Zoe notices Sue's shoes encased in a tidemark of mud, and she grins. 'She looks like she's hating every minute of it.'

'She got grounded for a week. Mum was furious, said she had never been so embarrassed. Before the mass took place, Sue tried to run away right through a field covered in mud. She was caught by a man walking his dog and seeing how Sue was dressed, he brought her right back to the church. That's the last photograph taken of my dad before the accident.'

'It must have been hard for your mum, two young kids to look after on her own and she was so young herself.'

'I don't know how she would have coped if it weren't for Gran and Grandad. Mum had to work, so Sue and I spent a lot of time at their house. My Grandad was like a father to me. He filled a massive hole. He was always there for me. He brought me up like I was a son to him, and when he died, it was like I'd lost my dad. I miss him. In a way, it brings it all back. Grandad, Soph and… well, Mum hasn't got long.'

Zoe looks in the box and tries to sound upbeat. 'There must be hundreds of photographs in here.'

'There's another three boxes under the stairs.'

Zoe hands Rob the photo album, and just as he is about to replace it in the box, a small envelope drops onto the table. He picks it up and turns it on his fingers, studying its yellow edges. 'I've never seen this before.'

'It must have been tucked in between the pages.'

'How intriguing.'

'It's an old envelope.'

'Well, aren't you going to see what's inside it?' Her voice is louder than she expects.

A small frown creases the side of his mouth and Zoe wonders what he is thinking. Rob runs his finger along the length of the envelope before opening it. He sits back in his chair and pulls out a photograph.

Zoe waits for him to speak. His silence seems an eternity. He gazes at Zoe. 'It's an old photograph of a family I don't recognise.' He says, mystified.

'Can I see it?' Zoe stretches out her hand.

Rob hands the black-and-white photograph to her. It is old and not what she is expecting. A couple, in their late twenties, are sitting together on two separate chairs, their postures stiff and formal. The woman is wearing a hat and a nondescript, long dress that almost covers her boots. She is in her twenties, her hair is long, her stare unswerving, her cheekbones prominent. She sets her mouth firm. The man's dark suit, waistcoat and white shirt seem worn and aged. And, at his side, a young girl of about three years of age stands, her hand resting on the adult's shoulder. It is the portrait of a family anticipating the flash of the camera.

There is something odd about the composition, and then it dawns on her. None of them are smiling. It was maybe the thing in those days; she thinks.

'Do you know who they are?'

Rob shifts in his chair. 'No. I've not got a clue. It was taken a long time ago.'

'The photograph must mean something to your mum, otherwise why would she have kept it?'

Rob thinks about this. 'I wish I knew.'

Chapter 3

Remembrance

It feels like a bright light has flooded his mind. It is uplifting, important. It feels worthwhile. To do nothing is not an option, this much he knows.

Rob has studied the photograph countless times that his eyes could have, by now, bord a hole in it. He peers into the eyes of the young man and wonders about the man that stares back at him through the grainy image. And his thoughts are always framed with a question - Who are you?

---

*

Set in an expanse of farmland and forest, the Georgian country house that is now Leyway Care Home comes into view. Rob's stomach always drops when he turns off the country road and swings onto the long driveway that curves through manicured lawns, tall hedges, and mature trees. He feels he has given up on his mum. He has handed her over to strangers, the caring professional. He knows his guilt is a normal reaction, and that she is now in a place with people that can care for his mum in a way that he, or others, could not. But whenever this building comes into view, he cannot help thinking he has abandoned her, and the dreadful feeling in the pit of his stomach is a constant reminder of this.

Rob parks his car. There are another six cars in the visitor's section of the car park. He checks his watch. It is almost two o'clock. It's always busy on a Saturday, more so on a Sunday, so he always visits his mum on a Saturday afternoon. Not that she is aware of what day it is, or the month. Most days now, she does not even acknowledge him. He often wonders if she is aware of who he is. On the few days that she is lucid, she will call him by his name and if he is lucky, she will say a few words in context before the darkness falls behind her eyes and she is gone from him again.

There are two nurses at the nurse's station. Both are familiar to him, although their names are not.

'Hello, Mr Webster.' A nurse stands to meet him. She is squarely built, in her thirties, he supposes, and he notices the skin at the edges of her lips crease as she smiles. 'How are you today?'

'I'm fine, thanks. And you?'

'I'm good.'

The other nurse, a younger woman, is studying a computer screen. 'It looks like Bill is with your mum. If they're not in the dayroom, he's probably taken her out into the garden. It's a nice day for it.'

'Thanks. I'll take a look.'

The day room is off a wide corridor with yellow and brown patterned swirls in the carpeting. Rob has always thought it a depressing floor covering that adds nothing to the ambience of the care home.

There are only a few people sitting in the dayroom, two women drinking tea, and a man, his chin resting on his chest, sleeping in front of a television. One woman appears to be listening intently. She nods and smiles, but the other is not talking to her at all, instead she is staring into her lap. A nursing assistant is standing with his back to the room and looking out of the window.

In the garden, Rob can smell freshly cut grass. The sun has broken through the clouds and is already warming the air. He sees his mum sitting on a bench looking over a fishpond. Bill is sitting beside her. She looks shrunken, a tiny version of the woman she has been, and he feels a sudden ache in his throat.

When he reaches them, Bill stands, as if now it is not his place to sit beside Rob's mum.

Bill smiles. 'Jeanie, look who's come to see you.'

Rob bends towards his mum and kisses her forehead.

'Hello, Mum.'

A flash of recognition brightens her eyes.

Bill turns to walk away. 'I'll leave you to it.'

Rob nods an appreciation and sits beside his mum, taking her hand in his. Jeanie returns her stare to the fishpond, retreating from the world around her.

It is enough just to sit with her, to feel her close to him. The familiarity of it sustains him in the absence of conversation.

The air seems heavy; the silence hanging thickly around them. It still catches his breath.

There were always words. His mum was an enthusiastic communicator. If she was not talking to someone, she was absentmindedly talking to herself. She was a tremendous presence that filled the space between people with her infectious personality.

Her eyes flick open and close again.

'Hello, Mum.' Rob tries to sound cheery.

She is not here, but she is. The contradiction, the bitter reality, torments him.

'Mum. I've got something to show you. It's a photograph I found in your house. An old photograph.'

'The fish have all gone.'

Jeanie's words startle him. They are unexpected.

'I liked to watch them swimming in the pond. Did you take the fish?' Jeanie's eyes skim the water.

Rob holds her hand. 'No, Mum. I didn't take the fish.'

'Well, someone did. Are you sure it wasn't you?'

'Maybe whoever took the fish will put them back again.'

'Yes, I would like that. Did you take the fish?'

Rob squeezes his mum's hand. 'No, Mum, I didn't take the fish.'

'Oh.' Jeanie looks at him. 'My son Rob is visiting today. Maybe he knows who took the fish.'

A heaviness bore into him. It feels like grief, the bereavement of a loved one. Rob takes an envelope from his pocket and takes out the small photograph. He shows it to his mum.

'Look, Mum, I've got a photograph.'

Jeanie stares at the pond.

'Do you know who these people are, Mum?'

She looks, but her eyes glaze, and her expression remains set.

'What about the woman? Do you know who she is?'

Jeanie leans in closer.

'I've never seen them before. Do you know who they are, Mum? I found the photograph in your house amongst all the others?' In his desperation, he is asking her too many questions. He knows this. It only confuses her. It is a gamble he thinks is worth taking.

Jeanie screws her face up.

'Try to remember, Mum.'

'He wasn't supposed to be there.'

'The man in the photograph?'

Jeanie stares at the pond.

'Where? Where was he not supposed to be?'

Jeanie leans a hand on the bench, and with an effort, she takes her weight until she is standing. She struggles to keep her balance and sways. Rob stands and takes her by the elbow.

'Careful.'

'I want to see the fish. I always look at the fish.'

They walk the short distance to the pond. Jeanie stares into the murky water. After a while, she looks up and turns to Rob with a questioning look in her eyes. 'The fish have disappeared, just like he did.'

Rob forces a smile. 'Where did he go?'

Jeanie runs her fingers along her forehead. 'An island.'

Rob seizes on the opportunity. 'Try to remember, Mum. I know it's difficult, but it's important.'

He can see she is growing tired. A few seconds pass. He must proceed with patience, yet he is unable to refrain from one more attempt. 'What was the island called?'

Jeanie touches his arm. 'I'd like a cup of tea and some biscuits. Chocolate biscuits would be nice.'

He is aware his mum is slightly swaying. A slight breeze has lifted, cold against his face. 'Come on, let's get you back to your room.'

She looks at him then and smiles. 'Corfu. That's what it was called.'

Chapter 4

Let the Past be the Past

There is a respectable turnout of family and friends. Not a bad send off for being a daughter, wife, mother, grandmother, and friend.

When the coffin arrives in the crematorium, Rob places a single rose onto the coffin. Beside him, Sue wipes away her tears with a handkerchief, as her rose falls from her hand. Gary has not travelled with her, nor have her children.

Uncle Bert bends stiffly and places his rose alongside the others. 'She always loved roses. Jeanie would appreciate the gesture. When it's my turn, don't bother with them. I hate roses.' He taps Rob's shoulder and turns to walk away.

After the service, Rob thanks the priest. 'I'll see you at the reception, Father. Nancy has done a good spread, as always.'

'A cup of tea would be grand and I'm partial to an egg mayonnaise sandwich. Nancy always puts wee bits of cucumber in them.'

'There'll be far too much.'

'There usually is. And your mother was fond of her.'

'Nancy said she wouldn't take a penny for her efforts. She wants me to donate what I would have paid her to a dementia charity.'

'They were good friends, Nancy, and your mother. They grew up together and never lived more than two streets from each other until Jeanie moved to Elie.'

'Nancy visited her regularly, even when Mum went into the nursing home.'

'It will be like she has lost a sister.'

'Yes. I suppose it will.'

At the faraway end of the function suite in the local hotel, a queue has assembled around an assortment of white and brown bread sandwiches: cheese, egg mayonnaises, tuna and cold ham, filling several tables along with miniature sausage rolls, several platters of Indian starters and slices of cold pizza.

Since arriving from the crematorium, Rob has met and chatted with almost everyone in the room, mostly close and distant relatives, and family friends. There are others he hasn't recognised, probably neighbours of Mum's from years ago, he thinks.

He recognises Nancy walking towards him. Now not occupied with preparing the buffet, she has discarded her apron and replaced it with a fitted black jacket. Rob pulls out a chair for her and she eases herself into it.

'Ah, that's a relief. I've been on my feet for hours.' She looks at Rob. 'How are you doing, my love?'

'I'm fine, Nancy. I'll just be glad when this is over. There were people at the graveside I hadn't seen in years.'

'Your mum would have been pleased with the turnout. She's probably looking down at us right now and smiling.'

'She would be if she could see all that food you've made. You've done her proud, Nancy.'

Nancy waves her hand dismissively. 'Nothing's too much trouble for Jeanie. She was the salt of the earth. A wonderful woman. I'm proud to have called her a dear friend.'

'She thought the same of you.'

'I can't believe how quick it was. I only visited her on the Tuesday and by the Friday she was gone.'

'It was a blessing. She didn't suffer.'

'We had some good times together over the years. It was the best thing that happened to her moving to the house in Elie. She was happy there. She loved it. The locals just seemed to adopt her as their own.'

'That's probably who the people are that I don't recognise here today. I never thought of that.'

'They will be. In fact, now that you mention it, I recognise some of them. See the older fella at the bar, the one with the tray of drinks. He was one of your mum's neighbours. He popped in on her a few times a week just to make sure she had enough milk and bread, stuff like that.' Nancy gives a rueful smile. 'Jeanie called him her personal shopper.'

'It's good to know there were people looking out for her.'

'You did too.'

'Not as often as I should have.'

'It's not as if you could just pop round as well. At least you made the effort to visit your mum. Not like your sister.'

'I just had to travel from Edinburgh, not London.'

'It broke your mum's heart that she didn't see a lot of her grandchildren. She never said so, but I knew her too well.'

'Your right, there's no excuse.'

Nancy's voice is quiet but sincere. 'You made her happy. She was so proud of you, Rob. You made up for your sister's disappointment. Where is she, anyway? I've not seen her.' Nancy lifts her head and looks around the room.

'She had to get her plane back to London. It's at five o'clock.'

Nancy shakes her head. 'I thought she'd at least stay for a few days.'

'I'm past caring. At least she turned up.'

'God! It's her mother's funeral. You'd think she'd stay for the whole day.'

Rob takes a bite of a tuna sandwich. 'Why do you keep doing this? It's not easy work.'

'What else would I do at my age? I've got a few good years left in me yet. I'm sixty-eight not eighty-eight. I need a purpose, something to keep the grey matter ticking over. It's not as if it's every week. Most of them are funerals these days. Which is a good thing. It guarantees a never-ending supply of customers.' Nancy laughs. 'And besides, Cara and Louise, my two granddaughters, help me out. They do most of the preparation. I just make sure it's up to my normal standards.'

Rob longs for the day to be over. He has still to collect his mum's things from the nursing home. The manager has phoned him to say they have packed his mum's clothes into bags and sorted out her belongings to be collected. Jeanie has always supported charity shops, visiting her favourites most weekends. Rob thought she would approve of his decision to donate her clothes to them.

'What's going to happen to the house in Elie?'

'Now there's a dilemma.'

'What do you mean?'

'Sue wants to sell it.'

'Oh! And you don't?'

'I'd rather keep it in the family. I think that's what Mum would really have wanted.'

'And what does her will say? That's what's important, your mum's wishes.'

'She knew Sue didn't need the money, but she knew my half from the sale would be life changing for me. I told her I didn't want the money. The idea of keeping the house in the family because of what it meant to her was more important to me. It defined Mum's sense of identity and her place in the world. It was a place she was at her happiest.'

'It's getting sold, isn't it?'

Rob nods.

'Have you spoken to Sue about this?'

'To be honest, I think Gary's putting pressure on her to move the sale along.'

'So, there's still a chance you can change her mind?' Nancy sounds hopeful.

'I doubt it. As they say, money goes to money.'

Rob sits a little straighter. 'When I was clearing some of

Mum's things from the house, I came across a photograph that... well, let's just say, it was not what I was expecting.'

'Oh! Why was that?'

Rob rubs his chin. 'It was an old photograph of a family. A man and a woman with a child. It's odd, I've no idea who they are. I know all my relatives and I've seen all the old photographs of the family, but not this one.'

'Oh, I see.' Nancy brushes her skirt with her hand. 'Did your mum know you'd seen the photograph?'

'At the nursing home, they often had sessions where they would look at pictures of the past that were relevant to the clients. You know, try to help them remember. I saw them do it with Mum a few times. So, I took the photograph on one of my visits to see if it would jog her memory.'

'Oh, really. And did Jeanie say anything?' Nancy inhales, unaware she is holding her breath.

'Not at first. She was tired and confused, and I was going to leave it at that.'

'That was probably best.'

'But she remembered.'

'She did, did she? What did she say?'

'Out of nowhere she said, Corfu.'

Nancy's eyes widen. 'Corfu. That's Greek, isn't it? I wonder where that came from.'

Rob stares at Nancy; he can tell she is flustered. 'The other thing she said was he shouldn't have gone there. I can only presume she means the man in the photograph.'

Nany draws in a wavering breath. 'Well, isn't that peculiar?'

'Is there something you're not telling me, Nancy?'

She sighs and reaches out, covering his hand with her own. 'I can't tell you. I kept her trust in life and I will keep it now that she is dead.'

'Why can't you tell me?'

'Just leave it. Walk away from it. It's just a photograph.'

Rob casts his eye around the function suite.

'There's no one here who would know,' Nancy says quietly.

'What about Uncle Bert?'

'Not even him.'

'I don't understand this. This isn't just an ordinary photo, is it? Why did Mum have this photograph and who are the people in it?'

'It's not for me to say.'

'You obviously know.'

'We have just said goodbye to the person who should have told you, and for all these years, she didn't. I'm not going to betray her trust today, of all days.'

Rob scratches his head. 'What does that mean?'

Nancy sighs.

'What?'

'I think it's best if you let the past be just that… the past.'

'I can't do that, not now. Mum has been keeping something from me, and from Sue, something that is making you uncomfortable. I don't understand why she would do that. That's not the woman I know.'

Nancy sighs again, this time deeper and longer. 'I understand Rob. I really do, but believe me, nothing good will come out of it.'

'How can you say that?' Rob can see how Nancy's face changes with his question. It is now dark with apprehension. 'What are you not telling me?'

Chapter 5

To do Nothing is not an Option

'Thanks for coming, Zoe.' Rob hands Zoe a mug of coffee and places a saucer with biscuits on the kitchen table. 'How was the drive?'

'It was fine. It's a lovely drive along the coast.' Zoe hovers her hand over the biscuits and then picks a white chocolate and raspberry one. 'Mm. These are nice.'

'I got them at the local shop and then when I got back to the house and put them in the cupboard, there was an unopened packet. Mum must have liked them too.'

'How did the funeral go? I'm sorry I couldn't make it. I'd hoped to get away a day early from the conference, but it was impossible.'

'Don't worry about it. I know you would have been there if you could. It went well.'

'I'm glad.'

'The crem was packed. Mum had arranged the whole funeral with the Coop several years ago, even down to what handles would be on the coffin. She wanted a religious service, but she also wanted a humanist speaker too. So, when we all got back to the wake, Bill did a moving eulogy. Mum had heard Bill at several funerals and said that she wanted him to do hers. Bill's the humanist, by the way. He was good. He got her down to a tee. About a week before the funeral, he sent me a template of questions to answer about Mum, her past, growing up, meeting Dad, all that stuff, right through her life. I had to ask Nancy about when Mum was growing up and their times together.'

'Did Sue help?'

'I asked her if she wanted to come up to Elie and stay at Mum's and we could share our memories and get something on paper, but she couldn't make it.'

Zoe stared at Rob. 'Surprise, surprise.'

'We spoke on the phone. It's done now. Actually, she was quite good at remembering things I'd forgotten.'

Zoe bites into her biscuit, ignoring Rob's praise for his sister. 'These biscuits are really good. I'll have to buy a packet for myself.'

Rob raises his eyebrows.

'I'm sorry. It's really none of my business. As long as she contributed, that's what matters.' Zoe takes one last drink of coffee and places the mug on the table. 'So, how are we going to do this?'

'Like everything in life, Mum has it organised. She left instructions in her will for all her clothes to go to charity shops, The British Heart Foundation, CHAS, Cancer Research…'

'That's a lot of charities.'

'You should see the clothes.'

Zoe smiles. 'We better get cracking, then.'

It feels like packing a life away, his mum's life. There are several cupboards full of her clothes: blouses, skirts, dresses, cardigans, tops, shoes, and jackets. He can still smell the distinctive aroma of her perfume on the collar of some of her jackets, forcing a ball of grief from his throat.

By the time they finish, ten black plastic bags bulge around their feet.

'We'll need to get th**ese in the car.' Rob checks his watch. 'Good. We've plenty of time. I'm sure Thursday is a late opening day. After we've finished at the charity shops, would you like something to eat?'

'Where do you have in mind?'

'Where they serve the best fish in Fife?'

'The famous chip shop in Anstruther?' Her eyes shimmer.

Rob laughs. 'No. This one's in Elie. It was Mum's favourite. It's called The Ship Inn. The fish is amazing and if we get a seat outside, the view is just as impressive.'

'Is it far?'

'No. Once we get back from dropping the clothes off, we can walk there in ten minutes.'

'Sounds perfect.'

The Ship Inn sits in a row of old houses, its white exterior and blue framed windows making it the centrepiece of the street. The outside seating area is opposite, across the narrow street. Rob had pre-warned Zoe that the tables were normally busy, so not to be too disappointed if they had to eat inside. To their relief, a couple are just leaving as they arrive. They weave through the tables towards the vacant one. When Rob goes to order their food, Zoe sits at the timber table in stunned silence, taking in the vast expanse of sand that stretches towards a shadowed headland where the sinking sun sprays the sky in a hue of caramel and a blaze of aureate cloud.

When Rob returns, his face lights up in response to Zoe's glowing smile.

'I can see why your mum loved this place so much,' she enthuses, scarcely containing her appreciation.

Rob sits opposite her. He has bought two glasses of red wine and places them on the table.

'It's a Merlot.'

'Lovely. I meant to ask you. How is work?'

'I'm in between jobs. I've left the college.'

Zoe leans forward. 'Oh! What happened?'

'It was no surprise, really. There've been cutbacks for about a year. I'd heard that the lecturers would be the first to go, not the curriculum heads. There was to be a restructuring. Basically, getting people to do the same job but for less money. To tell you the truth, I haven't been happy for some time. So, they offered me a severance package, and it was pretty decent, so I took it.'

'So, you'll be okay money-wise?'

'I only have to think of me these days, and I'm not leading the most lavish lifestyle. Besides, if I can't persuade Sue that it's a good idea to keep Mum's house, then there'll be the money from the sale.'

'Are you looking for a job? What's the lecturing market like these days?'

'To be honest, I'm enjoying the break. I've been busy with the funeral and the business of putting Mum's affairs in order. I didn't realise what was involved. There's so much to do. At least the funeral took care of itself.'

'Your mum made sure of that, as always.'

Rob smiles. 'She did. When her diagnosis was confirmed,

she made sure that everything was in place and organised to the letter before she lost the capacity to do so. She didn't want to be a burden, even when she was dead. Seeing how smoothly it all went, I'm so glad she had the foresight to do so.'

Zoe takes a drink. 'Mm, that's nice.'

'I thought you'd like it.'

'How are you, Rob? Really?' Zoe enquires.

'I'm doing okay.'

'Are you sure?'

'If anything, it's been a bit weird.'

Zoe knows this is a reference to Sophie. 'It's only to be expected. You're human after all.'

'On the day of Mum's funeral, when the hearse arrived, it brought it all back. I hadn't really thought about it. I was so preoccupied with what was going on. From when Mum passed and up until the funeral, I'd been living in a bubble. It was surreal. That morning, I just wanted the day to be over, and then, instead of seeing Mum, it was Sophie's hearse and Sophie's coffin I saw.'

'Oh, Rob.' Zoe shakes her head sadly.

Rob runs his fingers through his hair. 'Even after two years, it can still floor me.'

Zoe smiles fondly. 'I still think about Soph. In fact, I don't think there's a day that passes, I don't think about her.'

'Sometimes, after we'd visited Mum, we'd come down here. Sophie always ordered the fish and chips. She loved the view too.'

Zoe wipes her eyes with a napkin. 'I can see why.'

Their meal arrives, and they eat in silence.

Rob looks up from his plate. 'You're really quiet.'

'I can't eat and talk at the same time, and this fish is

amazing.' She points her fork at the white flesh. 'I want to savour every morsel.'

Rob smiles. 'I'm glad you like it.'

'I like everything about this place, the food, the view and...' she picks up her almost empty glass, 'The wine.'

'I'll get another. In fact, why don't I get a bottle? It will save me having to go to the bar again.'

A flash of horror crosses Zoe's face. 'I've drunk a whole glass of wine! I can't drive. What was I thinking?'

'It's fine. You can stay the night. Do you have to be back in Edinburgh tonight?'

'Well, no.'

'Then that's it settled. There're four bedrooms to pick from.'

'I'd hate to put you out.' She shakes her head. 'I can't believe I've just done that. I'm always so careful.'

'To tell you the truth, I never gave it a thought. It tells me you're relaxed and I'm glad you're here.'

'You're not just saying that because you're stuck with me?'

Rob smirks. 'Not if it means we can share a bottle of wine.'

For dessert they eat apple pie and cream, and once the server clears their table, another lights scented tea tree candles. It is dark now and yellow lights illuminate the windows of the houses perched above the sea wall that run the length of the beach.

Most people are relaxing, enjoying drinks now that they have finished their meals.

There is a burst of laughter from another table as Rob pours the last of the wine into their glasses and smiles weakly. 'I really want to keep the house. Do you know what I mean? Can you understand that?'

I know exactly what you mean, Zoe thinks. 'I can see why. This place... well, it grows on you.'

'For some, a house is just brick and mortar, but that house meant so much more to Mum. It was her life, as Elie was. She was truly happy here. It's funny, you know, but when I'm in that house, it feels like a warm cosy blanket is wrapped around me. There's just something about it.'

Zoe looks at him curiously.

'And I would say that even without all this wine inside me, if you're wondering.'

'I believe you.' Zoe laughs.

'That's why this whole business with the photograph seems surreal. I spoke to Nancy at the funeral.'

'And?'

Rob explains Nancy's reaction. 'She knows, but she's not going to tell me. This whole thing feels unreal. I've just found out my mum was not the woman I thought she was.'

'She's still your mum. That doesn't change. We all have secrets; some are just bigger than others.'

'This is starting to feel quite a big one, otherwise, why wouldn't Nancy tell me, and why is it only Nancy that knows?'

He can see her going over it in her head. 'Because whatever it is that ties your mum to that photograph, the only person your mum felt comfortable sharing it with was her lifelong friend.'

Rob remembers the moment he showed his mum the photograph at the nursing home. 'When Mum said *Corfu*, it was the first time I'd seen her smile in her whole time at that nursing home.'

'The photograph, or to be more precise, the family in it, has some kind of connection to your mum. That's why she had the photograph, but it doesn't explain Nancy's reluctance to tell you what it was. The question is what was that connection? I think that photograph was taken somewhere in Corfu and that could be where the answers lie.'

Rob frowns. 'I can't let this go now. I don't know.'

They finish their drinks, and Rob checks his watch.

'There're a few beers in the fridge if you want to head back?'

Zoe smiles. 'I could do with the walk.'

Rob looks at the sky and points Zoe's attention to a threatening bank of dark cloud. 'I think it's going to rain.'

They make it back to the house just as the first drops of rain fall. As they go through the house, Rob turns on a lamp in the hallway and in the kitchen. Zoe glances outside into the garden where the trees from the orchard loom in the dark, and then fade, as Rob adjusts the dimmer switch.

Rob retrieves two beer bottles from the fridge, plucks a bottle opener from a drawer and as he opens the bottles, suggests they sit on the sofa in the extension his mum had built, which she christened *the family room.*

'What's good in your life, Zoe?'

His question is unexpected. She keeps her eye fixed on the bottle of beer in her hand. She examines her fingers and her painted nails. 'I've got a good job, well paid, my own brand new flat, I can afford two holidays a year, my cars decent...'

'What about people, friends... is there anyone special?'

Zoe draws herself up from the sofa and Rob glimpses tiny muscles flicker at the edge of her mouth. 'Not since Greg left, but I'm over it and him.'

Rob thinks she sounds defensive, and he could kick himself for asking her such questions. He has only reminded her of what has gone wrong in her life, of course she would mention Greg. What was he thinking? That was it. He wasn't thinking.

'I'm sorry, Zoe. I shouldn't have asked.'

'It's fine, honestly. It's not as if you don't know all the details. You and Soph were great. You were both my rock. I'd never have got through it without the both of you.'

There is an awkward silence. The tables have turned and unexpectedly, Rob feels the throb of grief.

'Look, if the truth be told, Greg turned out to be one of life's bastards and bullies. It just took me sometime to figure it out. But we were both to blame for what happened,' Zoe continues, to Rob's surprise. 'We created our own little tsunami of destruction. Our rows were like a river of flammable material. It was very effective in destroying anything that was ever good about us. The worst of it was, when he drank too much, he used his fists and I struggled to hide the bruises. I might be small in stature, but I could also give as much as he gave. No one should live like that.'

His eyes haven't left her, and to her shame, she is enjoying the attention.

'Do you still see his family? Do they keep in touch with you?'

'I think there's a saying, when you divorce someone, you divorce their family, too. I never really got on with his sisters. I think they felt Greg was too good for me. They definitely made it plain they felt he was marrying below his station. Apart from Angela, she was the youngest sister. I always got on with her. She wasn't like her sisters. We still meet up now and again. He's bankrupt, by the way.'

'Greg!'

'His business folded. Obviously, his family blames me because of the stress I put him through with the divorce and the financial settlement. Ten grand for every bruise,' she says, bitingly.

A photograph of Sophie, Rob, and his mum catches Zoe's eye, sitting amongst a small gallery of framed photographs on a side unit.

'When was that taken, the one with your mum and Soph?'

Rob turns to look at the photograph. 'Just before she was diagnosed. It was out in the garden. We stayed here for the weekend... it was the last time she was here.'

Zoe touches his arm, and he places his hand over hers. It is a physical urge, an unexpected desire of affection. They stay touching, both stuck in the moment, not knowing what to do next, and then Rob slips his hand from her.

'It's getting late.' Zoe says. She moves to the edge of the sofa and yawns.

Rob wonders if it is exaggerated, a play at the moment that has just passed.

She smiles. 'Too much wine and beer. I'll certainly have no trouble sleeping tonight.'

'You can have the room upstairs. It's the second on the left. There's an en suite in that one. Mum used it as the guest room.'

'Thanks. I'll just go up then.'

'What would you like for breakfast?'

'I don't want to put you to any trouble.'

'Some toast with scrambled egg? I'll even put some cheese in it.'

'Sounds lovely.'

'See you in the morning, then.'

She rises and Rob can see she is hesitant. 'Thank you for a lovely evening. Goodnight, Rob.'

The memories of his day with Zoe swim in his head. He

stares at the photograph of Sophie and his mum, and he can't comprehend they are no longer with him: talking, laughing, touching, smiling, eating, sleeping, and breathing. He wants to believe they are somewhere, wherever that somewhere may be. And in his mind, they have found one another; they are together. It is a comforting thought, even just for an instant.

Rob is astonished that he has gone most of the day without mentioning the photograph and Nancy's reaction. Since he discovered it, the image has taken up so much space in his thoughts; it has wormed into his head.

Rob has studied the grainy photograph on countless occasions. He has peered into the eyes of the man and woman and speculated what lies behind the eyes that stare back at him.

The woman has high cheekbones; the skin taught across her cheeks. Her frame is slight and thin, her hair long and dark. There is an elegance in the way she sits, her back straight and her head held high. The man's hand rests tentatively on her shoulder. It is an intimate gesture, shared by two people who are at ease in each other's company and familiar with one another. There is a definite synchronicity. They are a couple. A family.

He has tried to imagine her voice. He has tried to savour every detail and catch glimpses of their story.

His mind floods in a bright light. It is uplifting, important. It feels worthwhile. To do nothing is not an option, this much he knows.

Why has his mum kept her secret from him? It hurts, especially since she can't answer his questions. He feels he suddenly does not know the woman he has known all his life.

At times, he is hesitant, but it is always short-lived and

always framed with a question - Who is this family and who is this other woman who was his mum?

Chapter 6

A Pivotal Shift

The morning sun washes the kitchen in a delicate light as Rob makes a strong coffee from a Nespresso machine. He remembers giving it to his mum as a Christmas present several years ago. He opens the glass doors that lead into the garden and sinks into one of the wicker chairs that surround a glass table. He feels a slight dampness on the cushion, which reminds him he forgot to take them indoors from last night's rain. Luckily, it had only been a light shower.

Rob takes a sip of coffee, revelling in its strong and bitter taste, as he spots several large snails stuck to the garden wall and he wonders if it has taken them all night to get to where they are.

He glimpses next door's black cat, prowling in the orchard as if it owns the garden. It used to eye him with suspicion, but now goes about its business, ignoring him.

A crow has landed on the wall and wipes its beak on the stone. A sudden noise startles it, and it takes flight in a fluttering of wings.

'I hope you don't mind; I've had a shower, and I made myself a coffee,' she says with an air of apology.

Rob looks up. Zoe is walking towards him, cup in hand.

'Not at all. You don't have to ask either.' He shifts in his chair, an accompanying warmth spreads through his chest at the sight of her.

Her hair is wet, and she has tied it in a bun. She walks barefoot across the stone cladding, smiling a good morning, as she sits next to him. He hasn't noticed before; her toenails are red, and she has a petite tattoo, a rose that sits just above her ankle.

'Did you sleep well?' he asks.

'I did. It's probably the best sleep I've had in weeks.'

Rob smiles. 'You should come more often.' Instantly, he regrets this. It is overfamiliar, and something this situation is not.

She smiles back at him, easing his worry. 'Thanks for the offer.' She leans back in the chair. 'This is a lovely garden. You really have to sit in it to appreciate how beautiful it is.'

'Mum loved it. She spent hours pottering about in it, weeding and planting. She even pointed the wall one year, all on her own. As her health failed, she was forced to get a gardener. I think he came every two weeks, just to keep on top of it. Unfortunately, Mum never handed down the gardening gene to me.'

'It would be a shame for it to not be kept tidy.'

'That reminds me. I need to get in touch with the guy that did the garden. I don't know if he's local, so he might not have heard about Mum. She kept all the important phone numbers in a little book she kept by the phone. His number is probably in there.'

'I remember when you bought that coffee machine for your mum. You were worried that she wouldn't be able to work it.'

'I certainly regretted it to start with.'

'Soph told me you must have shown her a hundred times before she got the hang of it.'

He is mindful of how often they mention Sophie in their conversation, and he wonders if it is deliberate on Zoe's part.

'I've heard nowadays they're putting the ashes of loved ones into lockets and other pieces of jewellery. It's become quite popular.'

Zoe screws up her face. 'I could never do that.'

'I don't think I could either.'

'Have you got you mum's ashes back?'

'They'll be ready to get collected tomorrow.'

'Have you decided what you're going to do with them?'

'Half of her is going beside Dad and the other half is going next to that tree. It was what she wanted, to be in her garden.'

Zoe sat staring at the tree. 'But you're selling the house. Have you told Sue what your mum wanted?'

Rob sighs. 'She thinks I'm making it up to stop the sale of the house,' he says with a trace of exasperation.

'Of course, she would.'

'If I dig the hole deep enough, no one will ever know.'

'Is it legal?'

'I don't know. I've never thought about it. There's only three people that know. Me, you, and Sue. And she's back in London. She's not going to be back up here. What about you, Zoe? Do you approve of it?'

'If that's what your mum wanted, then, of course, as long as it's a big hole, who's going to know?'

'Exactly.' He continues, 'And I promised her I would.'

'Then, the way I see it, you don't have a choice.'

Rob regards his empty cup. 'What about that breakfast I promised you? Are you hungry?'

Zoe raises an eyebrow. 'I thought you'd never ask.'

Zoe picks up her fork and takes a mouthful of the last remaining piece of scrambled egg. 'You really do make a good breakfast.' Zoe says, placing her fork and knife on the plate and dabbing the side of her mouth with a napkin.

'It's a secret family recipe.'

'Really!'

Rob smirks. 'No.'

'You had me there.'

'I do like to cook. I'm not Gordon Ramsay by any stretch of the imagination, but I enjoy it. The only problem is most recipes don't cater just for one. There's always maths involved, trying to work out the right amount of ingredients. Half the time, I end up just guessing and it still turns out okay, well, mostly. What about you? Do you like to cook?'

'Me! No. If I can get away with a microwave meal, I'm happy with that.'

'Now there's a challenge.'

'What?'

'Let me cook you something. Anything you want.'

'Oh, I don't know.'

'What's your favourite meal… well, microwave meal?'

'I'm not very adventurous with food. Let me see.' She stares at the ceiling. 'Shepherd's Pie.'

Rob raises an eyebrow.

'I told you. I like simple food.'

'Shepherd's Pie it is then.'

'You're really going to cook it. I thought you were kidding.'

'What are your plans for today?'

Zoe shrugs. 'I didn't expect to stay here, so I guess I need to get back to Edinburgh. I can't go about all day in these clothes. I need to change. What about you? How long are you staying here?'

'A few more days, at least. There's still a lot to do.' The thought of Zoe leaving deflates him and he wonders if she feels this, too.

For the first time since they have been together, there is an awkward silence between them.

Rob stands and takes the breakfast plates to the sink. He turns on the hot tap and squeezes the washing up liquid into the water. He feels her standing next to him. 'I could always come back.'

'You're thinking of that Shepherd's Pie I promised I'd make?'

'There is that, too. But seriously, if you want, I'd really like to come back.'

He turns to face her. 'I'd like that.'

She takes a deep breath. 'Me too.'

Get your copy:

vinci-books.com/skyfalls

ABOUT THE AUTHOR

Dougie lives in Dunfermline, Fife, with his wife, daughter, son and golden retriever.

Thank you so much for taking the time to read my novel. It really does mean everything to me. My novels are inspired by my favourite city, Edinburgh and my passion for Greece, her islands, people, landscapes, sea, light and ambience, all of which are important themes and symbols in my writing.

My books encapsulate themes such as love, loss, hope, coming of age and the uncovering of secrets. They are character-driven stories with twists and turns set against the backdrop of Edinburgh and Greece.

I never intended to, but seemingly I write women's contemporary fiction and since ninety-five percent of my readers are women, I suppose that is a good fit.

Since all my books are set in Edinburgh and Greece, you will not be surprised to know that I identify with a physical place and the feeling of belonging, which are prominent in my writing.

Edinburgh is one of the most beautiful cities in the world, it is rich in history, has amazing classical buildings, (the new town of Edinburgh is a world heritage site) and it also has vibrant restaurants and café bars.

Greece occupies my heart. Her history, culture, religion, people, landscape, light, colours and sea inspire me every day. There is almost a spiritual quality to it. I want my novels to have a sense of time and place, drawing the reader into the social and cultural complexities of the characters. I want my characters to speak from the page, where you can identify with them, their hopes, fears, conflicts, loves and emotion. I hope the characters become like real people to you, and it is at that point, you will want to know what is going to happen to the characters, where is their life taking them in the story.

The common denominator is, I want my novels to be about what it means to be human through our relationship with our world, our environment and with each other. Most of all, I want them to be good stories that you, as a reader, can identify with and enjoy.

ACKNOWLEDGMENTS

Heartfelt thanks to Sheona, my wife, for her continued support and constant encouragement. A special thanks to all my advanced readers. They know who they are. I couldn't do this without them, as they have given me invaluable feedback on all my novels. Also, immense gratitude to Emma Mitchell from Creating Perfection.

In researching this story, I am indebted to Mark Mazower for his superb and gripping account of wartime Greece and the Nazi occupation in his book *Inside Hitler's Greece: The Experience of Occupation 1941-1944*.

Also to Michael Matsas for his account, research and interviews on the fate of the Jews of Greece during World War II in the inspirational *The Illusion of Safety: The Story of the Greek Jews During the Second World War, New Edition Revised and Expanded*.